L I F E   L O N G

LIFE LONG

RONALD L. RUIZ

My thanks to the following individuals for their help and encouragement: Amanda Wilson, Stefan Ruiz, Jay Amberg, Sarah Koz, Ann Wambach, Annie Smith, Robert Brown, Allen Cetto, Jan McClellan, and Ren McClellan.

First Edition   ISBN 13: 978-1-937484-53-8
AMIKA PRESS   466 Central AVE #23 Northfield IL 60093   847 920 8084
info@amikapress.com   Available for purchase on amikapress.com
Edited by Jay Amberg & Ann Wambach. Cover art by Phe Ruiz. Cover photography by Stefan Ruiz & Deak Attila. Author photography by Amanda Wilson. Designed & typeset by Sarah Koz. Body in Espinosa Nova, designed by Cristóbal Henestrosa in 2010. Titles in Centaur MT, designed by Bruce Rogers in 1929, digitized by Monotype in 2000. Thanks to Nathan Matteson.

FOR PHE

I HAD gone to the Parker courthouse to take care of a ticket and try to get my car back. I saw the cop parked up ahead at the corner and I was extra careful at the stop sign. But I had no sooner crossed the intersection and started down the next block when he came after me. I stopped as soon as he put on his red light. I couldn't afford another ticket. I knew enough to stay in the car and wait for him to come up to me. I rolled down my window, and when he was next to me, I said, "Why did you stop me, Officer?"

"You don't know?"

"No, I don't. I was being extra careful."

"Well, you shouldn't even be driving this thing to begin with. It's a complete mess, an accident waiting to happen. I can probably cite you for ten different things."

"Yeah, but it's the only car I have, the only one I can afford."

He stepped back and looked at my car again and then at me again and then past me at the torn seats and the hanging pieces of roof cover. "Let me see your driver's license."

I gave him my expired driver's license.

"Sit tight. I'll be right back."

I watched in my rearview mirror as he went back to his car and radioed in. I thought of running but in the next breath realized how ridiculous that was, how much more trouble that would bring me.

He came back to the car and said, "Step out of the car."

"Why?"

"Because I said so, that's why.... You know, I've got half a mind to take you in. You've got a bunch of moving violations and parking violations that you haven't taken care of. But I'm going to give you one last chance. I'm going to impound your car and write you up for driving without a license and a faulty muffler. And if you don't show up in court this time, I'm going to get an arrest warrant out for you. Do I make myself clear?"

I nodded.

"I don't know what you're going to tell the judge but you brought this on yourself."

That's what brought me to the courthouse two weeks later.

As I was standing in the hallway trying to find my name on all the posted court calendars, someone standing next to me said, "How ya doing, Raymond?"

"Raymond" not Ray, grabbed my attention. I turned, and there stood Danny Bencomo, a cop I had gone to school with. He and his partner were in jeans and T-shirts, undercover cops now. Before I could say anything, he said, "Raymond, I want you to do me a favor. I want you to give your cousin Billy a message for me. Can you do that?"

"Sure, Danny, sure." The last thing I wanted to do was to be dealing with an undercover narc. And the next-to-last thing I wanted to do was to turn an undercover cop down. "Sure."

"You tell Billy for me that we know he's dealing and been dealing for a long time. Tell him we know he's a big-time dealer now. But sooner or later we're gonna catch him. Sooner or later somebody's gonna rat him out. That always happens. But for right now I want you to tell him that a lot of people on the street are OD'ing on stuff we know he's putting out there. It's bad shit. We've had two people die in the past week. Tell him he'd better clean his shit up because if somebody else croaks on us, we're gonna haul his ass in and charge him with homicide. Whether we can prove it or not doesn't matter. At least that will give cousin Billy another taste of what the rest of his life is gonna be like, sooner or later. Can you do me that favor, Raymond, and give your cousin Billy that message for us?"

Wide-eyed and scared I said, "Danny, I don't know anything about what you're talking about. Believe me."

"You may or may not. Right now we're not interested in you,

Raymond. It's your cousin Billy we're focusing on. I know how tight the two of you have been since grade school. So give him that message for us, will you?"

"Sure, Danny. But you've got to believe me, Danny, I don't know..."

"We're not interested in you, Raymond. At least not yet. It's Billy we want. It's Billy who's killing people."

Then they gave me two big glares and left.

I was terrified. I started to leave the courthouse to get to Billy. He was living just a few blocks away, but I remembered the cop saying, "If you don't show up this time, I'm going to get an arrest warrant out for you." That stopped me and I thought: *If I leave now, if I don't take care of this ticket now, they for sure will arrest me.* But Danny Bencomo had said they *might* be interested in me later. The cop was for sure and Danny was only for maybe. *I'd better stay,* I thought.

I went back to the court calendars. There were five sheets posted for the courtroom I was in, and my name was at the bottom of the last page. But I went in. The courtroom was packed, standing room only at the back and that's where I stood. The judge was already listening to people or rather pissed off at people. He was an old, cranky, bald-headed bastard. Mean enough looking and sounding that I was sure he was going to lock me up. But I didn't leave. Leaving was for sure.

Two and a half hours later with three of us left in the courtroom, he called my case. He had already put quite a few guys in jail and my chances of walking out of that courtroom didn't look too good. I was sitting but then I got up and went and stood where everybody had been standing.

He looked down at me and gave me a mean look and said, "Are you Raymond Lopez?"

"Yes, sir."

Then he read whatever was on his desk that told him about me. That took him a while. Then he looked down at me again, still mean-like. But now he was rubbing his chin. "You know, Mr. Lopez, there's a whole list of violations here that you haven't taken care of, haven't come to court for. Some of these I could put you in jail for for a long time. Why haven't you taken care of any of these?"

I didn't know what to answer or how to answer, and I just stood there staring down at the floor.

He waited and then said, "Mr. Lopez, I asked you a question. Why haven't you taken care of any of these violations?"

I could feel him getting not just mean but pissed off, but I didn't know what to say or how to say it.

"Mr. Lopez, I'm going to..."

"I've been sick."

"Sick? What have you been sick with?"

"Sick enough to be in the hospital for two months."

"What hospital?"

"Valley Medical Center."

"The county hospital here in Parker?"

"Yes."

"What were you sick with...? Mr. Lopez, look at me. What were you sick with?"

I hated talking about it. "They have a big, old, long name for it that I can't even say."

"Two months is a long time. What part of the hospital did they have you in?"

"I don't know the name of that department."

"What kind of illnesses were they dealing with there?"

"Mental."

"Were the doctors psychiatrists and psychologists?"

"Yes."

"Had you been there before?"

"No, sir, that was the first time, the only time I've been in the hospital."

"When were you released?"

"Three months ago."

"Are you taking any medication?"

"Yes."

"What kind?"

"Zyprexa."

"Do you take it every day?"

"Yes, I have to."

For a while he just looked at me. It wasn't a mean look now. And now I wasn't so sure that he was going to put me in jail.

"Are you working Mr. Lopez?"

"No. I can't get a job. They always want to know why I haven't been working and when I tell them I've been sick, and when they find out that it's been mental, they won't hire me."

"How do you support yourself?"

"I get disability and that's enough to pay for a room in this old lady's house and I eat a lot at McDonald's and Taco Bell."

He just looked at me again, nodding little nods to himself until he said, "What I'd like to do today, Mr. Lopez, is resolve all these matters before me so that you can walk out of here with a clean slate. Would you like to do that?"

"Sure, if you're not going to put me in jail."

"But in order to do that you're first going to have to admit your guilt to all the violations before me. In other words, you're going to have to plead guilty to all these violations. Are you willing to do that?"

"Sure, if you're not going to put me in jail."

"I will not put you in jail and you will walk out of here a free man. Are you ready to admit all these violations?"

"Yes."

"So how do you plead to all these violations? Guilty or not guilty?"

"Guilty. I did them all."

"Good. I'm going to order that the impounded vehicle be sold and that all the proceeds from that sale be applied to the moving and parking violations that were charged against you. In referring the disposition of these violations to the Department of Motor Vehicles, I am required by law to inform that Department that you are suffering from schizophrenia and taking medication for it.

That could mean that you'll have a difficult time getting another driver's license."

"Fine by me," I said elated.

I HADN'T even gotten to the courtroom door when the fear from Danny Bencomo's words returned. I had to get to Billy. I had to tell Billy before they arrested him and found out about me. But as I hurried down the courthouse steps on my way to Billy's, someone said, *We told you, you should never have gotten involved with Billy in Malaga.* "What?" I said and stopped and turned to whoever might have said that. But there was no one there. I panicked fearing who it might have been. "What?" I said again, hoping there would be no answer. But there was. Plain, clear, and loud. *We told you you should never have gotten involved with Billy in Malaga.* It was one of the voices and I was terrified. I didn't know what to do. I couldn't go to Billy. I couldn't let anyone see me like this. I had to take care of the voices. Now. But I didn't know how.

I sat down on the courthouse steps and thought. I was positive I had taken my meds that morning and still I had heard a voice. The meds weren't working. What to do? Go back to the hospital and tell them the meds aren't working? They would want to know exactly what I had heard and what it meant. There was no way I could tell them about Billy and me. And I couldn't lie about what I had heard either because then, not knowing what the truth was, they could never really help me. My thing with Billy had triggered it. Did that mean that every time I thought about Billy and me, that might trigger it again? And I couldn't tell anyone about my thing with Billy, especially after what Danny Bencomo had said. I couldn't live like this. I had to do something.

Then I thought of the old *curandero* Padre Ibarra had brought with him on his last visit with me at the hospital, telling me that the old man had helped many people with mental illness. The *curandero* didn't make much of an impression on me that day. No doubt it was because on that visit Padre Ibarra had given me the keys to the church in Malaga and I was all excited about that. The *curandero* didn't stay long that day but he did say that he would come again, and a few days later he did.

HE WAS a small, dark man who spoke and moved quietly. His dry brown skin lay in pleats of wrinkles on his neck and hands. He wore a starched and neatly ironed gray work shirt and pants that were a size too big for him.

"Padre asked me to look in on you and I thought that was a good idea. I hope I'm not disturbing you."

"No, no, thank you for coming." Aside from Padre Ibarra, he was the only visitor I had had.

"I came because I wanted to talk to you about mental illness hoping that some of the things I have to say will help you when you leave here. Would that be alright with you?"

"Sure." I would have welcomed anyone coming to visit with me and wanting to talk to me.

"For many years, I lived in the mountains of Chiapas in southern Mexico. I was a *curandero* there. There were no doctors or pharmacies in those mountains. I treated people with herbs and plants and advice that came from treating similar illnesses. There was mental illness in those mountains too, and I treated many of those people well enough, I suppose, so that after a while people with mental illnesses were brought to me or came to see me from great distances.

"But I want to be clear. I said I treated people with mental illness. I did not say that I cured people with mental illness. Because there is no cure for mental illness. That's right. No cure. It's a lifelong illness that can only be treated when it returns and return it does. They say that today the illness can be kept under control by having a patient take medication. But once a patient stops taking medication or won't take medication, the illness will take over whenever it wants. It is a lifelong illness.

"There were no medications in those mountains, and after a while I became convinced that the best thing I could do for anyone suffering from this illness was to try to make that person aware of the mind's workings. No one really knows what the mind is or where it is or how it works. We do see its workings, its products, all the time. We see its fears and worries, its joys and happiness all the time. It is with us and in us twenty-four hours a day, every day. It's always working, always producing new ideas, old memories, things to be avoided, things to strive for. It is working even when we sleep. It dreams. Because people suffering from this illness were always besieged with great fear and worry, I tried to make them aware that of all the things they feared and worried over, only a very few of those fears and worries ever happened. For all of us, sick or not, the multitude of fears and worries we carry with us seldom come to pass. That was the first thing I tried to do with a person suffering from mental illness. Then I tried to convince them to deal head-on with whatever fear or worry was seriously tormenting them. To say to that fear or worry, 'Happen! Go on happen!' Let all that fear and worry happen just as the mind is presenting it! Let it happen now! Because very little of those fears and worries ever happen and the ones that do are seldom insurmountable.

"Something as simple as that seemed to help. Help. Not cure. What it seemed to do was to stop at least some of the fears and worries before they reached a stage that they were out of control.... What do you make of all that, Ramón?"

"I don't know what to make of it. Because before I got sick, before I knew what was coming, I got sick, real sick, until the medication pulled me out of it."

He wasn't satisfied with my answer and he said that he wanted to show me an exercise he taught people so they could focus on the workings of their minds. He said it would only take five minutes. Did I want to learn how to do it? I really wasn't interested. The medication was working. But he had been kind enough to visit me, the only one besides Padre Ibarra, and I said OK.

He asked me to close my eyes for five minutes and watch how my mind moved from thing to thing. During those five minutes, he wanted me to concentrate and concentrate on how my mind moved from subject to subject. I closed my eyes and he repeated, "Concentrate! Concentrate!" I did, but all I saw was a big, flat, blank screen. When I told him that, he was clearly disappointed and he stopped talking about mental illness and the mind. Instead we talked about where he had lived and who he had lived with, about when and why he had come to the United States, and what kind of work he did or had done. Then he rose and shook my hand and wished me luck and said that if I ever needed help to contact him and he gave me an address and left. I was sure that I would never see the *curandero* again.

But he returned three days later, a week before I left the hospital. He said he had been thinking of me and felt it was very important that he try to teach me his coping skill again. By then, I was counting the minutes until I could leave the hospital and get back to my life out on the streets, and I would do anything to keep from counting. So I said "OK," and closed my eyes for five minutes to his "Concentrate! Concentrate!" This time I did see the mind creating thought after thought, each thought different and taking me to different things, times, and places. When I told the *curandero* what I had seen, he was elated and asked if I would try it one more time. Yes, it had stopped me from counting.

This time he said that he wanted me to label thoughts that were positive and thoughts that were negative. By negative, he said he meant any thought that could lead to fear or worry. I said I'd try. But new and different thoughts were rising so quickly that in the time it took me to try to label one thought, three more thoughts had passed, disrupting my labeling. When I told him what had happened, he said he understood and explained that what he wanted me to see with the labeling was that negative thoughts in the mind usually far outnumber positive thoughts. This interested me, and I tried labeling again, but with the same result. He said he understood, and after a repeat of the small talk of three days before, he left. I liked the *curandero* and I appreciated his thinking of me. Still I had no reason to try or even think about his exercises again. The medication was working.

But now, sitting on the courthouse steps, it made more sense to go to the *curandero,* rather than the hospital, to ask for help. When he saw me he said, "The voices have come again?"

I nodded. That was all I could say.

"Sit, sit," taking me by the arm to a couch. "Try to calm yourself."

I sat and nodded some more.

"When did this happen? Where?"

"I was...," and then the words left me.

"Just sit and try to relax. You're safe here. Nothing will happen to you here. Speak when you want, but only if you're ready."

It was late afternoon and outside, daylight was still strong, but the little front room was almost dark. Curtains heavy with dust and years of living blocked out much of the light at the rooms two windows. The old *curandero* was sitting across from me, saying nothing. I did feel safe, and gradually the terror ebbed away until I was able to speak. I don't know how much time passed before I spoke again, but it was a good while. Then I said, "I was walking down the courthouse steps when the voices came. I had gone there to take care of a ticket when all of a sudden a voice said that they had warned me about going into business with my cousin Billy."

"What kind of business is your cousin in?"

"Oh, he...helps people buy and sell things."

"What kind of things?"

"Oh, you know, mostly used things, secondhand things."

"What do you do there?"

"I'm kind of like an errand boy. I pick up and deliver things."

"What exactly did the voices say?"

"They were kind of like scolding me for being in business with Billy."

"Are you still taking medication?"

"Yes."

"Other than today, has anything like this happened since you've been taking medication?"

"No."

"Have you been to the hospital?"

"No."

"Why did you come to me instead of the hospital?"

"I guess I was thinking that if this could happen to me while I'm taking medication, then maybe I could use your system too, for fuller protection."

"That could be good thinking except for the fact that I have never treated anyone who's already on medication. My understanding is that once this happens to someone on medication, then the medication should be changed or the dosage should be increased. I think that's the best way for you to proceed right now. If after you've tried that and that doesn't work, then we can talk again."

"So what are you telling me?"

"That you should return to the hospital and report what's happened and ask for additional treatment."

"But it's late now."

"No, not that late. You've been here a little more than two hours. But you're calm now and I'm sure there are doctors on duty at the hospital twenty-four hours a day, every day."

I LIVED just a few blocks from the *curandero* and I made my way home without incident. The hospital was still not an option. I knew the people at the hospital had to report some things to the police, and they just might guess what Billy was doing and that I was connected to him. I was no longer living in Mrs. Ortega's house but rather, with the money that Billy was paying me, I had rented the two-room, spindly apartment that had been tacked on to the roof of her old garage in the backyard. It was just after eight when I walked up the driveway toward the garage. The front house was dark. Mrs. Ortega was already in bed and maybe asleep. Either way, she wouldn't be much help if the voices returned. I quietly went up the apartment stairs and immediately turned on the lights in the two rooms. Then I checked out the closet and the bathroom. No one there. I hadn't eaten since morning but I wasn't hungry, and I knew I wouldn't be able to sleep. I had to tell Billy about Danny Bencomo, but I couldn't let Billy see me in this condition.

If he did, he might get rid of me and I'd have to go back to living in the room in the front house and eating at Taco Bell and McDonald's day in and day out. I knew I had to calm myself and try to get some sleep.

By ten o'clock, I was in worse shape than I had been in the afternoon. Every creak in the old garage, every shift in the wind outside, or the brushing of a tree branch against a window, froze me with fear that the voices were starting. Waiting for them to come, expecting them to come, seemed as bad as their actual coming. I was losing it. I was about to break *without* the voices. Finally, sometime after ten thirty, after one more bout of fear, I hurried down the stairs and out to the sidewalk on my way to the hospital

Calm came over me when I entered the empty waiting room at the hospital. Somewhere behind the closed door to the rest of the Emergency Room, a bell signaled my arrival. I took a seat relieved, rehearsing and repeating what I would say to the doctor. A minute passed, another and then another and another, and no one came out to the waiting room and I could hear nothing and no one anywhere. I started to panic. I got up and opened and closed the entry door and heard a bell ring again somewhere behind the closed door. I waited. No one came. I waited some more. Then I jolted up and went to the entry door and went in and out, in and out, several times as the bell rang nonstop behind the closed door. Finally, a nurse appeared.

"What's going on out here?"

"I've been trying and trying to get somebody's attention out here! That's what's going on out here!"

"Calm down! Calm down, mister! We have a skeleton crew on tonight and we've been swamped. The doctor will be with you shortly."

"I don't know how much longer I can wait!"

"What seems to be the problem?"

"I'm hearing voices again! Three months ago I was in the psychiatric ward here for two months! You people gave me medication and it's not working and I'm hearing voices again!"

"Calm down and I'll get your file, and the doctor will be with you as soon as he can. What's your name?" Then she left.

I waited and waited for what seemed like forever. I knew the voices would get to me before the doctor did. I was about to start opening and closing the entry door again when a doctor did come and I told him about the voice that afternoon.

"Are you hearing a voice or voices now?"

"No."

"Have you heard them since this afternoon?"

"No."

"What exactly did the voices say?"

"They said that they had warned me not to get another ticket."

"Another ticket? What kind of ticket?"

"A traffic ticket."

"A traffic ticket?"

"Yes, but I had a whole bunch of them. So many that the judge was thinking about putting me in jail for a long time."

He looked like he didn't believe me. Then he looked at my file for a long time, and he said, "Well, there's no question you've had auditory hallucinations. But this recent one is strange indeed. When you were here, your doctor was Dr. Phillips, correct?"

"Yes."

"I'm going to increase your medication for a week. And I want you to make an appointment to see Dr. Phillips—the nurse will do that for you—a week from today. With this increased medication we should have a better understanding of what's going on here. Okay?"

"Yes, Doctor."

"How did you get here?"

"I walked."

"Walked?"

"Yeah, I don't have a car. But I don't live too far from here."

"The reason I ask is that I didn't want you, and don't want you, driving anywhere once you've taken the extra dosage. Just wait until you get home to take it. This extra dose will probably make you drowsy and put you to sleep quickly. Okay?"

"Yes, Doctor."

I WOKE from a deep sleep. Everything was silent and still. It took a few moments to know where I was—not in the front house but in the apartment above the garage. I listened. Nothing, no one. The sun was coming in across the room through the window to my left. That startled me. I sat up and looked at the window. That was an afternoon sun, a whole day after the courthouse and Danny Bencomo. I swung out of bed. I had to get to Billy. I had to tell him, warn him. I got dressed. But even though I was in a hurry I stopped and checked myself. My head was clear and strong, my breath was clean, and my eyes were sharp. That extra medication had worked. I didn't shower or eat. I had to get to Billy. I was about to leave when I saw that my hair was standing up and out in different directions. I stopped and brushed it. Not much luck. I combed it. No better. I splashed my head with water. My hair stayed down, and I brushed it further down more and left.

Billy's house wasn't far from the courthouse, maybe five blocks. Once I got past the courthouse and the jail and the police building and a few more county buildings, I could see it three blocks away, and I was sure the extra medication had stopped the voices. The house sat out there by itself in the middle of nothing. The city had torn down all the houses around it, but nobody knew why the city had left Billy's house standing there by itself. When I'd ask Billy why his house was the only one they hadn't torn down, he'd smile and say he didn't know and he didn't care. When I'd ask him how he got the house, he'd smile too but say, "That's personal information, Little Brother." He liked to look at me and smile and say, "That's personal information, Little Brother," about many things. He lived in that house alone and loved living in it. He used to say that no one could sneak up on him there, that he could see anyone coming on foot or in a car blocks away.

It was almost one thirty and hot when I got to his house. He must have seen me coming because the front door was wide open and the screen door was unlatched. When I knocked, he yelled from somewhere in the house, "Come on in, Little Brother, it's open!" I didn't go in. I didn't want to go in. I didn't want to talk about anything in that house, not after what Danny Bencomo had said. That house had to be bugged. Billy had to sleep and when his lights went out or he went out, what was to stop the narcs from bugging it then? We needed to talk, but not in that house.

I knocked again.

"Come on in, dammit!" he yelled. "Are you deaf? Come in! The screen door's not latched!"

I didn't move. I waited a few seconds and then I knocked again.

"Shit!" he yelled. And then I could hear and feel him coming on the old wood floors. When he reached me, he flung open the screen door and bracing himself on the doorframe shoved his upper body toward me until his face was inches from mine. Then he said, "Are you fucking deaf or have you just gone plain—"

And he stopped. He knew how much I hated the word. "Are you OK?" he said quietly.

"Yeah, I'm OK."

"Taking your meds?"

"Yeah."

"Then why didn't you come in? I was yelling like hell. You had to have heard me."

"We have to talk."

"Well talk. Come on in and talk."

"Not here."

"Why can't we talk here?"

I looked at him and shook my head ever so slightly, which stopped him.

BILLY CISNEROS and I had grown up together in Malaga. His mother and my mother were sisters. Even though Billy was three years older than me, we had been very close. We played together, ate together, and, at times, slept together. During the school year we took those long rides on the school bus together, to and from the Parker schools. But when my grandmother and I moved to Parker, I didn't see much of Billy anymore. The school I went to wasn't the school the school bus took him to. When I started taking care of the Malaga church on Saturdays, he was never around. His mother always said that he was working with his father at a ranch near Visalia. It was a long time before I found out that wasn't true. Actually he had run away from home and had gotten into some serious trouble with a gang and had been sent to the Youth Authority.

Growing up, people not only mistook us for brothers but for twins. Same build, same facial features, color, everything. But when he went to the Youth Authority and prison, and I got sick, there were definite changes. He came back buffed, huge, a body builder with a lot of extra weight that changed his facial features. He said he had to change in there, to keep them from making a punk out of him. I came back from my sickness skinnier than ever with a lot of lines all over my face. We didn't look like twins anymore.

"WHERE DO you want to talk?"

"Over in the park." The narcs couldn't wire a whole park.

"Which one?"

"The one on Calaveras Street."

"How do you want to get there?"

"I'll walk and I'll act like I'm saying goodbye. They're probably watching us with binoculars right now. You drive but wait a while before you start. That will give us a chance to get there about the same time."

"OK, I'll start toward town, which will make it impossible for any one to follow me without me knowing it."

"It'll probably take me fifteen minutes to get there."

"OK, I'll see you in fifteen minutes."

When I got to the park, Billy wasn't there. But then I didn't expect him to be there. Then it came to me, he was always late, always had one more thing to do before he got to me. While I was sitting on a park bench waiting for Billy, for the first time since meeting with Danny Bencomo, I asked myself why was I choosing to live in fear of the narcs when I already had so many other fears to deal with? Working for Billy didn't seem to make sense anymore. If I quit working for him all it would mean was that I would have to move back to that little room in Mrs. Ortega's house and eat at McDonald's and Taco Bell. That seemed much easier than worrying about the day the narcs would catch me with Billy and send me to prison. And I wouldn't have to worry about going to Malaga. Going to Malaga had been a big part of my life. I used to get satisfaction going there. Now I knew I would be worrying about going there every time I went.

MALAGA WAS what was left of a dusty little village eleven miles from Parker that Mexican farmworkers had built in the 1940s and '50s as shelter against the winters when there was no work in the fields. The houses were mostly lean-tos the workers had built themselves, and the roads were simply big dirt paths they had made bigger. The best and sturdiest structure in Malaga was a tiny church the workers had built from weathered brown planks they had taken from a torn-down barn on a nearby ranch. The church had three pews on each side of a center aisle that ran up to a small altar that had been set on the back wall with a gold-painted tabernacle mounted at the center. Behind the wall was a small room called the sacristy, where the chalice, the monstrance, and the priest's vestments were kept and where the priest changed for Mass. A door at the end of the altar on the right opened onto the sacristy. There were three plain windows on each of the two side walls, and above them were small plaques showing the twelve stations of the cross. Over the entry doors hung a crucifix with a blood-soaked Christ. The only other religious article in the church was a large, framed picture of Jesus with his flaming, bleeding Heart. The church in Parker had the same framed picture, but for some reason, the flaming, bleeding, thorn-bound Heart of Jesus in Malaga put a fear and dread in me that the one in Parker never did. Even as a boy, I avoided looking at the Malaga Jesus as best I could. In Malaga it always seemed that He was pointing and staring at me as if I were the one who had caused Him so much pain and suffering.

The priest, Padre Hugo Ibarra, had been sent from Spain to pastor the ever-increasing number of Spanish-speaking people in California's Central Valley. That was a huge assignment. His part of the Central Valley stretched from Bakersfield to Parker. Yet Padre Ibarra tried his best to say Mass in Malaga's little church twice a month. I lived in Malaga with my grandmother until I was fourteen, and for eight of those years, I was Padre Ibarra's altar boy whenever he managed to say Mass in Malaga. We left Malaga because my grandmother needed to be near the county hospital and its doctors in Parker. Padre Ibarra's rectory was in Parker, and for the next year and a half before my grandmother's death, whenever he said Mass in Malaga he would take me with him to serve as his altar boy.

When I turned sixteen, Padre Ibarra gave me a job as caretaker of the little church in Malaga. Every Saturday morning, regardless of whether or not Padre Ibarra was going to say Sunday Mass in Malaga, I took a local, southbound Greyhound bus to Malaga and the church fifteen minutes away. There I would sweep, dust, and mop the church and take care of the plants outside. Two years later when my grandmother died, Padre Ibarra found an old, church-going couple who agreed to give me a home until I graduated from high school, several months away. I was well on my way to my break then. When my break came, it so frightened the old folks that they asked Padre Ibarra to find me another place to live.

Before my break, the old folks had given me an old Chevy that I had finally gotten running. Two weeks after my release from the hospital while driving the Chevy, I came to a light-controlled intersection. The light had been green, but as I entered the intersection the light turned yellow and at the same moment I felt the Chevy's engine dying. I stepped down on the gas pedal not wanting to get stuck in the intersection. The Chevy started jerking, huge jerks, and was barely moving when the next thing I knew was that we had hit the rear fender of a flashy red car crossing the intersection on a green light. The red car spun around and skidded to a stop on the other side of the intersection. The Chevy had stopped dead in the intersection, and as much as I tried, I couldn't get it started. Out of the corner of my eye I saw the driver of the red car running toward me. I acted as if I hadn't seen him, and I filled my mind and mouth with apologies and explanations. But I could hear him cussing a wild streak as he came closer. When he got to the Chevy, he flung open my door and started pulling me out. Then he stopped and shouted, "Ray! Ray!" and hugged me. It was Billy.

A man came up to Billy and said, "I saw the whole thing, mister. This guy ran a red light and almost killed you. You want I should call the police?"

Billy turned to him and said, "Get lost, buddy. This is a family matter and it's just been settled. You call the police and I'll kick your ass." The man left apologizing.

We pushed the Chevy off the road, and Billy insisted that I go with him over to his house. "We got a lot of catching up to do," he said.

I must have apologized ten times but Billy always answered with, "Don't worry about it, Little Brother, I've got a body and fender man that will make it look like new in two days."

I had never been in such a luxurious car. It purred as we drove, and I had absolutely no idea what all those gadgets were for on the dashboard. And Billy's muscular build and full face also took some getting used to.

"So what have you been up to?"

"I had a nervous breakdown."

"That's what my mom said. She doesn't live in Malaga any more, but that's what some of the people there told her. So what happened after your breakdown?"

"They had me in the Parker County Hospital for two months, and they just let me out two weeks ago. What about you?"

"You feeling OK now?"

"Yeah, yeah. I got to be taking medication now but I'm alright. So what about you?"

"After you left Malaga, I dropped out of school and started running with some pretty bad people. One of them turned out to be a snitch and somebody murdered him. They couldn't prove who did it, so they gave all of us a bunch of time. I did three years in the Youth Authority and two years in prison."

"Wow."

"No, that turned out to be a good thing. I learned a lot in both places and met good people. Now I've got some good connections."

Billy drove to and through downtown and about half a mile later, I saw a huge clearing where houses used to be. "What happened to all the houses?"

"They got some really big planes landing at the airport now and to let those big planes land, they had to take the houses out."

A minute later Billy said, "That's my house over there," pointing to an old, beige stucco house two blocks away in the middle of nothing.

"You live there?"

"Yeah, that's where I live."

"But there's nothing there.... How'd you get that house?"

"That's personal information, Little Brother."

"You like living here all by yourself?"

"Not only do I like it, I love it!"

He parked his sporty, red car under the house in a space that took up a good part of his basement. I got out of the car and looked back at the smashed fender wondering how I was going to pay for that.

"Don't worry about it. Like I said, I got a great body and fender man that'll make it look better than new in a couple of days, and he owes me a lot of favors."

When I went in his house, I gasped. I had never seen anything like it. Big, stuffed leather couches and chairs on a soft, blue rug inches thick. Tables of glass on chrome. In the dining room there was a gigantic, polished wooden table with matching chairs and a bar stacked with a lot of different bottles. His bedroom was black. Black carpet, black velvet drapes that hung from the ceiling to the floor, hiding the only windows in the room. A black bedspread and black pillows covered the bed. One of the walls was painted black. Wall-to-wall mirrors covered the other two walls and the ceiling. The kitchen was filled with stainless-steel appliances.

"Jesus, Billy, where's all the money coming from?" I kept repeating.

He didn't answer until I asked, "Where you working, Billy?"

"I'm working supervising...facilitating."

"Supervising what? Facilitating what?"

"Merchandise."

"What kind of merchandise?"

"That's personal information, Little Brother."

"Billy, you just got out of the joint and you're involved again. How much time do you think the judge will give you this time?"

"Involved in what?"

"In drugs."

"Little Brother, you can search every inch of this house and basement and car and me. You can take a blood sample from me if you want, and I guarantee you that you won't find a trace of any drug anywhere."

"So where's all this money coming from?"

"I told you, I'm a facilitator. I facilitate things. I met a lot of good, savvy people over the past five years and I learned a lot. I learned so much that all I have to do is facilitate and not get my hands dirty in any way. So why don't you relax and have a seat. We're cousins, we're blood, and we used to be best friends, remember? I'd like to have that again. We've got a lot to talk about. Can I get you something to drink?"

"Thanks, Billy, but I can't. I'm on medication and those two things don't mix. If I don't have my meds, I'm gonna be in a real bad way again. I don't need that and I don't want that. Believe me."

"I can respect that.... Water?"

"Yeah, that's good."

We talked some that afternoon, but mostly we sat and listened to music. The sounds that came out of his new sound system were beyond me. I could hear *everything,* such as I had never heard or thought possible. We listened to some old *rancheras* that we had heard as kids, some rock music, and some music that Billy said was "instrumental" and that I liked. I started seeing Billy at his house a few days a week, and he like everybody else, asked me not to park my Chevy in front of his house.

Billy was always gone on Mondays and Tuesdays, something we never talked about. And after my break, I was taking care of the Malaga church again on Thursdays and Fridays. The other days of the week, I spent some time at Billy's.

THE THURSDAYS and Fridays at the church in Malaga came out of Padre Ibarra's third and last visit with me in the hospital. He had brought the *curandero* with him, and after he introduced him and said a few things about him, the *curandero* left. Then Padre Ibarra began, "Do you remember the last time I saw you here?"

"I don't remember anything of your first visit other than you and the nurse telling me later that you had been here. I don't think the meds had kicked in yet."

"No, I'm not talking about the first visit, I'm talking about the second visit. Remember what you told me then?"

I knew what he was driving at, but it was something I didn't want to talk about or remember. It was embarrassing to me now. "Not really."

"Well let's talk about it a little. Maybe then you'll remember. Do you remember what you said to me when I first came in?"

I looked down and didn't answer.

"You greeted me by saying that now you knew who I really was. I wasn't the priest I was pretending to be. No, I was your brother and I didn't want to admit it. You said that you weren't going to call me Padre Ibarra or Padre anymore because we were both born at the same time, right next to each other behind the church. When I asked you what church, you said the little church in Malaga. Do you remember that?"

I did. But I didn't answer.

"You said that from now on my name was Pedro and your name was Enrique. I didn't react so you took it a little further. You said that since we were in the United States and not in Mexico or Spain, you were going to call me Pete and I should call you Henry. I said that was fine, and then I said, 'Henry would you like to have some coffee?' And you said, 'Sure, Pete.'

"So we went to the little vending machine in the hallway, to that small table with two chairs next to it and we sat there with our coffee. I asked you how you were feeling, and you said, 'Fine.' And you said you were going to be leaving the hospital in a day or two because you were only there for a spider bite that had gotten infected but was all cleared up. Do you remember telling me that?"

"Yes, I remember that."

"Actually, you remember all of what I've said since I got here, don't you Ramón?"

"Yes, I do, Padre. I remember all of it." I couldn't hide anymore.

"Good, because your doctor says that the medication has taken effect and that more and more you're becoming your normal self and should be out of here in two or three weeks. He says that as long as you take your medication, you'll be fine and able to do anything and everything you did before. You know that, don't you, Ramón?"

"Yes, Padre."

"Good, because there's an important matter we have to talk about and I have to be sure that you understand what I'm asking, and that you're sure about whether you can or can't do it. That is, of course, if you're willing to do it.... There's talk that I may be transferred soon."

"Transferred where, Padre?"

"At this point only God knows that. The reality is that I may not be in this parish much longer."

"Where will you go, Padre?"

"That will be decided when it's decided. But what we're talking about has to be decided now. When you get out of this hospital I want you to start taking care of the church in Malaga one day a week just like you did before your illness. Will you do that for me?"

"Oh!" I was surprised and elated.

"What's the matter?"

"Nothing except I just thought that nobody in Malaga would ever want me near that church again, because of my break."

"No, I've talked to your doctor about it and he thinks it would be a very good thing for you to do again.... I've had some of the people who live there take care of it during your illness and I'm very dissatisfied with them. In fact, I've talked to the people in Malaga and told them that the doctor and I think it would be very good for you to return to your work taking care of the church there. I've explained your illness to them as best I could and said that everyone here thinks there is no chance that what happened there that night will ever happen again."

"But what if I go there and something happens to me there again?"

"Your doctor doesn't think that's a problem. He says that many, many people have their breaks in their homes and return there once they're on medication and stabilized, like you are now, without any problems. Besides I'm not asking you to go live there. I'm just asking that you go there for a few hours one day a week, like you have already been doing for almost three years, and then return here to Parker where you'll be living in a private home that the people in the hospital have already arranged for you."

"And where will you be, Padre, when I get out of here?"

"I may be here and I may be gone by then. I just don't know. And for that reason I'm going to give you the keys to the church now. These are the same keys you always got at the rectory on Saturdays before you went to Malaga. Keep them with you until the new priest comes to Parker, and then take them to him and tell him what you've been doing, and let him decide what he wants to do about the Malaga church. Will you do this for me?"

"Yes."

"You'll be needing money for the bus fare and the little extra spending money I used to give you for your work. If I'm not here when you get out, you'll probably find Mrs. Ramirez more at her house than at the rectory, and she will be the one who will be giving you the money for the bus and your work. Any questions?"

"No, but I'll do it."

"Good. The doctor thinks this will be a good thing for you to do."

Three days before my release, Amalia, the woman who brought me my meals and cleaned my room, said, with my breakfast tray in her hands, "Padre Ibarra died yesterday."

"What?"

"Yes, he had cancer but he kept working until he was real sick, and they say that all he asked the Bishop for was to let him go back to Spain to die. He took an airplane to Spain two days ago and they say that once the airplane landed in Spain and he was still in the airport, he collapsed and died."

TWO DAYS after I left the hospital, I went to Malaga. I took the morning local Greyhound there and came back on the afternoon local. Malaga was not a designated stop. If you were on the bus, you had to approach the driver at least a mile away and tell him that you wanted off at Malaga. Then he would pull off the highway onto a big patch of hardpan that had been cleared of dirt by years of buses arriving and leaving. If you were waiting for a bus going in either direction, you would stand on the edge of the highway and begin waving as soon as you could see one coming. The only sign of life near the hardpan was a little ramshackle building a block away with a crude, hand-painted sign that hung over it's door saying ABARROTES instead of GROCERIES. Doña Petra, a round little woman in her sixties, was the store's sole proprietor and clerk, and any time a bus stopped, she would post herself at her doorway to see who was getting off or on. Malaga's church and sixteen houses were on top of a small hill a block and a half from the highway.

It was late September the day that I arrived, and the heat and dust were still at their peaks and would remain there into October. When Doña Petra saw me getting off the bus, she spun around and disappeared into her store. When I reached the top of the incline, Don Rogelio Rodriguez was standing in the middle of the dirt road waiting for me. There were only two telephones in Malaga: one in Doña Petra's store and the other in Don Rogelio's home. He was a thin, dried-out, devout man in his seventies who had known me for many years.

"What do you want here?" he said.

"I don't want anything."

"Then what are doing here again?"

"Padre Ibarra asked me to take care of the church again."

"Padre Ibarra is dead."

"Yes, I know. But before he died, he asked me to look after the church the way I did for almost three years. And he told me he had told you folks that I would be coming out here again to take care of the church."

"Padre Ibarra was a sick man when he talked to us. I don't think he knew what he was saying and I don't think he really meant for you to come back here."

"Well," I said pulling out a ring of keys, "these are the keys to the church. Padre Ibarra gave them to me so I would take care of the church. I don't think anybody here has a set of these keys. Do they?"

The keys upset him. "I don't think Padre Ibarra gave you those keys. He knows what happened the last time you were here."

"Where do you think Padre Ibarra is right now?"

"He's dead."

"Is he in heaven or hell?"

"What does that have to do with anything?"

"You *know* he's in heaven, don't you...? So do you think he would for one second let me lie to you like this, or dangle these keys in front of you like this, if what I've told you isn't true? He would have already put a curse on me if I was lying about something like his church, wouldn't he? He would have had me struck down by now if I was lying. Wouldn't he?"

Don Rogelio's eyes swelled and he was breathing hard. He turned, and as he started to walk away, he said, "We don't want any more trouble here."

The little church was hot, stuffy, and dusty. I started by opening all the windows. As I did I saw at the back of the church in a corner, the old army duffel bag Padre Ibarra had given me. It was stuffed full of clothes and had part of a shirt and a sweater hanging out of the top end. I had been wearing that shirt and sweater the night of my break and that night wanted to return. But I had been extra careful to take my medication that morning. I knew then that without my medication, my mind had no walls. With it I could set up walls. I shook my head and said to my mind, "I don't want to think about that night. I don't want to think about that night." And I didn't.

It took me a little more than three hours to clean, dust, and mop the inside of the church and to sweep around the church outside and water the plants there. Several times I had to say to my mind, "I don't want to go back there." And we didn't. When I was finished, I walked back down to the highway with my full duffel bag. It was a long three-hour wait for the bus back to Parker, and during those three hours, as well as the three hours I had spent at the church, I neither saw nor spoke to anyone other than Don Rogelio.

That was how it was to be for the next three months: seeing no one, hearing no one, and speaking to no one. Some of the sixteen houses were vacant and would remain vacant until the late fall brought an end to the work in the fields. But some of the houses had people in them, people too old or too frail to work in the fields. And though I never saw or heard them, I could feel their eyes watching me, especially the eyes of the two sisters across from the church and the eyes of Don Rogelio in the house next to theirs, watching my every move.

After a month, it didn't matter how much they watched or didn't watch or how much they said or didn't say to me because it was then that I decided to catch the Thursday afternoon local to Malaga and spend the night in the church and catch the Friday morning local back to Parker. On those Thursdays I carried my duffel bag with me with enough food, blankets, and a change of clothes to get me through twenty hours. The reason for the change was mainly the situation I had at Mrs. Ortega's house. My room there was very small and cramped and Mrs. Ortega had little to do with me other than to collect the rent money. And aside from my room, I didn't feel comfortable in any other part of the house. She was wary of me and let it show. In Malaga the church was ten times the size of my room and I had it all to myself, as well as the garden that I had planted behind it. I slept in the sacristy behind the altar because it had no windows and was as private as I could be in the church.

One day, Billy offered to drive me out to Malaga the following Thursday.

"Why?"

"Because I'd like to see what it's like now."

"It's pretty sad looking. It looks deserted."

"That's OK. We grew up there and it's been years since I've been out there and I'm curious, that's all."

"OK."

The following Thursday afternoon, Billy drove me and my duffel bag out to Malaga. When we arrived, Billy said, "Wow! This place does look deserted—falling apart. It looks like a ghost town. Is anybody here now?"

"There's people here. The old ones and the frail ones who can't work anymore. And believe me, they're watching us right now, watching everything we do."

"How do you know that?"

"The store's still open and Doña Petra wouldn't be open if nobody lived here. And the first day I came back here, old Don Rogelio stopped me on the road and pretty much said they didn't want me here anymore."

Billy and his mom weren't churchgoers, and once we were in the church nothing interested him until we reached the sacristy. "What's that?" he asked, pointing to the floor and the trapdoor with a padlock on it.

"We keep the chalice and monstrance down there."

"What's a monstrance?"

"It's that big, gold leaf-like thing that the priest puts the Holy Host in and keeps it on the altar kind of like to remind the people that this is the House of God."

"Why are they kept down there?"

"Because they're both made of gold and probably the only things worth stealing here."

"Can I see them?"

I hesitated, thought, and then could see no harm in letting Billy see them. I unlocked the trapdoor, opened it, and knelt down next to the opening and pulled out the chalice and the monstrance, and I stood and showed them to Billy.

Billy looked at them briefly; then he went to the opening and knelt down next to it, lowered his head into it, and looked in every direction. When he stood he said, "Boy, there's a big space down there, five or six feet anyway. I bet you could put a lot of things in it."

"You could, but the only things worth stealing here are the chalice and the monstrance."

A few days later, Billy wanted to talk about the space under the trapdoor.

"Ray, how would you like to earn a few extra bucks every week?"

"Doing what?"

"Just taking care of a gym bag for me."

"Billy, I don't want to get involved with any drugs."

"Did I say anything about drugs?"

"No, but what's gonna be in the bag?"

"Money."

"Money? How much money?"

"A lot of money. But the bag will always have a lock on it. So nobody, except those who are supposed to know, will ever be able to tell how much money is in it. And it won't take much to see if anybody's been tampering with the bag or not."

"Whose money is it?"

"Some of it will be mine and some of it will not be mine."

"What's it for? Where's it coming from?"

"Some of it is my pay for being a facilitator. Remember when I told you I made my money by facilitating things? I don't deal drugs, if that's what you're worried about. I don't touch drugs. I just make things happen, and I get paid good money for it because I know how to make things happen in a way that very few people can."

"So how am I supposed to take care of that bag?"

"Well I can't keep the money here or put it in the bank. If I put it in the bank it wouldn't be long before the cops and the bank would say I was doing something illegal. If I kept all that money here, sooner or later the word would get out or someone would figure out that I must have a lot of money here and it wouldn't be long before some assholes would bust into my house and bust me and take every damn cent."

"So what am I supposed to do with all this money you're talking about?"

"Hold on. Let me tell you, let me tell you what I'd like you to do. Every Wednesday someone is gonna put one of these gym bags in a locker at the Greyhound depot and get me the key to that locker. You take the Greyhound to Malaga every Thursday afternoon, and before you go, you'll get that key from me. When you get to the Greyhound depot, you'll take the bag out of the locker and put it in your duffel bag and go to Malaga like you always do. And who's gonna be the wiser? Once you're at the church in Malaga, put the bag in the space under the trapdoor and lock it up again. No one's ever gonna guess that there are gym bags stuffed with money under the floor of a church in Malaga."

"Gym bags? How did we get to bags? I thought it was a gym bag, one gym bag, full of money,"

"Well, every week you do this, I'll give you one hundred dollars cash when you get back here on Friday."

"Every week? So how many weeks am I supposed to be doing this?"

"Well, let's see how it works. But to start with, you'll be taking a gym bag out of those lockers once a week for four weeks and keeping them under the trapdoor for four weeks."

"Then what happens?"

"Then on the Friday morning of the fourth week, I want you to put all those bags in your duffel bag. Four bags will fit in a bag like yours. I've already tried it. And leave the church with your duffel bag and the four bags inside of it. But leave fifteen minutes before you usually do and go to the bus stop like you usually do, but fifteen minutes early. As soon as you get there, somebody will drive up in a nice car and say, "Where's that duffel bag you're supposed to give me?" He'll open his trunk and you'll put the duffel bag in the man's trunk, and he'll drive off. Won't even take a minute."

"And who is this guy that's gonna drive up and take my bag?"

"I don't know. I don't even know what he looks like or what he'll be driving. But these people know what they're doing. He'll actually be parked somewhere close by so he can see when you get there, and then BOOM, he's right there."

"So what happens to my duffel bag if he actually takes it?"

"I'll have a new one for you when you stop by to get paid. Same size. It'll look like your old one but be a lot better quality."

"So how long is this supposed to keep going?"

"Well, let's see how it works first and then we can talk about that. So what do you say, Little Brother? Do you want to earn a hundred bucks a week for taking a gym bag from the Greyhound depot to the Malaga church? That's almost as much as you get for disability, isn't it...? So what do you say, Little Brother, are you in? Are you up for earning a hundred dollars for carrying a gym bag from a locker to the bus and from the bus to the church? A hundred dollars for fifteen minutes of work."

Billy was staring at me. The hundred dollars was whirling around in my head. The hundred dollars and all the things I could do with it. But I was scared. Finally, I said, "I don't know Billy... Billy, all the stuff you have here... You've only been out of the joint less than a year and you don't have a real job and yet you have all this money. Where's it coming from? What's it for? Anybody looking at all the stuff you got is gonna flat out think that you got something illegal going. Drugs, most people would say. So if I go in with you and you get busted, I could probably get busted too. And from what I hear, people with my kind of problem don't need to be getting locked up. That's the last thing they need."

"Ray... Look at me. I don't know what I have to do or say to convince you that what I'm doing is not illegal. True, I don't have a nine-to-five job. But what I do have are connections. I know how to get people together, how to make things happen. People pay me for that. Pay me good money for that. Now, what those people I get together do, after I've gotten them together, is none of my business. Nor do I want to make it any of my business. So how am I going to get arrested? For what am I going to get arrested? And I don't know how in the hell you're gonna get arrested either just for putting a duffel bag in a safe place."

I wanted to believe Billy. I wanted to work for my cousin and my best friend. And I wanted that money too. But I was scared. "Billy let me think about this. Let me think about it until tomorrow morning."

As I walked home my mind wouldn't let me be. That car, that house, that furniture and sound system, the clothes he was wearing and that gold watch, all for introducing one person to another?

Do you really believe that, Ray?

"Billy wouldn't lie to me," I kept repeating and repeating.

When I reached Mrs. Ortega's house, I saw the sign on the front lawn and stopped and looked at it. I knew what it said. I had seen it maybe fifty times before but I had never stopped and looked at it as I did then. I knew what it had to say even before I saw it for the first time. Because the woman at the hospital, who had made the arrangement for my room with Mrs. Ortega, had told me about it. "She also has a small apartment for rent. You'll see the sign on the front lawn when you leave here. It's a nice little apartment over her garage in the back. I looked at it. It would be perfect for you, Raymond. It has a well-kept kitchen, a bedroom, and a front room. But it would have taken more than half of your monthly disability check. So I told her that you wouldn't be interested." Now I looked at the three words on the sign, APARTMENT FOR RENT, again and again, and I also looked at the apartment over the garage and then the back porch of the house that had the tiny room I was living in.

The next day I said, "I'll do it, Billy, I'll do it. I'll take those bags to Malaga. But I'm going to need a hundred dollars in advance to make a deposit on an apartment."

"That's not a problem, Little Brother."

"You know when the new priest comes, I have to take the keys over to him."

"But nobody else has the keys to that church, do they?"

"I'm pretty sure they don't because I used to get the keys from the rectory, and Padre Ibarra always used to tell me not to lose them because they were the only set of keys he had. And those were the keys he gave me at the hospital."

"My mom tells me that the people in Malaga don't think their church will be reopened. They say that there are too many other people in too many other bigger churches in the Valley for one priest to take care of. Anyway we'll deal with that when the time comes, if it ever comes."

No sooner had I left Billy with a hundred dollars in my pocket, when my mind went to work again. How could I be storing bags of money in the House of God? That struck me and scared me. But only for a few moments, because I remembered what Padre Ibarra had said when he took me to the Malaga church that night until he could find me another home. "Live here as you would live anywhere else. There's no consecrated Host here. Only then does this become the House of God. Only then would I hesitate to let you live here even temporarily." But my mind wouldn't let up. How could I store money beside the chalice and monstrance? I brushed this one aside because neither the chalice nor the monstrance were holy until a consecrated Host was placed in them.

Besides, I had already planned to put the gym bags down there as far away from the chalice and monstrance as I could.

The first four weeks of moving the gym bags to and under the Malaga sacristy went smoothly, even though each bag gave me a new scare from Wednesday night to Friday morning. At the end of the fourth week, a well-dressed man in an expensive new car pulled up at the bus stop a minute after I got there and said, "Where's that duffel bag you have for me?"

"Right here," I answered.

"Good, put it in the trunk." He opened the trunk and I laid the duffel bag in it. Then he closed the trunk lid and drove off, just as smoothly as that.

THREE WEEKS later, I was sitting on a park bench waiting for Billy, wondering where he was. Waiting for Billy could irritate me, but on that Tuesday afternoon as I sat on a Calaveras Street park bench, I wasn't irritated. If anything, I was thankful because this time his delay had given me enough time to decide once and for all that I couldn't keep taking those money bags to Malaga. Seven weeks was enough. Whether Billy was lying to me or being completely truthful didn't matter. The fact was I couldn't stop being afraid of those bags and I didn't know just how much more fear I wanted to take.

When Billy finally arrived, he parked his big, red sports car just a few yards from me, and when he got out of his car, he was smiling and chuckling to himself.

"Jesus, Billy, did you have to park so fucking close to me?"

"What's the matter with you? Who gives a shit where I park?"

"We go through all this trouble to meet here to talk so that nobody can hear us or see us talking, and then you go and park right next to me."

"Look, we could have talked at my place. But you're so goddamn paranoid that you won't talk there. What the hell are you so afraid of?"

"Your place is bugged."

"Bugged? Where the fuck did you get that from?"

"I got that from Danny Bencomo. Remember Danny Bencomo from school? He's not just a cop now, he's a narc. And he says you're a big dope dealer and that your dope is killing people on the streets."

"What?" he said with a dry chuckle.

I told Billy about my run-in with Danny Bencomo at the courthouse. When I finished, Billy let out a big belly laugh. But there was nothing funny in it.

"There's not one goddamn thing that Bencomo punk can prove against me. He's just jealous, Little Brother. He sees me driving around in my fine sports car with a gorgeous woman cuddled up against me, and he can't take it. He knows I'm making more money in a day than he makes in a month. He'll always be on the city payroll, a civil servant all his fucking life. He'll always drive that shitty little Chevrolet of his or one like it and live in his little tract home all his life. And his wife will have to have her crappy job with the county to help support those three or four kids they have. I've put his ass down in every way possible. I've gone way beyond him and will keep going further and further beyond him and he can't take it. That's what I think of his petty bullshit about me being a big dope dealer and all the other lies he told you."

"Billy, I'm not saying that I believe Bencomo. You've told me a hundred times that you're not involved with drugs and I haven't seen any sign of drugs around you. If they had all that Bencomo said they had, I think they would have arrested you by now. That's not it, Billy. I just don't like being scared all the time. I plain don't like it. And I'm scared shitless that I could end up in jail, and that's no place for people like me. So I have to stop doing it. As innocent as you probably are, I have to stop being scared."

"Ray, do you think I would put you in a spot where you could be arrested?"

"No."

"And you hit the nail on the head. If they really had anything on me, especially about murders, they would've arrested me by now."

On and on we went until I said, "Billy, I guess I'm not making myself clear. I'm scared and I can't stop being scared doing the bags. It's not good for me to be scared all the time. If I break again, the shrinks are going to be asking me again and again what led up to the break. There's no telling what I'd tell them then, but for sure it would be about the bags of money. And they have to report stuff like that to the police. And no matter what you're doing or not doing, the cops will come after you about those bags of money."

That made Billy stop, and for a while nothing was said. Then Billy said, "Okay, Ray, you can quit. But just do me one more big favor. Just take one more bag to Malaga on Thursday and put the four bags in the man's car on Friday, and that will be the end of it. Because everything's in motion for Thursday and Friday and I can't stop it now. And if it doesn't go through, I could be in big trouble. So just do this last one for me, please."

"And that'll be it?"

"That'll be it."

"OK."

I didn't sleep well Wednesday night. I was still scared and wanted Thursday and Friday to come and be over as soon as possible. I'd wake up every fifteen, twenty, or thirty minutes and look at the clock. It had never moved slower. I got up way before 6:00. It was still dark, but I couldn't stay in bed any longer. I showered and dressed and shaved but it was only 6:10. I just wanted to get this thing over with. I tried to eat breakfast but the cereal tasted like paper. I wanted to go to Billy's house for the locker key as early as I could. The earlier the better, the fewer people there'd be on the streets and the fewer people who would see me walking across those empty blocks to Billy's house. But I couldn't wake him before 7:00. He'd blow a gasket if I did.

At 7:01, I was knocking on Billy's door. I couldn't feel or hear anything inside the house so I knocked harder. What if he wasn't home? What if he didn't have the locker key yet? How I wanted that day and the next to be over. I pounded on the door. Then I felt some movement and I heard him yell, "Stop pounding, god-damn it! Stop pounding!" I could feel him coming.

"Who is it, goddamn it?"

"It's me, Billy."

"What the fuck are you doing pounding on my door at this hour?" The door opened.

"Billy, I need the key to the locker."

"It's seven o'clock, goddamn it."

"Yeah, I know but I got to get going."

"Are you going..." He stopped himself, stared at me for a moment, and then turned and went for the key.

I waited looking around at everything and nothing, convinced that Danny Bencomo had his binoculars trained on us. Billy came back and started to hand me the key but I grabbed it from him instead and clutched it hard in my fist.

"What the fuck's the matter with you?"

"Nothing," I said, turning to go and saying as I left the porch, "I'll see you tomorrow around three."

I was back in my apartment at 7:23. My new duffel bag was packed and ready to go. I always caught an afternoon local, but that day I was going to go down to the depot in the morning and stuff the last of the gym bags in my duffel bag and catch the earliest morning local I could to Malaga. At the church I would busy myself with some of the many things that had to be done there. Better that than sitting in my apartment doing nothing except counting the minutes for the morning and early afternoon to pass.

As I was about to leave, my mind went to work.

What are you going to tell the man?

What man?

The man tomorrow morning at the bus stop.

Tell him what?

That you won't be doing it anymore.

Why should I tell him that?

Because Billy said that if this doesn't work, he's looking at some big trouble.

But that only had to do with today and tomorrow, not next week.

Don't you think you ought to at least tell the man that you won't be doing it any more?

Why?

Because he's used to dealing with you now, and if he sees somebody else at the bus stop next week, what's he going to think?

That's not my problem, that's Billy's problem.

Don't you think you should have talked to Billy about what to say or not say to the man, especially if he starts asking you questions about next week?

What Billy does is his business, not mine.

Not really. Like it or not, you're very much involved in this bags of money thing. You shouldn't have grabbed that locker key and run like you did. You should have taken a few minutes and talked to Billy about how to handle the man, what to say, and what not to say. Don't forget, he's your cousin and you say your best friend. You should go back to Billy and talk about this at least for a few minutes.

Talk to him where? His house is bugged.

You don't know that.

I'll bet anything it is.

Then talk to him out in the yard. It'll only take a few minutes.

On and on we went. My mind wasn't convincing me. On the other hand, I wasn't picking up my duffel bag and walking out the door either. Finally, I said, *OK, I'll go back and talk to him. It won't take that long.* It was just a fifteen-minute walk to Billy's and I didn't think we'd talk that much, so I could still get an early start to Malaga.

When I passed the last County building and could see Billy's house two and a half blocks away, I stopped, frozen. There were cop cars and cops all around his house. They had completely taken over his property and house, and I kept telling myself that I had to get out of the County Center before someone noticed me. I walked around the edge of the County Center as fast as I could without drawing attention to myself. No matter how I felt about Billy, at that point I did not want to be connected to him in any way.

I was just past Mrs. Ortega's driveway and about to go up the stairs to my apartment when I heard "Mr. Lopez, Mr. Lopez," the only name Mrs. Ortega ever used for me. I turned as she was coming out of her back porch door and waited.

"Yes," I said.

"Mr. Lopez, the police were just here."

"What?" My heart beat fast.

"They wanted to talk to you."

"About what?"

"I don't know."

"They knew you lived back here, but I told them you had just left. They asked where you had gone and I told them I didn't know but that I had seen you leave. They asked when you'd be back and I told them that you were always gone on Thursday until Friday afternoon. They asked what time on Friday you'd be back and I told them about three o'clock. They said they would be back then."

"That's all they said?"

"Yes."

"They didn't say what they wanted to talk to me about?"

"No."

"How were they dressed?"

"What do you mean?"

"Were they in plain clothes or in uniforms?"

"In uniforms, you know, those navy-blue uniforms."

"How many were there?"

"Just two... You can come over to the house and use my telephone if you want to call them."

"No, no. I have to get going. I have to meet someone soon. I'll call them tomorrow when I get back."

"Fine. I'll be here and you can use my telephone then."

"Did they go up to my apartment?"

"Oh, no. But they didn't ask, and I wouldn't let anyone go up there when you're gone. I really thought you were gone...with your duffel bag and all."

"My duffel bag?"

"Yes, you always take it and bring it back with you."

"Did they mention my duffel bag?"

"Oh, no. I just said that because it seems like I always see you take it when you leave and bring it back with you when you come back."

"Well, I have to get going now, Mrs. Ortega."

"But you'll be back tomorrow by three? Because that's when I told them you'd be back. And they said they'd be back then too."

"That's fine, Mrs. Ortega. But I really have to get going."

"Alright then, Mr. Lopez."

I SAT in my apartment and tried to calm myself, tried to make some sense out of all of this. The police were at Billy's. It had to be for drugs. Somebody else must have OD'ed and Danny Bencomo had said... They were busting Billy. There were so many of them and they were all over the place. Looking for something. Drugs. And now they had come here wanting to talk to me. They had to have been watching his place. They had to have seen me coming and going from Billy's all the time. They had to have been watching Billy's place with binoculars. Worse, they had to have seen me leaving Billy's place last Friday with that new duffel bag Billy had bought me, stuffed with old clothes. I looked at the duffel bag lying at the foot of the bed. What to do with it? It was made of a thick, heavy, olive canvas and actually stood up to my shoulders. It made me so noticeable anywhere I went.

I sat staring at the duffel bag. Why take it with me? Why go anywhere? I sat there in the stillness of the morning staring at the duffel bag, my mind blank.... No, I had to go to Malaga. I had to get rid of those gym bags, get rid of all that money. The chalice and monstrance were down in that space with the money. Sooner or later someone was gonna look for the chalice and monstrance and find all that money. And I, Billy's cousin, was the only one who had the keys to the church and the trapdoor. No one's gonna believe that I didn't know the money was there and what it was for. I had to get rid of that money. Then the man occurred to me, the man in the car. That money was supposed to go to him, and if it didn't then Billy, and now me, would be in big trouble. I had to get that last bag to him. And if I didn't get that money to him, he would probably get to me before the police did. Then I would have nothing to worry about, nothing.

I took the duffel bag and started for the depot. The cops wouldn't know I was going to Malaga. Only Billy knew that. And once I got the money to the man I would have nothing to worry about. Nothing. I would be out of the loop. I took every side street I could think of to get to the depot. But that big, damn duffel bag made me more than noticeable. I was getting a second look from everyone who saw me. But how else was I going to get four gym bags out of the church without anyone noticing? And tomorrow the man was going to ask me, "Is this duffel bag for me?" If I didn't have the duffel bag, what was I going to tell him? "No, these four gym bags are for you...." And it had to be four bags, otherwise there'd be big trouble.

At the depot, I used a side door and went straight to the lockers that were almost out of sight to anyone behind the counter. No one saw me. I matched the number on the key to the locker number and quickly opened the locker and took out the gym bag and stuffed it into the duffel bag and went out of the waiting room by that same side door without anyone behind the counter seeing me.

Cops routinely came into the waiting room to roust people who were sleeping on benches or the floor and didn't look like they had tickets. My thinking was that I couldn't afford to have any cop see me in the waiting room that morning with the duffel bag. I walked around the block, and this time I approached the depot from the big, covered hangar side where the buses arrived and left with passengers. There were signs along the outside wall saying that passengers were prohibited from waiting for buses in the hangar area. I paid them no attention. Two baggage workers saw me in the hangar waiting for a bus and said nothing. I asked the second one if he knew when the next local heading south would be leaving. He stopped and said he thought in about thirty-five minutes. I was counting minutes again.

I was the first passenger on the first southbound local that arrived. I took the front seat next to the window. It gave me a good view of everything on the streets. As the bus started and crept past the waiting room windows, I saw two cops in the waiting room talking to the man behind the counter who kept shaking his head no. I panicked. Was he telling the cops that he hadn't seen me? For the next fifteen minutes it occurred to me several times that the only person who knew I would be going somewhere on a bus was Billy. *Had Billy ratted me out?* Each time I was quick to shake the thought off. Billy would never tell the cops anything about me. The cops in the waiting room had to be asking the counter man something else.

For once when I got off the bus in Malaga, Doña Petra wasn't standing in her doorway, and there was no one else in sight. As I started up the hill to the church, I wondered if someone other than Billy, like the lady in the rectory, might have told the cops that on Thursdays I came to Malaga. If that were true, then it wouldn't be long before the cops would be in Malaga and find me and find all that money and say it was mine. But they would have to find me and they never would because the church was locked and it would stay locked and they would never think that I was in it.

Malaga's main street was a rut-carved, dirt road that ran north and south for two blocks at the top of the hill. If you turned onto the main street, the church was located in the middle of the first block on the biggest lot of the village, so that there was only one house on either side of it. Across the street, there were six houses. The one on the corner was vacant. Next to it was Don Rogelio's house. He lived there alone and tried to tend to everyone else's business in the village. Next to Don Rogelio lived two sisters, one a widow and the other a spinster. The house next to them was vacant. The last two houses had families in them who were gone during the day.

The only entrance to the church was in the front through two doors that were locked with a huge padlock when the church was closed. There were three windows on each side of the church that were kept locked when no one was in the church. But I had taught myself to unlock the back window that faced the hill by jiggling it. I had done this several times when I didn't want anyone, especially nosy Don Rogelio across the street, to know that I was in the church.

I stopped on the road directly across from the church's back window. Between me and the window lay the backyard of the house next to the church. It was always difficult for me to tell whether there was someone in that house. I looked at the house for a long time. I saw no sign of anyone but I couldn't be sure that there wasn't anyone in there. Finally, I decided that if the cops were on their way, I had no choice. I walked casually across the backyard prepared to say that I was just taking a shortcut if anyone stopped me. No one did, but I still wasn't sure that someone in the house hadn't seen me. I jiggled the back window open and boosted the duffel bag and myself into the church and closed and locked the window.

I was exhausted and I could feel the tension draining out of me. I stretched myself out on the bench farthest from any window. I fell asleep and I was awakened and shaken by a loud, rough noise approaching. It was a police car and it came to a stop just past the front doors. Two cops got out of the car and started toward the church. I ducked down and laid flat on the floor between two pews. They couldn't see me there, but I had left the duffel bag in the open under the back window and there was nothing I could do about that then. They came to the front door and one of them knocked.

"What're you knocking for? Can't you see this place is locked tighter than a drum?"

The knocking stopped. "So what do we do?"

"Let's take a look through the windows. You take one side, I'll take the other."

I stretched myself out as far as I could and as flat as I could beneath a row of pews and breathed as little as I could, until I heard them at the front door again.

"See anything?"

"No."

"You?"

"No."

"So what do you want to do?"

"I think we should try talking to some of the neighbors. See what they can tell us. Maybe they've seen him."

I heard them leave and then saw them knocking on the sisters' door across the street. I felt relieved. Those women were afraid of everything. They'd never get anything out of them. It was the widow who answered. She stood in the doorway the whole time with her head down, shaking it "No, no, no."

They came back to the door. "So what do you want to do?"

"I guess we're going to have to wait. Wait 'til he shows. The narcs want him big time and we can't go back without him. The other guy is saying that he doesn't know anything about drugs, that it's this guy who's got all the connections. He's saying that this guy's got all the money."

I wasn't sure what I had heard, but then I didn't want to hear what I had heard. Billy was saying... No, this had to be some kind of setup. But how would they have gotten here unless Billy had told them? And who else but Billy knew that I had the money? I felt sick, lying between those two pews.

"We better find a place to park where we can watch the door, but far enough away that he can't see us or at least won't notice us. Let's drive around and find a place."

They started to leave when from across the street came, "Officers, officers, can I help you!"

Oh shit! It was Don Rogelio.

"And who are you?"

"My name's Rogelio Rodriguez and I live across the street. I've lived there for thirty-two years. I pretty much know everything that goes on around here. So how can I help you?"

"We're looking for Raymond Lopez. He's supposed to be taking care of the church. Do you know him? Have you seen him today?"

"Oh, I've known Ramón since the day he was born. And he does take care of the church on Thursdays and Fridays. But you're a little early. It's not noon yet and he usually gets here on Thursdays around four o'clock in the afternoon. He takes the bus here from Parker and he stays overnight. Imagine that, staying overnight in a church like it's a hotel. And he leaves back to Parker on Friday around noon. What do you want him for? Is he in trouble? Or is there something wrong here?"

"We're not at liberty to say anything. But we really need to talk to him."

"Well, he'll be here almost as sure as I'm standing here around four o'clock, and for sure any time after four."

"What do you want to do, Frank?"

"We can stay here 'til four and find a place where we can watch the door. But that's a five-hour wait. Or come back at four. That's only a ten- or fifteen-minute drive. Let's call in and see what they want us to do."

They thanked Don Rogelio and went back to their car. Somehow, I had to get out of the church and Malaga without being seen. Then their car started, but I still didn't know if they were staying or going, until one of them said to Rogelio from their car, "We'll be back at four." Then they made a U-turn and went down the incline road.

I got up and sat down in one of the pews, dazed. Billy had to have told them. Billy had to have laid it all on me. Billy... I couldn't believe it. My head was bloated with numbness. But I knew that I had to get out of the church and Malaga without being seen.

But get out and go where? And what about the money? If I left the money, then someday it would be found and it could only have been brought here and put under the trapdoor by me. Maybe Billy had already told them that. Money from my drug trade, they'd say. And who wouldn't believe that? I had to get out of there. And go where? I still didn't know. No matter where I went, I was going to need some money—a lot more than I had—and all the gym bags had locks on them. But I had to get out of there before the cops came back. And what about the man tomorrow? I couldn't wait around for him. And then he and whoever he was connected to would be after me too. There had to be a lot of money in those bags. I remembered Billy saying that if tomorrow's deal didn't go through there was going to be big trouble. Big trouble for who? For me now. Because if the cops didn't get me, the man and his gang would.

I took all the old clothes out of the duffel bag and unlocked and opened the trapdoor and put two of the gym bags from below in it. The third one I sliced open with my knife and was stunned by the stacks and stacks of crisp, new, hundred-dollar bills bound by brown-paper wraps. I had to get out of there. I cut one of the bundles open and hundred-dollar bills slid in ever direction. Hurrying, I gathered some and stuffed them into my pants pockets. Then I put that opened gym bag into the duffel bag and packed the top of the duffel bag with as many old clothes as I could. I closed and locked the trapdoor and went out the back window and across the backyard and down the hill, hoping that Doña Petra wouldn't be in her doorway. I had to catch the first local going south because I couldn't go back to Parker. There was a huge eucalyptus tree half a block from the bus stop, and I walked to it without looking toward Doña Petra's doorway until I was behind it. She wasn't there. I waited and waited for a southbound local. It seemed like forever. More than once, I was sure a cop car was coming down the highway toward me. That didn't happen. Finally, I saw a Greyhound coming and I stepped out from behind the eucalyptus and waved and waved. The bus pulled over and stopped. But just as I was getting on the bus with the duffel bag, I thought I saw Doña Petra in her doorway. It didn't matter, I had to get on.

The bus driver said, "Where you going, bud?"

"Where are *you* going?"

"All the way to Los Angeles."

"That's where I'm going too, sir. To Los Angeles."

I DON'T know when it started or how it started or why it started. It was just there when Mrs. Adams came up to me during my last year in high school.

"Are you OK, Raymond?"

"Yeah, I'm fine."

"It's noon, Raymond. Everybody went out for lunch five minutes ago and you haven't budged. You've just been sitting here staring at the blackboard. Except there's nothing on the blackboard."

"Everything's on the blackboard."

"What?"

"I said everything's on the blackboard. Can't you see it?"

She turned and looked at the blackboard. "Stop it, Raymond, there's nothing on the blackboard. Are you OK?"

I nodded. I was OK.

She put her open hand on my forehead. "No. You don't have a fever, but you'd better get outside and get something to eat."

"I'm not hungry."

"You still have two more periods to go to and I know you'll be hungry then. You'd better go get yourself something to eat. Besides, I'm leaving and I have to lock up the classroom."

I heard her but it meant nothing. Everything was on the blackboard.

She shook me. "Come on, up, Raymond."

I didn't move.

"You were staring at the blackboard during class too. This has got to stop. And if you don't get up and I have to leave this classroom with you in it, I'm going to refer you to Mr. Stafford."

"For what?"

"For not paying attention to me in and out of class."

"And what's he gonna do?"

"He'll talk to you and if that doesn't do any good, he'll have a conference with your parents."

"I don't have any parents and my grandmother's too sick to come."

"She can't be that sick."

"Yes, she is. And besides, she doesn't speak English."

"Well, I'm going to get Mr. Stafford to come down here now."

"No, I'm getting up. I'm leaving. I'm going out to the yard." She had my attention now and the blackboard didn't.

I went out to the yard. It was loud and noisy. Students were laughing and talking to each other. I found a bench with the fewest students and I sat there and waited for the bell to ring. I didn't have any friends. But that didn't matter. Because by then I didn't need any friends.

In the hospital the doctors asked me when the craziness started. I said that it started with periods of just staring at things. That was a long time before the voices began and before Mrs. Adams called me on it. She was the first person who broke into my staring, made me stop, told me it offended people. I had been staring at home before that. How long before that I don't know. And how much time I would stare at something, I don't know. Because there was no one in my house to stop me like Mrs. Adams did. My grandmother was real sick and in bed all the time. She was more in bed than up, and when she was up she didn't care about anything except getting back to bed. So when the staring started at home and how long I would stare at something, I had no way of knowing.

The doctors were curious about what I was seeing when I was staring. "Everything," I would answer. "Everything I needed and wanted was there." That's why I could sit and stare for hours I told them.

"What do you mean by 'everything'?" they would ask again and again.

It was difficult to explain "everything," to give it a meaning. I finally settled on, "If I don't want anything or need anything, doesn't that mean that I have everything? When I was staring I was really satisfied with what I was seeing and with what I had."

"What were you seeing when you were staring?"

"Whatever I chose to look at. If I was staring at a tree, it was perfect. Everything about it was perfect. Its color, its leaves, the way it swayed in the wind. It was perfect and in a way, I guess, I was part of that perfection. If I stared at a wall, no matter how many times I had stared at it before, it still fascinated me. Even if I had already learned everything about it, it was like I had to learn about it all over again. Learn everything about it down to its pores. Learn how it was made, how it fit, and why it fit. It was like a living thing for me, one I really enjoyed being around."

The doctors wanted to know how long a staring spell lasted and how and why I stopped one?

I told them that I never measured how long I stared at something, but I assumed it could have been for hours. At my grandmother's house, when I started staring there was no one else there and nothing else to stop me. So I could stare and stare. What could stop me sometimes was my grandmother groaning or crying out for me. And also at times when I needed to eat or drink or go to the toilet. But it was when Mrs. Adams broke into my staring in the classroom and threatened to take me to Mr. Stafford that I first realized that it was something I had to hide from the others, that it was something I could be punished for, something to be ashamed of, something to deny and lie about if anyone caught me staring. So it was after Mrs. Adams, that others could make me stop staring if they just happened on me while I was staring.

One doctor asked me if during the time that I was doing all that staring was I reading anything, like textbooks, magazines, newspapers? I told him, why would I want to do that when all I had to do to read was to look up at all the words and sentences that were always floating past my eyes.

THEN MY grandmother died and everything changed. For two weeks I locked myself in our house and didn't go to school. I must have spent a good part of those days staring because staring at something was so much better than the world around me. I don't know what would have become of me if it hadn't been for Padre Ibarra. I didn't answer the door that first Sunday when he knocked to take me to Malaga with him to serve Mass. He knew I was there and he knocked and knocked. I could hear him knocking, but I must have been staring and that was so much better than anything he could give me then.

He came back the next day and knocked again. But this time he was knocking at the window just a few feet from me and *he* was staring at me staring. When I saw him at the window, that stopped my staring and I went to the door and let him in.

He said, "You missed Mass yesterday."

"I know."

"And you didn't clean the Malaga church on Saturday."

"I know."

"Why? What's going on with you?"

"My grandmother died."

"That was last week."

"I know."

"You were at the Mass and her burial."

"I know."

"You may know, but you can't keep living like this." He was looking around and the place was a mess, something I hadn't noticed until then. "Look at this place!"

I had already looked and I didn't need to again. It was a small, two-room house. Besides the bathroom, it had a bedroom, which had been my grandmother's, and another room that had been both our kitchen and living room, where I slept on a couch. It was all a big mess. I had let it go after they carried my grandmother's body out of her bedroom.

"You can't keep living like this."

"I know."

"So what do you plan to do?"

"I don't know. Maybe I'll just stay here."

"The landlord's not going to let an eighteen-year-old boy who's still in school and doesn't have a job live here by himself. How would you pay the rent anyhow?"

"I guess I could get a job."

"You can't do that. What about school, and your education?"

"I don't like school."

"What don't you like about it?"

"It bores me."

"And you're not going to get much of a job without a high school diploma."

"I know."

But I didn't care. That was the last thing on my mind. I hadn't been to school in two weeks and wasn't planning on going back. But I couldn't tell him that.

"You'll have to stay here for now, but I'm sure I can find you a family in the parish who's willing to take you in. A lot of people in the parish know you. They see you serve Mass with me here and know that you also serve Mass with me out in Malaga on Sundays. They know you take care of the Malaga church on Saturdays and that you go to school and have never been in trouble like your cousin. It shouldn't take me long to get you with a family. A week at the most. Are you OK with that?"

"Yes." What else could I say?

Looking around again he said, "But you'd better clean this place up. I wouldn't want the landlord telling anyone I'm trying to place you with about what this place looks like now."

"Yes, Padre."

He started to leave but then stopped and said, "Why didn't you answer the door on Sunday?"

"I must have been sleeping. I've done a lot of that since Grandma died."

"You weren't sleeping this morning. You were wide awake when I came to the window, just staring into space. What was that all about?"

"I guess I was thinking about Grandma. I've done a lot of that lately."

PADRE IBARRA placed me with Tony and Maria Alvarez. They were an old couple who always had friendly smiles for me when I served Mass on Sundays. They were very close to Padre Ibarra, and two days after he talked to me at Grandma's, they opened their home to me. Tony Alvarez had been a bartender who late in life found God. He had become St. Ann's self-appointed custodian. Now retired, he went to the church every day to work on whatever he thought needed work. In those days there was a convent in Parker that housed eight Mexican nuns, none of whom spoke English. Maria Alvarez was their official English interpreter and was involved in most of their activities outside of the convent.

The Alvarezes were childless and I think, at least in the beginning, they treated me like the son they never had. They gave me my own room complete with a radio and a table and chair for my studies. They also thought that because I was Padre Ibarra's altar boy and took care of the Malaga church, I had to be close to God. Dinner was when I spent the most time with them, and the subject of God and religion often came up. As long as I agreed with whatever they said about God and religion, I was sure to remain in their good graces.

After dinner, I was in my room with the door closed "studying," or so they thought. But I was staring. I always had a book open on my desk in case they came in without knocking. Since they couldn't read English, it didn't matter what book or what page that book was opened to. They were very proud of all the studying I was doing, and several times I overheard them telling people that I was studying to be a priest or a lawyer. Why they thought that, I didn't know. The truth was, I hadn't gone back to school after Grandma died. In my room, I would stare at the wall in front of me or at a tree outside my window or at anything in the room. Everything I needed or wanted was in whatever I chose to stare at.

When I left the Alvarez home in the morning "going to school," I walked and walked until I found a place where I felt comfortable sitting and staring and where I thought no one could see me. But then one evening at dinner, Tony Alvarez said, "Ramón, el Señor

Contreras told me he saw you walking out by the airport yesterday morning and that he honked and honked but you didn't pay any attention to him. I told him that you were in school yesterday morning and that he didn't know what he was talking about. Why would he be saying something like that?"

"I don't know. I was in school."

"I know you were. It's just like el Señor Contreras to make up things and spread them all around."

TONY AND Maria must have seen me staring at their old, broken-down Chevy in the backyard, although I don't ever remember staring at it, because one day Tony said, "You seem to be real interested in that old heap in the backyard?"

I liked the old car, but I didn't answer.

"Do you know how to drive?"

"I learned in school."

"Do you have a driver's license?"

"I got one through Drivers Education in school, but it might be expired by now."

"I tell you what. I'll give you that old thing if you can get it started and get it out of the backyard and promise not to park it in front of our house."

"I don't know much about cars."

"Come on, let's go out there. I'll show you how to start it and tell you what I think is wrong with it, and how you can get it moving once you get it started."

We went out into the backyard and Tony showed me how to start it, although he couldn't start it, and where he thought the problem was. Even though he tampered with that part of the motor for quite a while, it still wouldn't start. Then he gave me the keys and said, "Once you get it started and get it out of here and park it somewhere away from this whole block, it's yours."

I liked the car. I had never owned anything that big and with wheels. The places I thought I could go in it seemed endless. For days I came home "from school" and tried to start the car without much luck. Then one day, I got it started and drove it out the back gate onto the alley and half a block down the alley where it died on me and wouldn't start again. Tony Alvarez was shocked, but he insisted that I had to park the car a block away before it was mine. Try as I might I couldn't start it again in the alley. I had almost given up hope of starting it when Tony took me down to the Motor Vehicles Department and made me the legal owner. Leaving the department, I knew that I would be forever grateful to Tony. Months later when I was telling Billy what a good man Tony was, Billy snorted, "That old son of a bitch wasn't doing you no favors, Little Brother. Once that old heap was in the alley, on a public road, that sucker wanted his name off the pink slip, so that nobody could come after him when you or that old piece of shit fucked-up in the alley."

Even after the car in the alley was in my name, I still couldn't get it started. Then about a week later a big garbage truck pulled up behind me and honked for me to get going. My car wouldn't start. They honked and honked again, but my car wouldn't start. Then the garbage man on the passenger side of the truck came up to me, angry. "Hey, move this goddamn thing! We've got a lot of work to do in these alleys and we sure as shit can't do it with you blocking us!"

"I can't get it started."

"You better get it started or we'll push this fucking thing into the street."

"What if I can't get it started in the street?"

He didn't care and went back to his truck. I tried some more but it wouldn't start. They honked again. I tried again. It wouldn't start.

The angry man came back. "If you won't move it, we will! Move it or you and your piece of shit car are going out into the fucking street!"

It wouldn't start.

The truck banged into the back of my car, slamming me against the steering wheel. My car moved forward, slowly, then a little faster. We were a quarter of a block from the street, when there was a loud crash and a jolt that thrashed my head against the windshield. My car stopped and I turned. It looked like the front end of the truck was on top of my car's trunk. I got out of my car. The truck's front bumper had slipped over my car's back bumper, and now there was a huge dent all across the back of my car. Both the driver and the angry one came to my car asking if I was OK. "Yeah," I said. Then they began apologizing for the damage to my car, and when I told them that I had just gotten it and couldn't get it started, one of them got into the driver's seat of my car and the other got under the hood, and in a matter of minutes they had the car started and running. Then they drove the car out into the street, parked it along the curb, and smiling, said goodbye and drove on to the next alley. My car already had many dents and rusted-out parts, but the dent they left behind was the biggest of all. From then on whenever my car died in traffic and I couldn't get it started, as many people helped me as cursed me. By watching those who helped me, I was able to cut down on the number of times I couldn't help myself.

Parking was a big problem from the beginning. No homeowner wanted my old car parked near his or her home. Some homeowners became so mad after a day or two of seeing my car parked in front of, or near, their homes that they actually called the police. It didn't take long for me to start parking alongside parks or in Parker's little airport parking lot.

The police were an even bigger problem. The car's license plates and my driver's license had expired well before I was driving the old Chevy. Cops loved stopping me for the expired plates, which led to my expired driver's license and then any number of moving violations such as failure to yield, running a stop sign, and illegal left or right turns. Within a few weeks, a lot of the cops knew me and my car by sight. We irritated some so much that when they stopped us they began adding on violations for no muffler, loud muffler, bald tires, no signal lights, and a cracked windshield. I didn't have the money to pay for any of those tickets, so

I just ignored them, tossing them into the first wastebasket I saw after getting them.

Still, that old Chevy was my own space, a space like I had never had before. I could sit in it for hours and stare no matter what the weather was like or where I was parked. When I left the Alvarez house with my books tucked under my arm, it was with a sense of relief that very soon I could do exactly what I wanted without being interrupted or discovered. When the old folks asked where the car was parked, I said it was parked just a few blocks away where the people didn't mind and I could drive it from there to school and back.

I soon taught myself how to lower the back of the driver's seat so that I could lie down and stare up at the car's ceiling without anyone knowing I was in the car. But one day while I was staring at the ceiling, there was a rapping on my side window. When I looked up, there was a cop staring down at me. "Roll down your window," he said.

I did and he said, "What are you doing here? Somebody called in and said there was an abandoned vehicle parked in front of their house."

Thinking as fast as I could, I said, "A friend of mine gave me this car a few days ago. And while I was trying it out, it died on me here and I couldn't get it started, so I left it here for overnight. But I couldn't get back to it until today, and I've tried and tried to start it but it won't start. So I was just laying here resting, letting the starter cool off before I tried again, when you came."

He stooped and looked at the inside of my car and then at all the dents and rust on the outside and said, "You say someone gave you this car?"

"Yes, sir."

"You didn't pay any money for it?"

"No, sir."

"Alright, let me give you a push and see if it'll start so we can at least get it out of here."

He got into his car and came up behind me and pushed my car

until it started. As I pulled away, I waved to him and he waved back.

Three weeks later in another neighborhood, the same cop came up on me while I was lying down on the back of the front seat staring at my car's ceiling. This time he wrote me a ticket that was filled with numbers. As he gave me the ticket he said, "I'm leaving now but I'll be back in twenty minutes. If you're still here, I'm going to arrest you and take your ass into custody for a violation of Penal Code section 148, delaying an officer in the course of his duty. That's a misdemeanor for which you can go to jail for up to six months. Do you understand what I just said?"

"Yes, sir."

"Have I made myself clear?"

"Yes, sir."

I watched as he drove away and was finally out of sight, then I left. That was when I began parking along the sides of city parks and in the little airport parking lot.

As THE months passed, Maria Alvarez became even more proud of me. I could hear her telling her lady friends that she was convinced I was going to become a priest. My daily life was a sure sign of where I was headed. At Sunday Mass, she sat in the front row and beamed at me in my black cassock and white surplice. She told everyone that in all her days, she had never known a more disciplined, well-behaved, earnest, and honest young man.

But something must have happened that gave me the feeling that Tony Alvarez was suspicious of me or at least didn't trust me anymore. He started asking me questions at the dinner table that made me think he really knew something about me.

"Where are you working on your car?"

"At a friend's house."

"A friend? I've never seen you with a friend."

"This is a friend from school."

"What's his name?"

I stumbled a bit before I said, "Jimmy Jones. His name is Jimmy Jones. He's a white boy and he lives over on Clark Street on the other side of town where all the white people live.... That's probably why you've never seen me with him."

"How did you meet him?"

"At school. He's in my class."

"What are you working on in the car?"

"The motor."

"What part?"

"The front part. I don't know much about motors but he does. He does all the work and I just kind of help him by handing him tools and holding the light for him and cleaning up after him."

"Why don't you two work on the car over here?"

"Because you didn't want the car over here. You even made me promise that I would park it at least a block away."

"Why don't you invite him over here so Maria and me can at least meet him?"

"Because lots of kids over there don't like to come over to this side of town."

THE NEXT week I was pretty sure that Tony had found me out.

"What are you studying in school, Ramón?" he asked at the dinner table.

"What do you mean what am I studying?"

"Well, I didn't get much schooling in Mexico. But when I did go, we had subjects like mathematics and Spanish, you know."

I didn't like where he was going but I tried to remember as quickly as I could some of the courses I had taken. "Oh, I'm taking mathematics, history, English, and speech."

"Do you have a book for every one of those?"

Something was very wrong here. "Yes."

"And you take all your books to school every day, don't you?"

For the first time ever, I didn't like Tony Alvarez. "Yes."

"Then why is it that you always have one book open here when you're at school?"

"I don't understand." I really didn't understand and I was scared.

"Some days Maria goes into your room when you're at school,

to change your sheets or to open the window for some fresh air or to check the wastebasket, and she's always been seeing a book open on your desk."

"Sometimes I do leave a book open when I go to school."

"No, no. This is all the time. In fact, I've even gone into your room myself to check on the open book."

"I don't understand."

"Neither do we. What book do you leave behind?"

"Different ones."

"No, it's always the same one. We don't read or write English. But it's always the same book. We can tell by the cover and the picture on one of the pages."

"I don't know what the problem is."

"I didn't say it was a problem. It's just that we're trying to understand why it's on your desk open all the time when you're gone. Don't you use that book?"

"Oh, that's the speech book. I use it all the time."

"Then why is it always opened to the same page and you never take it to school?"

"What?"

"Page 182. It's always open to page 182. Even if we can't read English, the numbers are the same in English and Spanish. And the picture of two young people with skates is always there at the top of the page. It's the same page. Why don't you take it to school with you instead of always leaving it opened to the same page at the same place on your desk?"

"It's probably there like that to remind myself every time I sit at my desk that I have to study and not do something else."

"Like what?"

"Like daydream, I suppose."

My answers weren't satisfying him or me, and we sat there staring at each other until Maria Alvarez said, "That's enough. So Ramón leaves one of his books opened at the same page on his desk all the time. What's so important about that?"

"Maybe it's not so important. But wouldn't the teacher of his class not like it if he came to class all the time without his book?"

"We hardly ever use a book in speech class."

"I thought you said..."

"That's enough! That's enough! Can't we talk about something else?"

Maria Alvarez was upset. She seemed near tears. Her looks were apologetic for me and resentful for her husband.

The book Tony Alvarez was talking about was my speech text. I couldn't remember when I began leaving it open. But I did leave it open in front of me when I was sitting at my desk staring in case either of them came into my room without knocking. After dinner that evening I began taking my speech text "to school" every day. And I began putting other open texts in front of me when I was "studying" and closing them after I "had studied."

As FAR back as I can remember I had always been talking to somebody in my mind. When Billy and I were growing up in Malaga, we were always making his mom mad when she came home from work. Like one time we ate stuff out of the icebox that they were supposed to have for dinner, and another time we let the dog in and forgot to take him out when we went out to play and he pissed and shit all over the place. "Boy was my mom mad," Billy told me the next morning on the school bus. Then after school that day, I came home alone and bored and I remember having this kind of a conversation with my mind or someone in my mind.

I wonder what Billy's doing?

He's home alone. Remember the whipping he said he got and how his mom said that he couldn't play after school for a whole month?

Maybe I could go over there and we could do something inside and she'd never know.

I wouldn't do that if I were you.

Why?

Because he said that she's mad as hell at you too.

He never said that on the bus.

Yes, he did, two or three times.

But she didn't even know I was in the house.

Yes, she did, the neighbor told her. Billy told you that.

If I go over there and we stay inside, and I leave before his mom comes home, how is she even going to know I was there?

The nosy neighbor will tell her again. You can't get into Billy's house without the neighbor seeing you.

But I'm bored.

Too bad.

DOWN THROUGH the years that voice or that person in my mind or my mind itself always had the same tone of voice, the same know-it-all answers for everything. We talked a lot about Grandma getting sicker and sicker.

What if she dies tomorrow?

Why worry about something you can't control?

Yeah, but you're not eighteen and I am. I still got a couple of months before I'm nineteen. What do I do if she dies on me tomorrow or any day while I'm still eighteen?

You'll find a way.

A way! What the hell are you talking about? They'll put me in Juvenile or in one of those foster care homes.

Lots of people have been eighteen when everybody around them has died. They've survived.

Survived! Doing what?

You can get a job somewhere and make enough money to support yourself while you're still in school.

That's easy for you to say, you're not eighteen.

THEN ALL of a sudden the voice changed. It was louder, stronger, more forceful, like he was really a person who knew everything and was really there. We still had conversations but he was always right. The strength in his voice made him right. Then he began talking to me even when we weren't having conversations, warning me and warning me about so many things and then after warning me, ordering me to do what he said.

You got to watch Tony. He doesn't like you. He wants you out of his house. He wants you in jail. He's out to get you. You know that as well as we do. He's out to get you. Watch him!

How do I watch him?

Watch everything you say around him. Because he'll twist it. He'll turn it around on you. He'll tell the police that you said something you didn't say. And they'll take you to jail.

The police?

Something will happen here. He'll set something up here, some crime, and then he'll call the police.

Like what?

Like he'll say that you tried to poison him and his wife. And no matter what you say to the police, he'll turn it around on you. Remember at the dinner table, how he turned your words around about your open book? And what was he doing in your room? She's the one who cleans, not him. He had no business in your room. He's spying on you. You have to be very careful around him. You have to avoid him. Watch him!

I can't avoid him at dinnertime. I have to eat. And it's really the only time I see him during the day. So how do I avoid him and still eat?

You can come home late. You can say that you're not hungry now and could you eat later? Or you can tell her that you have to eat earlier because you have too much homework to do. Or you can eat real fast and leave the table before he gets a chance to start talking to you. Those are some of the things you can do to avoid him. But you do have to avoid him because he's out to get you!

I took to eating real fast and asking to be excused from the dinner table because I had an extra lot of homework to do. After a few of those dinners, Maria knocked on my door. I leaned over my open book knowing it was her and said, "Come in."

"Is there something wrong, Ramón? You're eating so fast that I think you're going to make yourself sick. And you never even look up at us as you eat. It's just eat, eat fast, so you can leave us. Have we done something to offend you? It's like you never come out of your room anymore."

"You don't understand..."

By then whenever I was talking to another person, the voice was always there, whispering to me, guiding me, not letting anyone, which was most people, take advantage of me.

"The school year's ending and they're piling all this homework on us that always has to be done by the next day."

She's not really concerned about you. She's covering for her no-good husband. She has to know what he's up to. She's probably part of it too. I wouldn't trust her. Don't say much more to her. Get rid of her.

"But Padre Ibarra said on Sunday that there were three weeks until school was over, not the next day."

Now she's dragging Padre into to it, too. She's part of it, no doubt about it. They're pretty clever. They think you would never think she was part of it. Now you have to be careful when you talk to her too. Don't tell her anything more. Get rid of her.

"Please, Mrs. Alvarez, I have to do my homework. I have so much of it."

"OK. OK."

Less than a week later, on Sunday after serving the last Mass in Parker and before driving out to Malaga with Padre Ibarra, I came out of the sacristy to collect the wine cruets. The church was usually empty by then. But on that Sunday Tony Alvarez was quietly talking to Doña Espinoza, the head of the Guadalupana Society, in a side aisle. When they heard me and then saw me, they stopped talking and looked at me as if they had been talking about me. Then Doña Espinoza said real loud, "I have to get going, Don Alvarez," and moved quickly past him down the aisle. Tony Alvarez kept looking at me awkwardly and then, without saying anything, turned and followed her down the aisle and out of the church.

They were talking about you, Raymond, talking about you. That was pretty obvious, wasn't it?

Why? Why were they talking about me?

Because old man Alvarez knows how close you are to Padre Ibarra. He knows that not much can happen to you in this community as long as Padre Ibarra likes you the way he does. But if more people than just him, people that really count, like that Espinoza woman, start telling him what you're really like, then he won't stand by you once the shit hits the fan and the police come after you.

Come after me for what?

Like telling everyone you are going to school when you're not. Remember last year how they put that Hernandez kid in Juvenile for playing hooky from school? And you've missed way more school than he did. And what about that dollar fifty you found in the collection basket in Malaga and spent on yourself and never turned over to Padre Ibarra? That's stealing anyway you look at it, stealing from the church to make it worse. If Padre Ibarra and everyone in this community found out what you're really like, they'd lock you up right now.

But Tony doesn't know those things about me.

That's what you think. And even if he doesn't know he sure as hell is suspicious. Remember how he wouldn't let up about that open book in your room? You forget too fast, and you can't be forgetting at all because that asshole is after you. And already you're forgetting about in church, and your Tony and that Espinoza woman. Plain as day, they were talking about you.

How do you know that?

Come on now. Didn't you see how quietly they were talking? They didn't want to be heard even though there was nobody else in the church. But they knew you were back there with Padre so they had to be quiet. And then you came out and you had to have seen their reactions when they saw you. You can't lie about that, Raymond. Boom! They stopped talking just like that. Why? Because they were talking about you. You saw how uncomfortable they were then when they saw you. And then she got out of there as fast as she could. She knows you, right?

Yeah.

She's always around the church, right?

Yeah.

Always talks to you when she sees you, right?

Yeah.

Think about this now. Has she ever, except for just now, not talked to you when she saw you? Think about it.

No.

But today for the first time when she saw you she didn't say a word to you, right?

Right.

And you saw the way she took off, right?

Yeah.

They had to be talking about you, talking bad shit about you, right?

Yeah.

And old man Alvarez was just as bad, wasn't he?

Yeah.

But you're used to that.

Yeah.

Look, I'm just trying to help you, Raymond. That old puke is after you. You have to watch out for him. I'd stay as far away from him as I could if I were you, Raymond.

THAT SAME Sunday, Padre was real quiet on the drive out to Malaga. He hadn't said a word when we reached the overpass. Usually he hadn't stopped talking by then. And the more I thought about it, I realized he hadn't said much that morning before and after Mass in Parker either. "Are you ready?" That's all he had said to me before each Mass. "You'd better hurry with those cruets; we're going to be late in Malaga." That's all he said to me after the last Mass. I looked over at him before and after the overpass, but he looked straight ahead.

Does he know about the dollar fifty?

Of course he knows. Why else would he be so quiet? On top of that you can bet that old man Alvarez is working on Padre.

But one other time I found a dollar on the floor of the church and I showed it to Padre Ibarra and he told me to keep it because it would be impossible to know whose it was.

Yeah, but that's real different. No telling who the money on the floor belonged to. But the money in the collection basket, that's the church's. Somebody put that money in the basket for the church. You don't need to know who put that money in the basket. When that person put that money in the basket he was giving that money to the church, not to you, Raymond. *That's why you haven't told Padre about it, 'cause you know you stole it.*

For the rest of the way to Malaga I snuck glances at Padre Ibarra. He hadn't said a word, and he just kept looking straight ahead, never over at me as he usually did. He seemed cold, like he didn't want me to be there with him.

Did he know? Did he know?

Of course he did.

But who could have told him? I was the only one that knew there was a dollar fifty in the basket.

Maybe he planted it there to see if he could trust you. And now he knows. No wonder he's not talking to you.

When we pulled up to the church in Malaga, Padre Ibarra turned and looked at me and said, "Ramón, I'm very sorry that I've been so disconnected to everyone and everything this morning, but last night I was told that my mother had died in Spain yesterday."

The voice said, *I don't care about why he was so quiet this morning. You'd be a fool not to think that old man Alvarez and his stooges haven't been working on him.*

DINNER AT the Alvarez home was served at 5:30. There was often talk of God or of St. Ann's Church or of Tony as a young man. We were usually finished with dinner between 6:00 and 6:15. Once I began eating as fast as I could with my head down, I was leaving the table between 5:35 and 5:40. I was in the second week of my fast-pace eating when Maria prepared *albondigas*...my favorite dinner. I slurped down my first spoonful of broth and was bringing half a meatball to my mouth when a force slammed my hand and the spoon back down into the bowl, splattering soup and meatballs everywhere. Stunned, I looked up and saw Tony bent over toward me from his side of the table with his hand flat next to mine.

"I've had enough of this!" he scowled. "Get up and get out of here! You're not eating another morsel at this table until you can sit and eat with us and look at us like we're human beings. Get up and get out, I said!"

Tony's eyes were bulging and his mouth was quivering. Maria was crying and pleading, "Antonio, please calm yourself. You're going to have a heart attack. Ramón, please go to your room."

As I rose, he began shouting again. "This is my house and everything in it including this table and the food on it I've earned with the sweat off my balls! And I will not be disrespected in it by a little street worm! You will not get another piece of food from us, no breakfast, no lunch, no dinner, until you are ready to show us some respect at this table and everywhere else in our home!"

Maria cried louder.

I closed the door to my room and stood there trying to sort out what had happened.

What did I tell you? I told you he'd come up with something. Trust me, this is just the beginning. He'll roll this into something. All of this just because you were eating fast and not looking at him. The man's a lunatic, a God-fearing lunatic. One of those. Just wait and see what this becomes.

I had not expected this. I stood by the door hoping to hear Tony change his mind. Instead I heard, "Stop your sniveling, Maria! That little bastard's going to learn a few things from me."

"Antonio, please calm down. Your blood pressure's going to give you a heart attack."

"Don't tell me what to do, goddamn it. Especially about something very ugly that's happening in my house."

"You're swearing, Antonio. You're taking God's name in vain."

"Don't you tell me what words to use and not use! I'm much closer to God than you and that little fairy in there combined!"

Tony wouldn't stop. On and on he went.

What's the matter, Raymond?

I guess I didn't expect him to get so mad. Besides, I'm hungry now. I have to eat. I have a little of Saturday's money left. But that will only last me a day or two. And then what?

You can go out there right now, Raymond, and apologize to Tony, kiss his ass, tell him how sorry you are for not looking at him at the dinner table. Tell him you're ready to sit down with him at his table like a good little boy and look at him and listen to him all night long, if that's what he wants. Can't you see how this thing is escalating? First he says you have no friends. Then you're lying about your open book. Worse, you're probably not going to school. Now this. You're eating fast and not looking at him and disrespecting him. Now you can't eat any of his food. What's next? So now more than ever you have to stay away from him because next he'll be accusing you of a crime. Can't you see that, Raymond? He's out to get you.

But I'm hungry. I have to eat.

We understand that but...

It was a new voice, a second voice, a softer, higher voice. A woman's voice?

Right now we have to deal with what's just happened. There are ways to get you out of here, but we have to deal with this first. His wife is part of the conspiracy too. All her crying and being upset is fake, it's part of their plan. That way you'll think she's on your side. They want you to trust her. That way it'll be easier to destroy you. But we're not about to let that happen.

Maria's part of the conspiracy too? I hadn't thought of that. But it makes sense.

Of course she is. Are you trying to tell me that she doesn't know what her husband's up to? Who told him about the open book in your room? She did. Who was the only one who was supposed to be going into your room? She was. Yet she took him into your room to show him the open book. When you started eating fast, who kept piling on the food from the beginning, so that you'd have to eat faster and faster making it so obvious what you were doing and making him angrier and angrier. That was her role. And now you want to go out there and apologize to them for what they've done to you? They want to destroy you and this is just the beginning.

What do I do now?

What you do now is do what we tell you to do. We're much better able to deal with them than you are. We've seen a lot of these conspiracies. For now, just listen to us. They'll make another move before too long.

Even though there were two of them then, more and more their voices sounded the same. It was getting harder and harder to tell them apart. But then there was no need to tell them apart because they were saying the same things at the same time, making their message louder and clearer, louder and clearer.

Raymond, we know what's going on in your mind. What you don't want to understand is that we're part of you. We live in your mind. Part of your mind is us. Everything that goes through your mind goes through us. We hear it, we see it, we know it. And because of that, we're here to guide you and protect you.

Yeah, but I'm hungry. When do I eat?

Wanting to eat and being hungry are part of the mind too. The more you think about eating and being hungry, the more you will want to eat and the hungrier you will feel. For sure you have to eat and we will see to it that you eat. But you don't need as much food as you think you do. For now you have enough food in your body to keep you going for days. So stop thinking about food and eating and being hungry and you'll see the difference. For now, we have to wait, wait and see what they're up to next, how they're going to try to get you to do something that will put you in jail like Billy and then in prison like Billy.

We waited. The voices were loud and clear. There was no denying them. Those old bastards were going to come at me again. We had to wait and see. I sat by the door waiting. I don't know how long I waited but it didn't matter because I knew the voices were there with me, waiting. I could feel them. They were part of me.

Then the knock came, just as they said it would.

Wait! Don't answer! Let her think you're asleep!

They knew it was Maria before I did.

She'll knock again.

And she did.

Wait 'til she says something and then answer and tell her you were asleep!

"Ramón, Ramón." Her voice was low and muffled, as if her mouth was pressed against the door. "Ramón, Antonio's asleep. I brought you some *albondigas*. I warmed them up. I know how much you like them."

Tell her you're not hungry.

"I'm not hungry." And at that moment, I wasn't hungry. They were right, hunger was a state of mind.

"But you haven't had anything to eat since those tacos I gave you for lunch."

Don't answer her. She's part of it too. Let her grovel... She's not really groveling. She's part of it. It's just a big act. They've decided to use her to get to you. They think she can get close to you. Don't answer.

"Ramón, I can't talk very loud and I can't stay very long. Antonio's gone to bed and I think he's gone to sleep. I don't know for sure. If he has, I don't want to wake him. That would just make things worse. I know he's been hard on you lately but he's not a bad person. And I think all of this could be straightened out if the three of us could sit down with Padre Ibarra and have a frank talk. What you don't understand is that Antonio resents all the time and attention that Padre Ibarra gives you and what little he gives him. Antonio's down at the church every day. He works there all the time, and no one pays him a cent for all his work. He says Padre Ibarra has nothing to do with him except for finding more work for him to do. On Sundays he sees how much Padre Ibarra cares for you. And he knows you can go to the rectory whenever you want and get whatever you want. Padre pays you for taking care of the Malaga church. None of that seems right or fair to Antonio. But nobody's ever brought that up with Padre. Like I said, I think we can straighten all this out by the three of us talking to Padre."

Don't say anything. Don't answer her. Tony's sent her here. If you talk to her she will go on and on until you go out there. If you don't answer, she'll leave.

After another minute or two, Maria left.

I slept a strange sleep that night because even though I didn't hear the voices during the night, nor did I dream of them, I somehow knew that they were there with me, watching out for me.

The next morning, the moment I opened my eyes, the voices started.

We've got to get out of here as soon as we can! So get up and get ready to go! They've had all night to plan and they've come up with something new for sure, something they don't think will fail. The sooner we leave, the less time they'll have to put their new plan into action, the less time they'll have to make it work. Let's leave long before you usually leave.

I washed, dressed, combed my hair, made my bed, and straightened my room in a matter of minutes.

Make sure all your books are in your backpack.

They are.

Because you're leaving so early today, they sure as hell will come in here looking for proof that you're not going to school.

Maria was already in the kitchen when I opened my door. She heard it and came to the kitchen door. When she saw me, she backed into the kitchen for a moment then met me as I was passing the kitchen door.

"Good morning, Ramón. Did you sleep well?"

I stopped and looked at her.

Don't answer. The bitch is part of the plan.

I turned away and left her.

"Why are you leaving so early, Ramón? I know you must be hungry and I got up early to make you a real breakfast. It's almost ready and if you'll wait for just a minute, I can make some tacos for you."

Tell her you're not hungry.

I stopped and turned, "I'm not hungry."

"How can you not be hungry? You haven't eaten anything for two days. Please, I made you some eggs and *chiles rayados*. Wait just a minute and I can have everything in some tortillas for you."

"I said I'm not hungry, damn it! Can't you just leave me alone!"

She stared at me open-mouthed, shaking her head. "Ramón. Please don't curse in my house. What's wrong with you? Why are you acting this way? What have I done to you? What have we done to you?" Tears welled in her eyes.

She's faking it. Move it. You're not getting anything out of this. She's just trying to set you up.

I started for the back door. "Ramón! Ramón!" I heard her behind me but I didn't stop. I went through the dining room and in and out of the back porch, down the steps into the backyard.

Great! Great! Let's get the hell out of here.

I was no sooner in the backyard when I heard, "Hey! Where in the hell do you think you're going?" It was Tony coming toward me from the cellar and I stopped.

Don't stop, goddamn it, don't stop! Let's get the hell out of here!

But I stood frozen waiting for him to approach me.

He was angry. His unshaven face was raw-red, and he stumbled as he walked. I had never seen him in that condition. But Padre Ibarra had told me that he had had a bad drinking problem until he found God, and that when he was drinking he had been a mean drunk who had caused many problems in the parish. When he reached me, I could smell the alcohol on his breath and see the hate in his eyes.

"Where the hell do you think you're going at this hour of the morning, you little punk?"

Don't answer, Raymond. Anything you say he'll turn around, and that will give him an excuse to get angrier. He has to be pissed off. They weren't ready for us leaving so soon.

I didn't answer.

"I said where in the fuck do you think you're going?"

Don't answer.

"I'm going to school, that's where I'm going."

"School at this hour! Bullshit! Didn't I tell you that you weren't getting another ounce of food from us until you showed us some respect? And you haven't showed us shit yet. So where's the food that she gave you? I could smell her cooking it from here. What you don't seem to understand, Mr. Schoolboy, is that everything in this house, including the food she was just cooking for you, I paid for by working my ass off. So she has no food to give you because she can't give you what belongs to me. *Comprende, idiote!* Now give me that goddamn backpack. I know my food's in there."

Don't give him anything. He'll find a way to use anything you give him against you.

I stared at him. I wasn't afraid of him. In his condition, he was pathetic.

He yanked the backpack off my shoulder and frantically unzipped it. He struggled to separate the books inside of it. Finally, he dumped the books on the ground and then looked through the empty pack and then shook it and shook it. "Where is it? Where is it? Where's my food?" he demanded, throwing the empty pack on the ground.

Don't answer. Every time you answer you give him another reason to keep us here.

I stooped and began putting the books back into the backpack. He stooped too and began patting and feeling my legs and thighs. "Get your filthy hands off of me!" I shouted and shoved him away from me. He landed on his butt and for a moment looked around as if he didn't know how he had gotten into that position. Then he struggled to get up and walked unsteadily away, muttering to himself.

THE PARKER Municipal Airport was a mile and a half from the Alvarez home. I'd parked my car there the day before. As I walked to it that morning, the voices were loud and ecstatic.

We've been telling you that they're out to get you. You saw it for yourself this morning, didn't you? They had a new plan. The old one didn't work. The old woman got up extra early this morning. She was already cooking you a big breakfast and probably a big lunch too. She was cooking all right, even though she had heard him tell you that you couldn't have any more of his food. She was gonna get you to sit down and have that big breakfast, nice thing that she is. And as soon as you did, he was going to call the police because you were eating something that wasn't yours, something that you had been forbidden to eat by him. Eating that food would have been theft, and the cops could have carted you away to the jail and Juvy right then and there. That was their new plan. That's why we had to get you out of there early. You saw for yourself.

Over and over they repeated that. The repetition didn't bother me. They were my friends and they were there to protect me.

It had rained during the night and when we got to my car there were puffy, white clouds everywhere. I pulled down the back of the front seat and lay down looking up at those clouds. The voices stopped. They let me be, let me enjoy those clouds. I don't know how long I stared, but after a while I was hungry again and the hunger was starting to hurt.

I'm hungry.

You're not hungry. You just think you're hungry and that's because you've been eating too much. You have to get used to eating less. It's good for you.

Hey! I haven't had anything to eat since yesterday at noon. That's twenty-four hours and I'm hungry.

The less you eat, the closer you will be to us, the clearer and more open your mind will be.

But you guys don't eat. If I don't eat, I'll die.

We're not telling you not to eat. We're just telling you to eat less.

Yeah, but I'm hungry right now and I need to eat.

So where you gonna eat? You can't eat at Tony's.

I've got to eat something.

So where you gonna eat?

At Taco Bell. I've got money.

You've got money?

Yeah, from Saturday.

I drove to Taco Bell, parked, and started to get out of the car.

You can't go in there.

Why not?

Because Tony and his old bitch have probably told everybody by now that you're not going to school, and when anybody in there sees you they'll probably call the police.

But I'm hungry.

Shut up and listen to us! Get in the car line over there and get your food there.

I parked behind some cars and waited until I could order two tacos and a large Coke. When my order came, I paid the woman and drove to the far end of the parking lot and parked.

What are you doing?
I'm gonna eat.
You can't eat here.
Why not?
'Cause yours is the only car parked here for miles. Everybody can see you here and everybody will wonder why you're parked here and they'll naturally look this way and see it's you and call the police.

If I park where all the other cars are parked you're gonna say that I'm parked too close and everybody can see me there. I just wanna eat.
We know that. You've said it enough times.
So where am I gonna eat?
At the park.
Which park?
The big one.
Frank Ball?
Yeah.

As I was driving to the park I thought several times how good my car was running. After one of those times the voices said, *Yeah, it is running good.*

That took me by surprise. I hadn't been talking to them and I guess I wasn't convinced that everything I thought ran through them. I wondered if my car could make it to Malaga eleven miles away. *Sure it could,* they said.

I parked inside the park and ate my tacos and drank my Coke. Finished, I lowered the back of my driver's seat and looked up at a tree across the road. Whenever I took to staring, the voices never seemed to interrupt me. I don't know how long I lay there staring but it was long enough for a park worker to rap on my window and say, "Hey pal, I don't know what you think you're doing here, but you can't sleep in the park, in or out of your car. You better get moving."

Let's get out of here before this asshole calls the police.

I started the car and drove out of the park. It wasn't 2:30 yet and it was still a good while before I could go back to the Alvarezes'. What to do until five?

Let's go to Malaga! Let's go to Malaga!
Yeah, but I don't know how much gas I have. My gas gauge doesn't work.
Get some gas. There's a gas station right down the road.

I pulled into the gas station wondering if it would be better to take the highway or the back road to Malaga. A man came up to the car and asked if I wanted gas. "Yeah," I said and nodded. The highway would be faster, but the back road would be safer. But if the car died on me, there would be more cars on the highway and more cars to pull over and try to help me, or would their drivers just ignore me?

The man came back to the car and said, "That'll be twelve dollars and forty cents."

"Wait, twelve forty?"

"Yes, twelve forty."

"Why?"

"Because I filled it up. I asked you if I should fill it up and you said, 'Yeah,' so I filled it up."

"I don't have twelve forty."

"How much do you have?"

"Let me see...a dollar twenty-four."

The man took a deep breath and then blew air out of his pursed lips slowly but loudly. "Well, I'm gonna have to get the boss down here. But I'm taking your license plate numbers down and if you take off before I get back, I'm gonna call the police." He took the numbers down and then started back toward the office.

What did you do that for?
Do what?
Tell him to fill it up. We heard you say, "Yeah."
I didn't say, "Yeah, fill it up."
Listen, you stupid piece of shit, we heard you say, "Yeah, fill it up."
Now look what you got us into. From now on, you do as we say!

They were screaming.

Did you hear us, goddamn it? We won't tell you again! Understood?
Yes, yes.
Now let's get the fuck out of here!

But they have my plate numbers. The car's registered to me.

We don't care who's got what fucking numbers! We said, let's get the fuck out of here! Now do it! Or do we have to bear down on you!

Their voices were a roar. There was no denying or defying them. *OK, OK.*

I turned the key in the ignition. The motor rolled over and over. But it didn't start.

Get this fucking thing started and let's get the fuck out of here!

I tried again. The motor turned over and over but wouldn't start. I tried again. The motor stopped turning. It was dead.

You sorry, stupid son of a bitch!

They were furious and I was scared.

Let's get out of here and make a run for it!

But they'll find out who I am.

Will you shut the fuck up and get going!

I reached for the door handle, but I was going nowhere. A big, burly, gray-haired man was standing on the other side of the door looking down at me. The other man repeated, "It's twelve dollars and forty cents, and he told me to fill it up and now he says he's only got a dollar and twenty-four cents."

"Is that true?" the big man said, looking at me with steel-gray eyes.

I shrugged. Part of it was true and part of it wasn't.

"Give me the keys and get out of the car."

I gave him the keys and got out of the car. He squeezed into the front seat and turned the ignition. The motor stood silent. He looked at me angrily. "Tell you what, smarty pants, we're keeping this heap of shit here until you come up with twelve forty.... Harry, let's push this thing over by the trash cans where it's out of the way." Then he turned to me again and said, "Now you get the fuck off my property before I make you sorry you even came near it."

I stood and watched as the two men pushed the car toward the far end of the lot.

Are you deaf or something! Let's get the fuck out of here before they call the cops! Did you hear us? Before they call the cops! Let's go!

But I stood and watched until the hood of the car reached the trash cans, and then I turned and walked out of the gas station and onto the sidewalk beyond it.

You really are acting stupid today. First you tell the guy to fill it up when you only got a dollar and then you stand there waiting for the cops to come after the man told you to get off his property! What is wrong with you! We don't know why we're wasting our time with you!

I walked for a while until I realized that I didn't know where I was going.

That's right! Where are we going? We've got a couple of hours in front of us and we can't just keep walking around and around and we can't go back to the park. They just threw us out of there.

I got to get off the street where people can see me.

It's about time you started thinking again about what we've got to do.

We were about three blocks from the irrigation ditch and the water was at its lowest.

That's right! You're right! The irrigation ditch. We could sit on the inside of the bank now and no one could see us from the street.

The water was clean, cool, and colorless, and it kept silently running and running. I sat and watched it. It had everything it needed to have. The voices let me be.

But when the shadows of the trees behind the other side of the bank crept up on me they said, *You gotta go back.*

I didn't want to go back. The ugliness back there at the gas station fell heavily on me. *Go back where?*

Don't act stupid. To the house. Where else are you gonna go back to? Where else do you have to go back to?

How can I go back when I knocked the old guy on his butt?

You gotta remember who you are.

Remember who I am? Who am I?

Who you are to them is all that matters.

And who is that?

To them, you're Padre's favorite youngster. His altar boy. The kid that serves two Masses with him here in Parker on Sundays and then goes out to Malaga with him to serve another Mass. You're the holiest kid in town.

Worse for them, now you've seen Tony drunk and not only do they have to respect you, but they also have to be goddamn afraid of you. Because if you ever tell Padre that Tony was drunk, their life here in Parker is over. They have to be scared shitless of you.

I might be that to them, but who am I?

Who do you think you are?

I don't know.

We can tell you who you are.

Who?

You're the youngster who's gonna to turn the table on those Alvarez assholes, who's gonna put their conspiracy around their own necks.

So what do I do or say when I walk back into that house?

You don't say a goddamn thing to either one of them. You just walk in there like you own the place and go to your room and close the door like you don't want to be disturbed.

I'm gonna be hungry. I'm already hungry. And don't tell me I should be eating less because all I've had to eat is two tacos in a day and a half. And I'm not sitting down to dinner with them.

You don't ever have to sit down with them again. Just remember who you are to them and walk up to that refrigerator in the kitchen and help yourself to whatever you want and take it to your room and eat it there. Trust us. Do like we say. And they won't say a word because they know who you are and what you can do to them.

They know who I am, but who am I?

Let's not get into that again. We just told you who you are.

I sat on that bank thinking and nodding to myself. It all made perfect sense. I looked at my watch: ten to five. We had better get going.

I WENT through the alley to the back gate. I wanted to do what I always did even though the voices were hollering, *Don't go through the alley! Don't go through the back door! Use the street! Go through the front door like you own the place! Who's gonna stop you! No one's gonna stop you! Show them who's running the place now!*

I opened the gate and stepped into the backyard. There was no sign of him. But he had to be somewhere. He was always home by this hour. All was quiet. I passed the spot where I had pushed him off me, where he had fallen on his butt. I went up the back stairs to the back porch door and for a moment thought of knocking. *Are you fucking crazy? This is your place now! You don't need to be knocking at your place now!*

The back porch screen door was unlatched. I went in and the old porch floor creaked loudly. They had to know there was someone else in the house. It was 5:10. They had to know it was me. Yet there wasn't a sound anywhere. I moved through the dining room. Then at the kitchen door I saw her standing, looking at me.

Don't say a fucking thing to her! You don't need to be talking to her. This is your place now!

She had a small, tight, frightened smile and she said, *"Como estás, mi'jo?"*

Don't answer her! You're not her fucking son! She's part of it! She's part of it too!

I stepped past her and then stopped. I was hungry. I turned and went back to her and brushed by her into the kitchen and went to the refrigerator and opened its door.

"What are you doing, *mi'jo?* I'm cooking dinner for all of us."

"I don't need your stinking dinner. I'll take what I want from here."

Stop talking to her! Don't talk to her! That's what they want! They want you to talk to her! So that you'll tell her where we're at!

I took out some cold chicken *mole* and tortillas and refried beans and a carton of milk. Then I turned and showed her, "This is my dinner. And I don't ever need and want you fixing my dinner or anything else for me to eat again. Do you hear me? Do you understand me? I'll take whatever I damn please and I'll fix whatever I damn please, and I'll eat in my room whenever I damn please. Do you understand?"

She was still in the doorway, but now she was crying, kneading her hands in her apron and shaking her head in hurt and disbelief.

"Now get the fuck out of my way!"

Give it to her Raymond! Tell her like it really is!

They were hooting and hollering, jumping and dancing as I made my way to my room with my food.

Once in my room, I slammed the door shut as hard as I could, wanting to bring the drunk out of hiding.

That chickenshit! He's not showing himself. He heard everything and probably saw some of it. But he's afraid of you now, Raymond. He knows you've got him by the balls. He knows once you tell Padre who he really is, then his whole, holy fairy tale is over.

I was hungry. I stuffed myself as the voices watched, saying nothing, not even that people ate too much food. But then they said, *Listen! The two of them are talking out there. They haven't given up. They're planning again.*

I couldn't hear anything.

Move your table over here next to the door. They're talking in low tones. They don't want you to hear. Listen!

I moved the little table that I had been using as a desk next to the door and listened. I thought I could hear them mumbling but wasn't sure. Every now and then I thought I heard her sobbing.

She's not really crying. That's just a cover. What they're really doing is planning. They really want to get you, don't they?

Yes, they did. Yet try as I might I couldn't hear anything other than her sometimes crying. Then the old floor said someone was coming, and the faint knock on the door said it was Maria. *"Mi'jo, can I come in? I'd like to talk to you."*

Don't answer! Don't answer. Keep her out there.

I didn't answer and the silence was thick.

"Mi'jo, please, we need to talk."

More silence.

Then, *"Mi'jo, Antonio and me have talked. We know you're a young man now and that we can't keep treating you like a little boy. Antonio takes back everything he said and did at dinner yesterday and this morning. You don't have to eat dinner with us anymore. You can eat whatever you want, whenever you want, and you can fix it yourself. Or sometimes, if you want, you can eat something I've cooked. And you can eat anything and everything in your room* like you're doing now. We can still have a good life together if we can just talk about these things. Please let us talk to you. Open the door, *mi'jo.*"

Seconds passed. She tried the door but it went flat against the table and I pushed hard on the table against the door.

"Please don't make us come in there. Antonio wants to talk to you too. Really he does. He knows what he did and said was wrong. Please open the door. We just want to talk to you face-to-face and tell you how sorry we are that this happened."

She tried the door again but the table held.

We could hear her leaving and the voices were laughing and laughing, and then I was laughing too. When we stopped laughing, the voices said, *Did you hear her saying, "Don't make us come in there?" You heard that, didn't you, Raymond. They're threatening us. They think they can force their way in here. They're in for a big surprise. Raymond, move that table and put your bed up against the door. Put the headboard against the door.*

I can't move that bed by myself.

Yes, you can.

How?

Piece by piece. Take the mattress off and then the spring off. Then you can move what's left.

If I drag it across the room, that'll make a lot of noise and they'll know what I'm doing.

Then take the sideboards off and carry them to the door one at a time, and move the headboard that way too.

I did what they told me and though the mattress and spring were heavy and awkward, I was able to lift them across the floor without making any noise. Then I put the bed together again against the door without making any noise.

Then we looked at the bed against the door and we laughed and laughed until we stopped to listen and wait. We couldn't hear anything but we knew they were planning something, so we waited. But every now and then the voices would point to the bed against the door and we would laugh some more. As the room darkened, instead of the pointing the voices would say, *Please don't make us come in there,* and we would laugh again.

When the room was dark, Tony came to the door. "What the hell is going on in there! Stop that laughing! Stop it! You're driving us crazy! It's late. We need to go bed. We need to sleep." He tried the door. It wouldn't open. We laughed. He pushed against the door. It wouldn't open. We laughed. He grunted against the door. It wouldn't open. We laughed.

He started crying and slobbering. "Ramón, please stop laughing. You're driving us crazy. We can't sleep. We tried to go to bed but then you laugh that long, loud laugh of yours and we can't sleep and we can't stay in bed. Please stop. I'm so sorry I said what I said and did what I did. Please stop."

He sat against the door crying.

Let the sorry son of a bitch cry. He deserves it.

But he's probably trying to peek through the keyhole.

Let him peek. It's dark in here.

And we laughed more. When he left the door, we laughed again.

The voices said to wait until they had a chance to get back into bed again and try to sleep before we laughed again.

We waited until we heard Tony in the bedroom and then we laughed loud and hard again. When we stopped we could hear Maria screaming.

Let's wait even longer this time. Let them think they can go to sleep, let them even fall asleep for a little while, and then we'll laugh and laugh.

We waited and as we were waiting there was suddenly light in the room. I looked around and saw that light was coming through the window. I jumped over to the window. Tony was on a ladder coming up the side of the house with a flashlight in his hand that was shooting light up through the window onto the ceiling. When he saw me he screamed, "What's going on in there? Open the window! Open the fucking window before I break it open!"

Pull the shade down! Pull the shade down!

I lowered the shade and it blocked the light. Moments later he was rapping at the window, "Open it! Open it!"

Let him rap! Don't answer! Don't say anything! If he busts that window and tries to get in here, give him a good shove backward and the crazy asshole will flip over and bust his head wide open.

He stopped rapping. All was quiet. I thought he had gone back inside and was waiting for him to get back into bed when there was an explosion at the window. I ran there, stepping on shattered glass everywhere. I raised the blind. Tony was on the ground and had thrown a rock through the window. The lower half of the window was one huge hole and Tony was coming up the ladder again.

He's coming up the ladder!

Toss that fucking ladder over! Kill that sorry son of a bitch!

I grabbed the two ends of the ladder that were propped against the windowsill and started pushing them away from the house.

"Don't Ramón! Stop, Ramón! You'll kill me!"

I struggled against his weight. But little by little, my end of the ladder was moving away from the house. Now, Tony was going down the ladder as fast as he could. And the lower he got, the easier it was for me to move the ladder. When I had the ladder almost straight up and down, I gave it a hard push and it started tipping over. Tony must have jumped off the ladder because all of a sudden, it flipped over.

You should have pushed harder, sooner, and killed that sorry son of a bitch! Keep the blind up and watch the window, and if he props the ladder up again, wait until he's almost up here and then push. But let's do some more laughing.

This time the voices sang, *Up the ladder he goes and down the ladder he goes. Up the ladder he goes and down the ladder he goes.*

And we laughed and laughed until we couldn't laugh anymore, and then we decided to wait until it seemed like they had gone to bed before our next turn.

There was no next turn, because before we could sing again, there was a knock at the door and a voice said, "Ramón, open the door. It's me, Padre Ibarra. What's going on in there?"

The voices said nothing. As quickly as they had appeared, so too did they disappear. And now my world was just Padre Ibarra and me.

"Ramón. Open the door."

"Yes, Padre. Just a moment, please." I tugged the bed far enough from the door so that I could open it. When I did open it, Padre Ibarra looked at the room and at me in disbelief. Tony was standing behind him, and Maria, in a bathrobe, was standing behind Tony crying.

"What is going on in here, Ramón? What happened? Why all of this?" looking in every direction.

"He hit me."

Padre Ibarra turned.

"You're lying. I did no such thing."

"I'm not lying. You're the liar. He hit me, Padre, at the dinner table. He spilled the *albondigas* all over the table and then sent me to my room."

"That's not true."

"Not true? Ask Maria. Padre, ask her if I'm telling the truth. Ask her who's lying."

Maria screamed and ran from the room.

Padre turned to Tony, "Antonio is that true?"

Tony was looking down at the floor shaking his head no.

"And that's not all, Padre. He said that from then on, I couldn't eat anything in his house, no food, no nothing. And where was I supposed to eat?"

"Antonio?"

"He wouldn't look at us when we were eating."

"No, no. What you said was that it was because I wouldn't look at *you.*"

"He showed me no respect, Padre. He just kept eating and eating and wouldn't look at me."

"I had a lot of homework and I was eating fast so I could start on it.... And that wasn't all of it. He had been snooping around in my room when I was at school. Then he said that I couldn't be going to school because I went without my speech book that I had left open on my desk to the same page every day. He was trying to prove that I wasn't going to school. He said I didn't have any friends so how could I be going to school. That wasn't true because I was working on my car at my friend's house after school."

Then the room was silent and Padre turned to Tony who was still looking down at the floor, but he wasn't shaking his head anymore. Padre took a deep breath and looked away.

Still, I wasn't about to let Tony get away with anything. "You haven't heard the rest of it, Padre. You really haven't. This morning at seven o'clock on my way to school, Tony stopped me in the backyard and he started feeling up my legs and my thighs..."

"What?" Padre looked at Tony again.

"I wasn't feeling him up. I was just trying to see if he was taking any of my food from my house."

"Liar! See, first he says that he didn't tell me I couldn't have any of his food, now he says that he was just checking to see if I had any of his food on me. Which is it Tony?"

Padre closed his eyes and rubbed his brow.

"But the best part, the part that proves everything that I've been saying, is that when he was trying to feel me up at seven o'clock this morning, he was drunk! Yes, drunk! The man who parades around here and everywhere acting like he's so holy, telling everyone that he hasn't had a drop of liquor in years, was drunk.... Ask him! Ask him!"

"That's enough, Ramón, get your things. I've got to get you out of here."

"I brought my things in a box and I don't know where the box is."

"Antonio, get him a box."

IT WAS after midnight when we left the Alvarez home in Padre's car. He stopped at the rectory and came out with some blankets and a pillow, a bag of groceries, and a duffel bag. "Take your things out of that box and put them in this bag." He started the car and said, "I'm taking you out to Malaga and you're going to spend the night in the church. It may only be for tonight, but it could be longer. I have to find you a new place to live. If that's going to take a few days, then I'll arrange for one of the church folks out there to feed you. In the bag is enough food to get you through tomorrow at least."

"But how can I sleep or live in the House of God, Padre?"

"There's nothing consecrated out there right now. So it's just like any other building and a church in name only. It's only when I consecrate something out there like I do with the hosts every Sunday or take something out there that's been consecrated that it becomes a House of God. So there's no problem with you staying there tonight or for a few days, if need be."

It was a little past one in the morning when we turned onto Malaga's main, dirt-pocked road. Padre's car rattled and the car lights bounced around in every direction. Lights in houses across from the church were turned on and I saw curtains moving. As soon as Padre parked in front of the church and got out of the car, the house lights went out.

Padre went up to the church and opened the doors and then looked back at the car. I wasn't moving. Sleeping and living in the church was not something I wanted to do, especially after the way I lied at Tony's. He motioned to me but I paid no attention. He came back to the car and said, "Ramón, get your things and get into the church."

"I don't want to sleep in there. I don't want to live in there. That's the House of God."

"Ramón, I've already explained. There is nothing consecrated in there. The tabernacle's empty. The chalice and monstrance are in the sacristy under the trapdoor. This is like any other building. Get your things and come on in."

"What about the picture?"

"What picture?"

"The big one of Jesus with His Chest cut open and His Heart on the outside of His Body, burning and bleeding with a crown of thorns around it."

"That picture's not consecrated, it's just a picture. Get your things and let's go in. I'll take the blankets and the pillow and the groceries. It's late and I have to get back to Parker."

You better listen to him. You better do as he says. He's your only friend now and you don't want to lose him. You don't want him joining the conspiracy too.

What conspiracy?

Tony's conspiracy.

That's in Parker. That's Tony and Maria's conspiracy.

What makes you think the church people out here don't know the church people in Parker? Sure as shit they all know by now what happened in Parker tonight. You're going to need him to protect you here, just like he did at Tony and Maria's.

"OK, OK. I'll go in but I'm not sleeping or living in the church part. I'll sleep in the sacristy."

"Sleep and live where you want. It's late and I have to get back to Parker and get some sleep. I have to be in Newhall in the morning."

As I got out of the car Padre said, "Here's a flashlight. It can get pretty dark out here at night. There's a strap on the duffel bag that let's you carry it on your shoulder. Here, I'll show you. See, that frees up your hands, the easier to use the flashlight."

I took the flashlight but didn't turn it on. There was enough moonlight to get me to the church doors, and once inside, I could get to the sacristy without a light. And I wouldn't have to see that flaming, bleeding Heart. In the sacristy Padre said, "You know, we woke a lot of people up when we came. I'm sure the two sisters across the street are terrified. They're always terrified. I'm sure they're still awake trying to figure out what's going on over here. I think we'd better go over and talk to them now. Otherwise God only knows what they'll do once I leave without you."

We walked across the street to a small, wood-framed house and Padre knocked on the screen door. No answer. No lights, no sounds, no sense of movement within. "They're afraid of everything," he said softly. "The older one was married for a while until her husband ran off with another woman. The younger one, the spinster, never married. She had a very sheltered life, living with her parents until they died and then she came to live with her sister."

He knocked again, harder. "Señora Gutierrez. It is me, Padre Ibarra," he said loudly. "It is important that I talk to you." No answer. He was taking tiny steps back and forth that were moving him nowhere. He looked at his watch but couldn't see the hands or the numbers. He was getting angry.

You better calm him down.

How am I gonna calm him down?

Well you better hope that he calms down because you're the one that's going to live with these people, not him.

Live with these people? What are you talking about?

After Tony gets through talking to all these church people, who do you think is going to want you living near them?

Padre will set them straight. He'll tell them about Tony.

What's he going to tell them? Tony's been with him for years, taking care of the church without being paid a nickel and never having had a drink in all that time. Now all of a sudden he's drunk and feeling you up. Who's going to believe that? You'd better...

Now Padre pounded on the front wall so hard that the porch shook and a light went on in the house. "Who is it?" came a voice from within.

"Open the door, Señora Gutierrez. It's me Padre Ibarra. I need to talk to you."

A sliver of light opened at the edge of the door.

"Open the door!"

You better calm him down.

"Oh, it's you, Padre." And the door opened. A short, stout, dark woman in a bathrobe stood looking up at the man on the other side of the screen door.

Padre looked at his watch and said, "Mrs. Gutierrez, it's almost 1:30 and I have to get back to Parker, but I think it's important that I talk to you about this young man," pointing to me. "You know him don't you?"

She looked at me and the face of a figure hunched behind the stout woman rose up and looked at me too. It was a thin, wrinkled, white face that hunched down again as soon as she saw me looking at her.

"Yes, I know him. He's the one that comes on Saturdays and takes care of the church and the yard and serves Mass with you when you say it here."

"His name is Ramón..."

"Hey, what's going on over there? It's 2:30 in the morning and people are trying to sleep!" It was Rogelio Rodriguez, the nosy old neighbor, who came limping out of the darkness.

"Ah, Señor Rodriguez. It's probably a good thing that I talk to you too. This is Ramón..."

"I know who he is. He's here every Saturday and some Sundays."

"Ramón's going to be staying in the church tonight and maybe for a few days until I can get him settled in Parker."

"Why out here and not in Parker?"

"His grandmother died..."

"Yes, but that was some time ago. Why can't he be where he's been in Parker since then? Why bring him out here in the middle of the night? I don't think I like this."

"I don't care what you like. I'm the pastor of this church, and I'll let someone stay there a few days if that's what I want to do. And I don't have to explain anything to you. It's almost 1:30 and I have to be on my way. Ramón will be staying in the church maybe for a few days. Does everybody understand that?"

They could see that Padre was angry and the stout woman and the old man nodded and the hunched woman remained hunched.

"OK, Ramón. Let's go back and close up the church."

You'd better be nice to your priest friend. It looks like you may be needing him down the line.

As we entered the church again, Padre turned on the lights.

And I shouted, "No! No! Don't do that!" and I turned to see what I didn't want to see, that big red Heart out in the open on fire and bleeding and Jesus pointing to it with one finger and at me with the other. "No, no, turn the lights off."

"Calm down, Ramón. I just want to make sure everything's as it should be before I go."

You're losing it, man. He's going to go. Don't let him see you like this.

"Everything looks OK and I'm going now," he said, turning off the lights. "I'll see you about noon tomorrow." He stepped outside and closed the door and I hurried to the sacristy.

What is the matter with you and that picture?

I don't know. I've never liked it and it's bothered me before but never like this. I just knew it was going to scare the hell out of me even when I was in Padre's car.

We're gonna get you over that right now, aren't we?

They started laughing.

Now get on out there where the picture is and turn on them lights.

I don't want to go out there and I don't want to turn on those lights.

We don't give a damn what you want. We're telling you what to do.

They were still laughing.

Please don't make me do that.

We said get your ass out there! Turn on those goddamn lights and stare at that damn picture until we tell you not to!

I had to do what they said. I had to look at that Heart. I had no choice. They were my friends, my only friends.

Go!

Slowly I went to the light switches on the front wall of the church.

Turn them on!

I turned them on.

Look at it! Look at His Heart!

I did. It was the blood dripping and the thorns cutting and the flames burning that made me turn and run out of the church screaming. I ran to the sisters' house across the street, screaming. I pounded on their door and begged for them to let me in, but they wouldn't answer. I ran toward Don Rogelio's screaming. He had come out of his house and when he saw it was me, he opened his arms for me and I ran to him but knocked him down and ran over him and out onto the road screaming. I ran up and down the road screaming. More people had come out of their houses. One of them chased me and finally caught me and wrestled me down to the ground and then sat on me as I was screaming. I kept twisting and kicking, crying and screaming, but he wouldn't get off me. Finally, a sheriff's patrol car arrived and the two deputies cuffed me and tied my legs and put me on their back seat and drove me to the hospital

I WAS in the hospital for two months. The doctors put me on fifteen milligrams of Zyprexa for the first two weeks I was there and then lowered the dosage to ten milligrams a day for the rest of my stay and, they said, for the rest of my life to make sure I didn't have another break. The voices were the first to go and then the staring and the ability to see everything, everywhere, and in anything. By the second month, I was beginning to be what they called my "normal" self.

LOCAL buses were the means of transportation for many people who lived in the small towns and unincorporated areas in the southern half of the Central Valley. Those buses ran from Parker to Bakersfield, making many stops along the highway when they were waved down by prospective passengers standing on the roadside or when asked by passengers to stop and let them off. They were old buses that had once serviced the express runs and had since been replaced by newer models.

The bus driver said, "Where you going, bud?"

"Where are *you* going?"

"All the way to Los Angeles."

"Then that's where I'm going too, sir. To Los Angeles."

"Los Angeles? I never had anyone take a local all the way to Los Angeles. Shoot, it takes me more than double the time it would take one of them expresses to get to Los Angeles."

I turned to see the reaction of the other passengers, mostly Mexicans. They were stone-faced, except those in the first rows who had seen and heard everything.

"You might want to take the next local into Parker instead and then take an express from there."

"I don't want to go back to Parker and take an express from there." I was nervous. We needed to get going. Parked there, we were drawing attention. I couldn't see Doña Petra's store but she had probably already called Don Rogelio and told him she had seen me get on a bus heading south, and he was probably talking to the Parker cops right now.

The driver was looking at me as if I wasn't making any sense. Then he said, "Suit yourself, mister, but I wouldn't even know what to charge you. I ain't never had a fare from here to Los Angeles and I wouldn't know what to charge you until we got to Bakersfield. That's my first and only stop at a station from here, and one of them clerks would have to figure that out for me."

I took a hundred-dollar bill out of one of my pockets and held it out to him. There were murmurs from the folks nearby. "Here take this for now. That ought to get me to Bakersfield from here, and when we get there, you can give me my change and tell me how much more the fare will be to Los Angeles."

The bill took him aback for a moment, but then he looked down at the floor too. "I think you dropped something down there."

I looked. Next to my shoe was another crisp, new, hundred-dollar bill that must have slipped out of my pocket when I pulled out the first one. I bent down and picked it up and the murmurs were louder as I stuffed it back in my pocket.

The driver still hadn't taken the bill from my other hand, and there was fear and suspicion in his look. "What you got in that big bag of yours, mister?"

"My clothes."

"You sure that's all you got in there?"

"I'm sure." I was fearful too. We still hadn't moved and the Parker cops had to be on their way. More than that, he might not let me stay on his bus. Then what would I do?

"Well, I'm gonna have to put that big bag of yours down below in the baggage section. There's only one seat left on this bus and that bag of yours won't fit in one of the overhead compartments, and you and that bag won't fit in one seat either. And like I said, there's only one seat available on this here bus."

"I only need one seat. I can sit in that seat and stand the bag between my legs."

"No, that won't do. That won't be very safe. I'm gonna have to put that bag down below in the baggage section."

"Look," I said picking up my duffel bag and showing it to him, "I've gone up and down on a lot of local buses around here and the drivers always tell everybody getting on the buses that they'll have to keep their bags with them, that they can't store bags below on local buses. Now you're trying to tell me just the opposite. So what's made you change your mind?"

He didn't answer. Instead he kept looking at the top of my bag, which was now pointing right at him, and at the hundred-dollar bill I was offering him. And there was more fear in his eyes. Finally he nodded and took the bill and said, "You'd better take the only seat I have left, and you'll have to wait 'til we get to Bakersfield for your change."

I turned and looked for the seat. The only empty seat was next to the aisle in the last row on my left. I started down the aisle. No one looked at me. They looked straight ahead or had their eyes closed, faking sleep. Still I worried that some of them had seen the two hundred-dollar bills and I worried about what they would think, or worse, what they might do.

The man sitting next to the empty seat was looking out the window. His head was bald and shiny brown. As I was getting my bag and myself into the empty space he didn't turn and look at me. Then as I was about to sit, the bus shook its way back onto the highway and I lost my balance and landed hard on my seat, bumping him. He didn't turn, even after I said, "Excuse me." Annoyed, I lifted the duffel bag onto the edge of the seat between my legs, high enough so that I could rest the top of it on my shoulder next to him and shield my face and head from him. That didn't make him turn either. It didn't matter I told myself. What he was looking at out that window was just his little world. He would never be part of the world that all that money in my bag was putting me in.

The bus started down the highway, stopping every few minutes, it seemed, at the edge of villages or in the middle of nowhere letting people off and on. And Los Angeles kept getting farther and farther away. On the other hand, after several of those stops without cops jumping on the bus to arrest me, I began thinking that maybe the cops didn't know I was on that bus. Or maybe they would be waiting for me in Bakersfield. And then I would think that with all the people getting off, there were fewer and fewer of them that had seen me with the two hundred-dollar bills, and maybe none by the time we got to Bakersfield. But Billy had said that tomorrow's drop-off was a very big deal and if anything went wrong with it, there was going to be a lot of trouble. There had to be a lot of money in those bags. And I kept seeing the man there tomorrow at noon, all dressed-up standing next to his big, new car waiting and looking for me at the Malaga bus stop. And when I didn't show, there were going to be a lot of dangerous, angry people looking for me. By noon tomorrow, I had to be far, far away.

After several more stops, I lowered my duffel bag and stood it next to me halfway in the aisle. Then I turned to the man next to me. He was looking straight ahead now. The wrinkles on his neck and hands said he was probably in his sixties. The starched and freshly ironed work shirt and work pants were too clean, too presentable for him to be going to work. I had vowed not to talk to him, but by then I had no choice. None of the local buses I had been on had toilets and this one was no exception. I poked him and he half turned and I said in Spanish, "Does this bus make any stops before it gets to Bakersfield to let people get off for a minute or two?" He looked at me as if he didn't understand my question and then answered in Spanish, "I don't know."

I turned from him. It was a waste of time trying to talk to people like him. My bladder was aching. I crossed my legs forcing the pain back. But I thought I could feel a leak. I re-crossed my legs, squeezing them together as hard as I could. I shifted my weight onto one buttock. That helped, but not for long. The last thing I wanted, the last thing I could afford, was pissing all over myself and the seat and the floor and my duffel bag, piss running all over the floor and people smelling it and making a commotion and tracing it back to me. I had drawn enough attention to myself with the two hundred-dollar bills. Now everyone would remember me and could ID me to the cops. "Yeah, the guy with the duffel bag. The guy who pissed all over himself and the bus. Yeah, that's him alright."

I bent over. I crouched. I cupped my knees and brought them to my chest. My eyes were watering: with tears or piss? I worried. I held everything at my chest, held it and held it. The man next to me had gone back to looking out the window. He didn't want to be involved. Yet, as intense as the pain and my efforts were, as fearful as I was that I would ultimately piss all over myself, somewhere in the corner of my mind were the images of cops waiting for me in the Bakersfield bus station and the well-dressed man in his new car starting to hunt me down.

I was still holding myself when the driver stopped the bus, got out of his seat, stood and turned and loudly said, "Bakersfield! We have fifteen minutes here! Fifteen minutes! Bakersfield!"

I started to stand but felt a squirt of piss on my thigh and sat down and clutched my knees to me again. The man next to me said, "Excuse me," and shifted past me without another look or word and was gone. The bus emptied and I was still gnarled in a knot in my seat.

The driver studied me from the front of the bus and then said, "Hey, bud, this is Bakersfield. This is as far as you go with me. If you still want to go to L.A. you can catch an express here. Come on, up with you. We gotta go inside and figure out your fare from Malaga to here. Come on, get up."

"I gotta piss real bad."

"I don't care what you have to do besides getting up and outta my bus. So get up.... We've got station police here that'll come and get you up if you don't get your butt up quick and get outta my bus.... You want me to call them?"

"No! No! No!" The word "police" blotted out my need to piss. I got up but as I picked up my duffel bag, I felt a stream of piss run down the inside of my leg. I moved bowlegged down the aisle with piss coming out of the bottoms of my pant cuffs.

"Jesus Christ!" the bus driver said when he saw the stream of piss. "Hold it! Hold it!"

"I can't! I can't!"

"Get your butt outta my bus! Hurry! Hurry! Hold it! Hold it!"

I was moving as fast as I could and holding it as best as I could but the piss wouldn't stop coming. "I'm trying!" But at the bus door I stopped and looked in every direction for cops.

"What are you stopping for? Get your butt to the restroom!"

There were no cops. I hobbled down the bus steps still pissing.

"Get yourself cleaned up in the restroom and over to the waiting room as quick as you can. We've got to straighten out your fare and I've got to get back here and get this bus cleaned up before we start loading people on it."

I stood over the commode in the restroom for several minutes somehow trying to guard against a repeat of what had happened on the next part of my trip. It took me that long to realize that what I was trying to prevent was futile because my pants were sopping wet with piss, my socks and shoes were squishing with piss, and even the bottom part of my duffel bag was wet. No one was going to let me on their bus in that condition. Then the bus driver yelled at me through the restroom door, "Come on, get a move on! We've got to straighten out your fare and I've got to get my bus ready for all those people waiting inside!"

In the waiting room people stared at me. Someone must have told them what had happened, and it didn't help that my faded blue jeans were now a deep, dark blue down the inside of each leg and that my old sneakers were a two-tone tan and the darkest brown. I kept my eyes down as much as I could all the way to the ticket counter.

"So you're the young man who had all that unfortunate trouble on the southbound local that came in a while ago?" said a soft-spoken man in a short-sleeve shirt and tie from behind the counter.

I looked at him but before I could answer, the driver, who was standing next to me said, "This is him alright and like I told you, he wants to go to L.A., but he ain't going with me. I'm just here to make sure he gets his change from the hundred-dollar bill he gave me toward a fare from Malaga to here."

"Yes, and I've calculated that fare to be sixty-two dollars and thirty-two cents. And here's your change," as he moved some bills and coins toward me. "Is it true that you want to go on to Los Angeles?"

"Yeah."

"Well, you won't be going there on Jim's local."

"Why?"

He turned to the driver and said, "Jim, you'd better check on your bus's condition before you start boarding your people. I can handle this."

The driver nodded and walked away.

The man turned back to me and said calmly, "The local you were on was sold out for southbound destinations even before you arrived here. To make matters worse, because of your unfortunate accident, and I know it was an accident, we're not able to use the two rear seats where you were until they've been thoroughly cleaned up in a day or two. So two people who have already purchased tickets will have to be turned away. There is an express bus to Los Angeles that will be leaving here in two hours and fifteen minutes and I can put you on that bus."

"Two hours and fifteen minutes?"

"Yes, that bus will actually arrive in Los Angeles almost an hour before the local you were on does."

I looked around the waiting room. No police. If they knew I was coming to Bakersfield, they would have been here by now. But the longer I waited in Bakersfield, the longer they would have to come.

When I turned back to the man he said, "What I'm about to tell you is just a friendly suggestion. If you're going to continue traveling, you should change your clothes and shoes. I assume you have clothes in that duffel bag of yours? But I was told that your bag was soiled too, so you might very well need to buy some new clothes and even a new bag. There's a sporting goods store two blocks from here. I'm sure you can buy a fresh change of clothes there and even a new bag pretty inexpensively."

I tried to think but the smell of my clothes and my duffel bag was getting stronger and stronger and that was all I could think of then.

"By the way," the man continued, "if you decide on taking the express to Los Angeles, your duffel bag will have to be checked into the baggage compartment under the side of the bus."

"Why?"

"Those are our regulations. A bag that size has to be checked into the baggage section because it won't fit in any of the overhead compartments in the bus."

I tried to think again but couldn't. Checking the bag in with the bus people, plus the smell that was reeking from me and my bag, was making my mind one big swirl.

"I guess I should also tell you that if you decide to shop at the sporting goods store or anywhere else around here, you'd be best off avoiding the use of hundred-dollar bills for your purchases. This is a poor part of town, and use of big bills will only bring you negative attention."

"But I only had two."

"That's fine. I'm just saying that it's not a good idea to be buying things with hundred-dollar bills in this part of town."

I stepped away from the counter, walked a few steps, and for whatever reason, stopped in the middle of the waiting room. My mind was swirling so much that I was terrified by the sense that the voices were returning. I wanted to take another Zyprexa, but I had taken one that morning. And I had been warned against taking more that fifteen milligrams a day, and the pills I had were all ten milligrams. I looked back at the counter and the ticket man was staring at me. Some of the people in the line at the door were staring at me too. I had to get out of there. If the cops showed up then... I looked in every direction and went into the restroom.

I went to the farthest stall and closed and locked the door. I put the duffel bag on top of the commode's tank and sat on the commode with my pants lowered down around my shoes. I had to calm down. I had to think. I listened for anyone who might have followed me. No one entered the restroom for several minutes, and when two men did, they loudly used the urinals and left. The cops hadn't come. If they were coming, they probably would have been there by now, and the well-dressed man wouldn't start looking for me until tomorrow. That calmed me. I had two hours to decide what I was going to do.

The first thing to think about was the duffel bag. If I was going on to L.A., the clerk had said that it was too big and had to be put in the baggage compartment. I looked at the duffel bag. There had to be a way to cut down its size. Then it occurred to me that the gym bags themselves were taking up space. If I could put all the money in the duffel bag and get rid of the gym bags, that had to reduce the size of the duffel bag.

I stacked the four gym bags against the back stall wall. Because each bag had a padlock, I would have to cut the bags open. I had already cut into a bag in Malaga, and now I took out all the loose, hundred-dollar bills that had fallen from the one bundle I had opened earlier. These I rewrapped with the bundle's band, and I put it and all the other bundles of bills into the empty duffel bag. I sliced open the first gym bag that had come into my possession and was stunned to find there were only bundles and bundles of banded pieces of white paper the size of dollar bills and nothing more. The second bag also had only bundles of white paper. The fourth bag was filled with bundles of hundred-dollar bills. I checked and rechecked the bags to make sure that I wasn't hallucinating. Maybe it was a good thing I wouldn't be giving the well-dressed man all four bags the next day.

The two bags with the real money and a few of the old clothes that didn't stink filled less than half the duffel bag, and it sagged badly. People would wonder why I was using such a big bag for such a small load. More than that, the bag, like me, stunk. The sporting goods store the ticket man had recommended seemed like a good idea.

With four gym bags under one arm and the duffel bag strapped over the opposite shoulder, I went to the restroom doorway and watched until the ticket man was busy with a customer. Then I slipped out into the boarding area and walked along until I found a garbage bin. I tossed the four gym bags into it and headed in the direction of the sporting goods store.

In the store I tried on several gym suits, choosing one that I thought made me look like an athlete. I took all the bundles of bills out of the duffel bag and put them in a brown, traveling gym bag. I took a few bills out of the rewrapped bundle and put that bundle on top of the others where I could easily reach it. The gym bag was less than half the size of the duffel bag, which I left in the dressing room with all my old clothes. Then I went up to the sales-clerk and told him I was going to buy the gym suit I was wearing, as well as the sneakers and socks and underwear that I had on and the traveling gym bag I was carrying.

The salesclerk studied me for a moment and then said, "Well, we'd better find out what all that comes to first." He was a tall, gray-haired man with tired eyes and a long paunch under his white shirt. He started to add up the items and said, "I kinda wish you hadn't worn all these things until we were sure you had enough money to pay for them."

"I got enough money."

He nodded and kept adding. Then he said, "That all comes to a hundred and seventy-two dollars and seventy-six cents. And if you're going to use a credit card, I'm going to need two forms of current identification and at least one of them at least should have a current photo."

Unzipping one of the pants pocket I said, "I'm paying cash," as I fingered in that pocket for two bills. Separating two bills from the others, and then placing them on the counter I said, "Here's two hundred dollars. That ought to cover it."

The two bills took him by surprise. With a puzzled look he took up the bills and examined them, turning them over and over again. Then he set one down and held the other one up to a light bulb, looking at every corner of it on both sides. Then he set that bill down and took the other one and held it up to the bulb too. Then he rubbed each one of them with his thumb and forefinger. He looked at me again, still puzzled, and said, "Well I guess I have to give you some change."

He opened the cash register and looked up at me again, still uncertain. "The people at the bus station must have sent you here."

"Yeah, they did."

"I thought so. I didn't think you were from around here.... Where you going?"

"Los Angeles."

"Live there?"

"No."

"Looking for work there?"

"Nope."

"Got family there?"

"Yep."

"Kind of a vacation-visit then?"

"Yep."

He sorted out my change in the cash register and started to give it to me but stopped and instead said, "Now what I'm about to say, young fellow, I hope you don't take it in a bad light. It's just that you can't go around handing and spending hundred-dollar bills like they're dollar bills. There are a lot of bad actors around everywhere these days, especially in this neighborhood, who may just see you flashing those big bills real casual like and decide that they need them more than you do. So I'd be careful with them if I was you."

"See, it's not my fault. I just got out of the hospital and my first disability check was out there waiting for me. I took it to the bank to cash and the woman there gave me mostly hundred-dollar bills."

"You were in the hospital and now you're on disability. Sounds pretty serious to me. But I don't want to get into that."

"Neither do I... I better get going. I've got a bus to catch."

IN THE waiting room I got in line behind two men. When I got to the counter the ticket man said, "Whoa! I almost didn't recognize you in your new clothes. So what have you decided?"

"First of all, if I buy a ticket to Los Angeles, I want to be sure that this traveling bag is going to be with me in the passenger's part of the bus all the way to Los Angeles. It's less than half the size that my old duffel bag was."

"I don't see that as a problem."

"Then give me a ticket on your Los Angeles Express," I said putting down a hundred-dollar bill.

The man looked at the bill for several moments and then at me for several moments before he said, "This is the fourth hundred-dollar bill you've passed around here in just a few hours. In all the years I've worked here, I've never seen anything like that."

"What do you mean fourth? I've just given you two hundred-dollar bills."

"No, sir. Bob Donovan over at the sporting goods store called me a few minutes ago and said that you paid with two of them over at his store. Now they may or may not be part of a disability check, but I just want to warn you, my friend. You can't go around using hundred-dollar bills like they was dollar bills. Sooner or later someone's gonna take notice of that and try to take advantage of that."

It was too late to start thinking about that.

THE INSIDE of the bus was dimly lit when I boarded and there were only a few vacant seats left. I chose a seat next to the aisle closest to the toilet. All the passengers seemed to be Mexicans and the man next to me in the window seat was no exception. He looked up at me when I stopped at the empty seat beside him. He had a wide face with a thick, black, bushy mustache and dark eyes. He measured me for a moment and didn't say a word, and then he turned and looked out the window at the night.

"Is this seat taken?" I asked trying to ingratiate myself.

He half turned and said, "I haven't seen anyone sit in it yet," and turned back to the window.

No accent. *Born here,* I thought.

I was standing in the aisle gripping my bag's two handles with two hands looking up at the overhead bin trying to decide how to open it. I set the bag down on the open seat, keeping one hand on the handles. I reached up and felt along the bottom of the bin until I found the latch. I clicked the bin open and then felt with my free hand to see if there was space for my bag. The bin seemed empty, and I raised my bag and put it in the bin rearranging it several times to guard against it sliding when the bus was in motion.

The bin didn't seem to have dividers, and the last thing I wanted was to have it slide down and out of the bin onto someone's lap or into the aisle.

I closed the lid and sat down. But I was no sooner sitting when I thought of a better way to protect against its moving. I got up and moved it around several times, but I couldn't see exactly where it was, so I stood up on my seat to see rather than feel for the best place to put the bag. Even as I was standing on my seat I moved it several times trying to find the best place for it. Until the man in the seat next to mine said loudly and angrily, "Sit down, boy, goddamn it! The bus is moving! Sit the hell down!" Others turned and looked in our direction. I stepped down into the aisle and into my seat embarrassed and offended. But I saw then that the man was very thickset and muscular. There was no way I was going to respond to him. I sat in a gloomy silence as we rode out of Bakersfield.

We rode in silence for many miles until he said, "What you got in that bag, youngster?"

"What?" as if I hadn't heard.

"I said what you got in that bag of yours up in that bin?"

I panicked and looked straight ahead, not wanting him to see my fear. "Nothing" was all I could say.

"Whad'ya mean, nothing? Who do you think you're talking to, youngster? Some idiot? The way you fooled with that thing up there tells me that you've got something that's pretty damn important to you up there."

"I got my clothes in it, and I was just worried about it sliding around and falling on other people, that's all."

"Yeah, right."

We rode on, but now I was worried that I had fooled around with the bag so much that he knew there was something in it worth having, worth him having. And if he decided to take it what could I do? Yell and scream that it was mine? Let the bus driver and cops decide whose it was? And once they saw what was in it, I'd be on my way to the Parker jail.

After a while the man said, "Where you headed, youngster?"

"Los Angeles."

"We're all headed to Los Angeles. Where you going to in L.A.?"

The question stunned me. I had never been to Los Angeles and I didn't know anyone in Los Angeles. My sense had been that I was going to keep going, that I had to get as far away from the police and the well-dressed man as I could. "I'm not going to Los Angeles."

"Where you going?"

Again I panicked. I didn't know where I was going and I didn't know how to answer. He was already suspicious of me, and now he was looking at me and waiting for me to answer. And search as I could for an answer, I couldn't find one. What somehow seeped out of me was, "I don't know."

"You don't know?"

I nodded and repeated, "I don't know."

The man leaned close to me and in a soft voice said, "Are you running?"

"Running?"

"Yeah, is somebody after you, like the police or somebody?"

I looked at him. Our faces were inches apart. I must have been trying to look into his eyes but in the bus's dim light all I could see was darkness.

"Don't worry, I'm not a cop. There's no fucking way I could ever be a cop. Believe it or not, I just feel for you. You remind me of me, thirty-five years ago. But as green as I was then, I was never as green as you are now. You don't know the first thing about running. If I had the time and situation, I'd take you under my wing right now and show you a few things. But I don't have either. You might say I'm kind of running myself.... You're running aren't you?"

"Yeah."

"I knew there was something weird about you from the minute I first saw you."

"How could you tell? It's pretty dark in here."

"No, the first time I saw you, you were in the waiting room."

"In the waiting room?"

"Yeah, when you were in line to buy a ticket. You really stood out."

"What?"

"Only the poor people in this country travel by bus. A lot of them don't own a car. Can you imagine not owning a car in this country? Or if they do own a car, it's too old or beat-up to make it to L.A., or it's cheaper to ride the bus than buy gas for that car of theirs."

"So?"

"And there you were standing in line in a shiny, brand-new running suit and expensive new running shoes. I'll bet there hasn't been a person in line all day long, or all week long, decked out as good as you were then."

"Yeah, but you don't understand."

"What don't I understand?"

"I lost my other clothes and had to buy new ones."

"Yeah, but if you had enough money to buy the clothes you're wearing now, you had enough money to buy new, everyday clothes and not these expensive clothes that all the people in these lines couldn't buy even if they wanted to. So right away you got my attention, and then you got my attention for another reason."

"What was that?"

"That new traveling bag you were carrying. It wasn't that big, but the way you were carrying it said it was real big for you. It's the kind of bag that everybody holds loosely with one hand. But you were holding it with two hands, and it was pressed tight against you, even when you moved. That told me right away that you had something in that bag that was real important for you, money or something. That was just my guess. And then on the bus you came down the aisle holding it the same way, and fussing with it and fussing with it in the bin. There's something in there alright. But don't worry I'm not interested in copping your new bag. I've got too many other things that I have to tend to right now. And whatever's in there is always going to mean a lot more for you than it ever will for me. So where you going again?"

"I don't know."

"This bus is only going to L.A. You know you got on a bus headed for L.A., don't you?"

"Yeah, I knew that."

"So you must have at least thought of going to L.A., didn't you?"

"It wasn't like that. I got on the first bus I could get on and it was going to Los Angeles. The only thing I was thinking about then was getting out of where I was."

"People coming at you from every direction?"

"Yeah."

"Cops and maybe other people too?"

"Yeah."

"I've been there. I know the feeling.... So you're not thinking of staying in L.A.?"

"No, I think they could trace me to Los Angeles way too easy."

"Well, we're gonna get into L.A. late and there won't be many buses going anywhere 'til morning. That should give you some time to think things over."

"I don't think I'll be hanging around in the waiting room until morning. Way too many cops in those places for me."

"That's not what I'd be thinking about if I were you. Bus depots are usually in a creepy part of town and L.A. is no exception. People wandering in and out of depots or walking those streets at three or four in the morning are usually pretty hungry. As soon as they see you with your brand-new gym suit and your brand-new running shoes, you'll become a target. Maybe that bag you got up there is all you got but one way or another they'll end up with it. There are some cheap hotels around that L.A. depot, and if I were you, I'd get in one of them for the night as quick as I could. First thing in the morning, I'd catch me a cab out to the nearest Walmart store and buy me some everyday clothes and shoes in the working man's section and get me a regular suitcase, nothing fancy, that I could put that traveling bag in. And two changes of clothes. If you wanna travel poor, you gotta look poor. But all of that will give you enough time between now and the time you leave Walmart to decide where you're going."

Then he turned from me and sat upright and looked out his window at the night. I would have liked to keep talking to him and maybe find out something about him. But he had made it clear, without having said so, that we would talk only when he decided to talk, and it seemed then that he had said all he had to say.

But about a half hour later, he leaned toward me again. "Have you decided where you're going yet?"

"No, I haven't. All I've been able to think about is getting in and out of Los Angeles. Are you going to Los Angeles?"

"Yeah."

"Do you live there?"

"No, but I have a lot of friends in East L.A. and South Central. Guys I did some time with."

"But is Los Angeles your hometown? Is that where you're from?"

"No, it's hard to say where I'm from now. Over the past thirty-five years I've lived in and around many places in California, courtesy of the State of California. But you're Mexican, aren't you?"

"Yeah."

"Speak Spanish?"

"Yeah."

"Then you should think about going to Mexico."

"Why?"

"Because I don't think you've done anything bad enough to have the U.S. Government come after you down there. And any private party that's after you is gonna get lost in a sea of brown faces down there, especially if you give up wearing brand-new gym suits and brand-new, expensive, running shoes and look more like the people all around you."

"Where in Mexico would I go?"

"I wouldn't go to any of the border towns like Tijuana or Juarez. There's too much heat on both sides of the border with the drug gangs on that side killing everybody in sight, and the Border Patrol on this side stopping and questioning anybody and everybody that looks like a Mexican. It used to be that you could cross into Mexico on foot whenever you wanted without a passport or visa or anything, just walk right in. Not anymore. Not anymore. The Mexicans have their military guarding their borders asking for a passport or a visa and putting all your things through a metal detector."

"I don't have a passport or a visa, so how do I get into Mexico?"

"They say that the farther away you get from Tijuana and Juarez the easier it is to cross, especially in little places like Agua Prieta. But those little places are hard to get to, especially if you're traveling by bus. What I've heard is that it's still easy to cross in Laredo. There you can walk over the Rio Grande on a big bridge and not get hassled on the Mexican side because there's so many Mexicans who cross back and forth every day to work over here in the mornings and then cross again to go back home in the evenings."

"Where's Laredo?"

"It's in Texas."

"Where in Texas?"

"Way down near the southern tip of Texas."

"How do I get there? By bus?"

"How else? But I wouldn't take a bus traveling along or near the border because they say the Border Patrol is stopping buses everywhere down there and getting on the buses looking for illegals."

"So how do I get to Laredo?"

"I'd go to Dallas from here and from there drop down to Laredo."

"Where's Dallas?"

"In the middle of Texas."

"How do I get there?"

"From here you take a bus to Phoenix and from there take one to Albuquerque. From there take one to Dallas and then take one down to Laredo."

He straightened himself. That was all he had to say and he looked out at the night again.

He had been helpful and I felt close enough to him then to lean over and extend my hand and say, "My name's Ray. What's yours?"

He turned, annoyed, and pushed my hand away and said, "Did I ask you what your name is?"

"No."

"Then what made you think I wanted to give you mine?"

"I just thought..."

"I don't care. Whatever you thought was wrong. When you're running you don't give your name to nobody. That'll just help anybody looking for you to find you." He turned back to his window.

We rode on in silence. Gradually I began seeing more and more lights, enough to make me think we were either nearing a little town or the outskirts of Los Angeles. Then the lights became so many that it had to be Los Angeles.

The man leaned over to me again and said, "I don't know where you're going or what you'll do when you get there. But when you get there try to be satisfied with that. Because if you're not, the chances are that you'll just end up doing more and more running, and you'll never stop until it's too late. And believe me, a life of running isn't much of a life at all."

Then he stood and said, "Excuse me," and brushed past my knees out onto the aisle. I thought he was on his way to the toilet stall behind us but he moved instead down the aisle to the front of the bus. That made me think that he thought so little of me that he wanted to find another seat. I lost sight of him and after a few moments the bus slowed and stopped. I looked out the window and saw only houses. We weren't at any depot. Then the bus started up again and I saw that we had been at a railroad crossing. On the tracks I saw the figure of a man walking rapidly away from the bus.

A little while later I saw buildings and businesses. Los Angeles. Not long after, the bus was pulling into the bus yard and I remembered the man's advice that I stay in the first hotel I saw near the bus station. The bus slowed and turned into a loading slot and stopped. When I stood up to get my bag, I saw that police had surrounded the bus. I sat down without my bag. I didn't want the bag anywhere near me. Maybe they wouldn't see it. Maybe it had slid down to other passengers far enough away so that they could never tie it to me. There was a loud murmur on the bus. There had to be others who didn't want any contact with the police. Illegal aliens at least.

The driver opened the door and three young men in combat uniforms jumped up into the bus. They spoke briefly with the driver then all the lights went on and a handsome, sturdy, dark-skinned man spoke loudly in English and Spanish. "OK! Everybody stay seated! We're Los Angeles and State Police officers and we want everybody to get their identification out. We're going to be talking to each and every one of you to find out who you are and what you're doing here. Anyone who doesn't cooperate with us will be taken into custody until he or she does cooperate with us." Another, louder murmur. "Calm down, calm down!" And the three talked to the driver again.

I knew they had caught up with me. All the bus people along the way had been able to identify me and the duffel bag and now the traveling bag. I went over and over in my mind what I would tell them. First, no matter what Billy said, he was lying. No matter what he said, I knew nothing about his drug operation and was in no way involved in it. The bags I let Billy hide in the church, I did as a favor to him as my cousin. I took the bags and ran because I was afraid of what the other people in his organization would do to me once they found out that Billy had been arrested. I knew they would come to the church looking for me and the money. Leaving with the bags was the only way I thought I could protect myself.

The cops divided the bus into three sections. The lead cop took the back section. He didn't come straight to me, rather he started with the people four rows in front of me. Why, I didn't know, especially if they were after me. The questioning was going pretty fast and I couldn't figure out what they were doing. Maybe they weren't after me after all. Then some of the cops looked into some of the bins and that did scare me. I couldn't make out all of what the cop was asking the people in front of me but none of it seemed to be about me.

Then he was standing next to me looking down at me. "Where's your identification?"

"The only thing I have is an expired driver's license and I don't carry that around with me."

"What's your name?"

"Jimmy Ramirez."

"Where you from?"

"Sacramento."

"Where you going?"

"Los Angeles."

"Why?"

"To visit some cousins of mine."

"The driver said there was a man sitting next to you for most of the trip down from Bakersfield."

"Yeah, there was."

"Who was he?"

"I don't know."

"Do you know his name?"

"No."

"Some of the folks here said that he yelled at you, that he was angry with you. Did he know you that well to be angry with you?"

"No, I never see the man before in my life. He just yelled at me at the beginning of the trip."

"Why did he yell? What was he angry about?"

"Just because I had put my bag up in the bin and was trying to rearrange it."

"In this bin?" he said, pointing.

"Yeah, at first I was trying to make sure it didn't slide all over the place. But I couldn't quite reach it. So I got up on my seat and I was rearranging it when he yelled at me to sit down. I could tell by his voice that he was pissed off at me so I sat down. He didn't look like anybody to mess around with."

"What did he look like?"

"The light wasn't real good in here then. But he looked real muscular and serious."

The cop opened the bin and reached into it, and I thought I was going to have a stroke. I could barely breathe. I closed my eyes and lowered my head and gritted my teeth.

"Is this your bag?"

I didn't look up.

"I said, is this your bag?" Louder.

I looked up and nodded.

He held my bag up higher, turned it, looked at it from different angles, shook it, and put it back in the bin.

My heart was beating so fast I didn't know if I could talk.

"Did he have any luggage with him?"

I shook my head. That was all I could do.

"None at all?"

I shook my head again.

The bin was still open and he looked in it some more. My head was aching and my heart was beating wildly. He wiped his brow and stroked his chin and thought. Then he said, "Did he talk to you? Did he say anything to you besides 'sit down'?"

"No, in fact I tried to shake his hand, to get on the good side of him, and introduce myself. I even asked his name. That pissed him off some more. He told me to put my hand down and that he didn't give a damn what my name was, that he hadn't asked me for my name and that he wasn't about to give me his name."

The cop nodded to himself, stopped and said, "So you don't know who that man was?"

"No."

"His name is Alejandro Rios and for many years he was the leader of one of California's biggest prison gangs. He's a violent, dangerous man convicted of two murders and guilty of many more. He was paroled out of prison just last year after many, many years in there. Once outside, he went back to his old ways and is now leading a vicious drug gang out here. Some say he's still running what goes on with his old prison gang. You're lucky you sat down when he told you to sit down.

"Have a nice visit with your people."

He turned and signaled the other cops to go and he left. Then one by one the passengers filed out. I was the last one out of the bus, trying not to, but carrying my traveling bag with both hands.

It was 11:30 as I walked into the waiting room with Alejandro's words bouncing around in my mind, "If you're gonna ride the bus, you better look like a bus rider." The waiting room was less than half full but it seemed like all of them noticed me and looked at me hard. "If you're gonna ride the bus..." I hurried out of the waiting room into the street putting both hands on my bag's handles.

The sidewalk was busy. People were shuffling in both directions, but no one was in any hurry and the ones who noticed me took a second look. A smelly old man in dirty clothes tapped me on the shoulder. "Hey, youngster, how about helping a guy out who's down on his luck. Loan me a dollar and the Lord'll be with you." When I looked at him, I saw beyond him half a block down on the other side of the street big, black, bold letters painted on the side of an old building—HOTEL. I brushed past the man and stepped into the street. A car honked and brakes screeched. I looked over my shoulder at a driver cursing me, and I hurried even more toward the painted sign.

It was a hotel. I could see a dimly lit lobby and counter, but there was no one anywhere in sight and the front door was locked. I knocked on the door. I pounded on the door. No movement anywhere, nothing. I pounded again. Someone passing behind me said, "Hey, boy, can't you read English?" He was pointing to the bottom half of the door. *"No hablas ingles, cabron?"* he added and smirked as he moved on. The sign said: LOBBY HOURS 7:00 A.M.– 11:00 P.M. NO ONE WILL BE ADMITTED AFTER 11:00 P.M. I saw a doorbell button on the inside of the door paneling. I pressed on it and pressed on it. Nothing. There were a couple of young hoods watching me from the street corner less than half a block away. I kicked on the door and then I saw the head of a man peer out from behind the counter wall. I rapped hard on the glass portion of the door. That brought out a thin, dried-up old man in a worn, gray cardigan sweater from behind the counter.

He came a few feet toward me and pointed to the sign on the door. *"No puedes leer el señal?"*

I pounded some more.

"You no read English?"

I pounded again.

"You have a room here?"

"No, but I want a room here."

"I can't let nobody in after eleven o'clock."

"I have plenty of money. I'll pay whatever you want."

That made him think. He tilted his head and looked at me from different angles. "You alone?"

"Yes."

"No girlfriend?"

"No."

"No boyfriend?"

"No."

He thought some more. Then he said, "I have only one room, single bed, nothing else. Forty dollars." He watched me. "You have forty dollars?"

"I have fifty dollars. I'll give you fifty dollars for the room."

"You have fifty dollars? Show me."

The change from the clothes and the bus tickets amounted to more than fifty dollars. I sorted out two twenty-dollar bills and a ten and held them up to the glass.

He came closer and looked at the bills. "Okay, let me get the keys."

Once I registered, he came around the counter and said, "Follow me," and started toward the back of the building and a dark stairwell. As we climbed the first flight of stairs he said, "I put you on the third floor. That way there won't be no hanky-panky with your girlfriend or boyfriend climbing through the second-floor window in the back. I know you young people."

When we reached the third-floor hallway, he pointed down the hall to our left and said, "The last door on your right is your toilet. The door across from it is your shower. Make sure you knock before you go into either one of them."

He led me to the second door on the right and unlocked an old wooden door with a long key. He opened the door partway and turned on a light that came from a small, bare bulb that hung down from the high ceiling. He motioned me into the room and

I stepped in next to him. "This is your room and here's your key. And remember that the front door is locked and you don't have a key for it. So you can't leave the building until after seven o'clock in the morning. And don't try to find me for anything because you won't find me." He handed me the key and said, "Sleep good," and left.

It was a long, narrow room with walls that ran up maybe twenty feet. There was nothing in the room except an old dresser and across from it a single bed that looked like a cot. On the dresser was a pitcher half filled with water and a glass next to it. The floor was wide, smooth, worn, wooden planks with a three-by-four rug next to the bed. A window at one end of the room opened and looked out into blackness. A short chain that fit into a metal slot on the back of the door hung on the wall next to the door.

I fastened the chain in the slot and then took my bag with me to the bed where I sat and thought. That day had been the longest day of my life, and finally in that bare room, I felt safe. The police hadn't been waiting for me at the bus station. And even though police had actually questioned me on the bus and handled my bag, they had no idea who I was or what was in my bag. The well-dressed man hadn't even started looking for me yet, and he would never find me now that my name was Jimmy Ramirez. Tomorrow couldn't be anything like today.

I knew I had to keep moving. Los Angeles was way too close to the Parker police and to Billy and all his friends, whoever they might be. With all that money in my bag, those friends would probably never stop looking for me. Funny, but I still didn't know how much money was in the bag. I hadn't counted it yet; I hadn't had a chance to count it yet. And I didn't feel safe counting it there in that room. There could be cameras in the walls or the old man could be peeking in on me.

But my biggest problem was where to go tomorrow. The man on the bus seemed to know what he was talking about, but I didn't know any of those places, least of all Mexico.

Then there was the problem of my medication. I took the pills out of the vial and counted. Eight. Eight days before I needed more. But that shouldn't be a problem. The vial had all the information I needed to get a refill and there were two refills left. All I ever had to do was hand the vial to the pharmacy people and sit and wait for my refill. What worried me more was that I had wanted to take two pills this day—one in Bakersfield and then one tonight like the prescription said. Even though the doctors had warned me not to. There had been times that day when I had thought for sure that all the stress I had been going through would bring on the voices and I couldn't deal with them again. Never. Just the thought of the voices scared me. I got up, took the vial out of my pocket, went to the dresser, and took a pill.

I fell asleep sitting on the bed thinking. I woke up sometime during the night still sitting on the bed with my bag next to me. It seemed like I should have gotten up and turned off that bare bulb, but all I could do was roll over onto the bed and cover myself and my bag with a blanket and go back to sleep.

When I woke in the morning, the first thing that came to my mind was the gym suit. I had to be the only person in Los Angeles wearing a gym suit. I thought of taking a shower but there was no way I was going to walk down to the shower and back and undress and dress in there with my bag in the room. Necessity made me run down to the toilet and back in my gym suit, but that was necessity. The man on the bus said to have a cab take me to Walmart to buy some everyday clothes, which made a lot of sense.

When I got down to the lobby, I asked a different clerk to call me a cab. I guess I had seen people do that in the movies. But this wasn't the movies and the clerk didn't like that. "We don't do that here. If you want a cab, *you* go find one. I'm not your servant." Then he added, "You checking out?" I nodded and he answered, "Good."

Outside I saw three cabs parked in front of the bus depot. I waved to one and he drove me to a nearby Walmart. People in Parker were always talking about the Walmart there, but I had never been to it. This one was enormous. I had never been in a store that big and never before seen so many Mexicans in one store.

One of the workers showed me where the men's clothes were and I bought two sets of jeans and flannel shirts, a pair of boots, socks, a jacket, underwear, and a tan baseball cap with CATERPILLAR printed on the front. Then I bought a black canvas suitcase with rollers like the ones I had seen people using in the waiting room at Parker and Bakersfield. It was big enough to hold my traveling bag and all the new clothes I wasn't wearing.

In Parker I had heard men who had come up from Mexico on the bus talking about how they had hidden their money on themselves while they were riding on the bus because there were thieves everywhere. On the bus when you were asleep, at different bus stops, when the bus was stopped, robbers who got on the bus with guns and took everything they could see from everyone. So after I had paid at the registers, I went back into the store to the men's dressing rooms. There I put on my new clothes and put the ones I wasn't wearing along with the traveling bag into the black suitcase...but not until I had taken a few hundred-dollar bills from the rewrapped bundle and hid most of them in the underwear and socks I was wearing. I felt like a different person when I walked out of that dressing room. I left the gym suit and the running shoes and the jock strap behind.

As I was passing the book section in the store, I saw packets of maps on a rack. I chose one that showed all of the U.S. and part of Mexico. I knew Los Angeles was too close, but I didn't know where to go. The man on the bus sounded like he knew what he was talking about, but I knew nothing about those places or even where they were. I wanted to study a map before I bought a ticket.

I had a cab take me back to the bus station. The driver left me a few doors from the depot. As I got out of the cab, the smell of food drifted to me, and it occurred to me that I hadn't eaten anything in a day. I looked around and thought the smell was coming from a Mexican restaurant across the street.

It was a small place with four stools propped against and under a counter, and four tables with four chairs each set a foot or two apart from one another. There was no one in the restaurant other than a woman who was cooking something on the other side of the counter. It smelled like *menudo*. But it didn't matter what it was, the smell made me hungrier. The woman had her back to me and after a few moments without turning said in Spanish, "Can I help you?" without turning.

"Yes, I'd like some breakfast," I answered in Spanish.

She turned and saw me and answered in English, "Tell me what you want and I'll fix it for you."

Her face was thin and her nose was sharp and her skin was a deep bronze. She reminded me of the Gypsy women I had seen pass through Malaga years before. "I'd like some huevos á la Mexicana with chorizo and beans and tortillas."

She saw my suitcase and said, "Are you coming or going?"

"I'm going. But I could use something to eat before I go."

I went to one of the tables and took out the map and looked for Dallas and Laredo. It took a while but I found both in Texas. Then I looked for Phoenix and Albuquerque. That took a while too. On the map it looked like going from Los Angeles to Dallas was a straight line with both Phoenix and Albuquerque on that line. From Dallas down to Laredo seemed like a straight line too.

The woman brought my breakfast and setting it on the table asked, "Where you going?"

"I'm thinking of going to Mexico."

"You have people there?"

"Yes, my grandmother always talked about her people there."

"Where?"

"In Guanajuato."

"Oh, Guanajuato!" she said sitting down. "I know Guanajuato. It's a beautiful place. An old colonial town, high up in the mountains with perfect weather. As a girl, I used to go there all the time. There's not a prettier place in all of Mexico. Are you traveling alone?"

"Yes, I wanted to visit Guanajuato before I started working. My grandmother died last year and left me some money, not a lot, but enough to do some traveling."

"Going to see your people down there?"

"Yes."

"Taking the bus are you?"

"Yes."

"Don't cross at Tijuana or Juarez."

"Why not?"

"Well, on that side of the border the *narcotraficantes* are killing everything that moves. It's terrible. They kill people or cut them up for no reason at all. On this side of the border the Border Patrol is stopping every bus on the road along the border or close to the border and making everybody show their papers. And if you don't have papers, you're going to jail until you can prove you're legal here. And if you can't prove that, they dump you on the other side."

"How would you go then, if you were me?"

"I'd go to Dallas and then down to Laredo. They say it's still pretty easy and not dangerous to cross either way down there."

A couple came through the front door and the woman rose and excused herself. The clock on the far wall said 11:14. In forty-six minutes, the well-dressed man would be waiting for me alongside the highway in Malaga. I ate as quickly as I could and in a few minutes hurried across the street to the depot with my suitcase.

The waiting room was filled with people everywhere but no cops. Just then I had to find the men's room. I saw the sign over a doorway across the room, and with my suitcase in hand I squeezed my way in that direction. There were signs on either side of the doorway that said in English and Spanish: RESTROOM FOR THE USE OF PASSENGERS ONLY. VIOLATORS WILL BE PROSECUTED.

There were five occupied urinals on my right as I entered, with lines of two and three men behind the current users. I got in the shortest line and tried to be patient, but my mind kept reminding me of yesterday's bus ride. Next to the urinals were several closed stalls and across from them several washbasins. There was water everywhere around those basins: water on the floor, water on the spaces around the basins, water dripping down from the basins, water on the big mirror above the basins, fresh water and dried water that blotted, streaked, and caked the mirror. At the farthest basin a man stripped to his waist was bathing himself with what looked like a T-shirt. There was water all over his pants and shoes and puddles on the floor around him. I watched him and the cracked ceiling above me as intently as I could, trying to hold off my need.

When I finally reached the urinal, it was plugged, brimming with urine. I looked down at the floor and saw how it had been draining itself. I tried flushing but water and urine poured over the edge hard and fast. I jumped back and picked up my suitcase and looked down at my new, hour-old boots and saw that they had been hit. The man behind me was losing patience. "Come on, man. Hurry it up. You shouldn't have flushed that goddamn thing in the first place. Piss and get out of there." I got as close and as far away as I could from the urinal with one hand on my suitcase and a careful eye on my new boots and the bottoms of my new pants. But it wasn't far enough because my boots were splotched again, as were my pants.

I went to the basins to wash my hands. The porcelain was grimy brown and black. There was no soap so I just rinsed my hands. There was no paper in the dispenser and the electric dryer next to it didn't work, so I dried my hands on the seat of my new pants and went back to the waiting room.

It was packed, people everywhere. Still no cops. Most of the people were Mexicans, with some blacks and a few whites. People were sitting in every seat and on anything that looked like a seat. People were standing in the aisles, and along two walls men and boys were sitting on the floor with their backs against the walls. I looked for the ticket windows and found four near the door I had first come in. But three of them had "closed" signs in their openings. The open window had a line at least twenty feet long that ran all the way to one of the side doors. I didn't want to get in that line but above the ticket windows a clock read 11:28. The well-dressed man was probably starting to drive from somewhere to meet me outside of Malaga, and a plane from Parker to Los Angeles took less than an hour. I had to get in that line.

I went to the end of the line and got behind a Mexican man and his family. Only the man was in line but his wife and his mother-in-law and four kids were on either side of him with their suitcases, backpacks, and two big cardboard boxes bound with rope. Again I told myself to be patient, that sooner or later I would get to the ticket man. But the line wasn't moving. It was 11:42. Only eighteen more minutes and the well-dressed man would be waiting for me outside of Malaga. And a few more minutes after that he'd be zooming up the hill to the church in that big, new car of his. He'd go to the church. But not if the cops were there. If he stopped what would old Rogelio tell him? Probably that I hadn't been to the church and the cops were after me. In less than an hour he could be in Los Angeles. Maybe he'd be here before I got to the ticket window.

A tall, older black man got in line behind me. After a few minutes, he poked me, and when I turned, he smiled and said, "You been waiting here long?" I nodded but I wasn't smiling. His smile got bigger and he nodded back and said, "If you're gonna travel by bus, you'd better get used to it."

"Why can't they open at least one of the other windows?"

"Because they don't have to. Most of the folks here have no other way to travel and Greyhound knows that. Why would they pay another clerk to open another window when they know that we'll wait as long as it takes to get a ticket? Are you gonna walk away from this line because you don't want to wait anymore? I don't think so. You see, you've got no other way to go. They know that and you know that."

I looked at the clock: 11:52. He was still smiling. I didn't like his smile, I didn't like him. There was no glee in that smile, no happiness. Instead he was laughing at me because he could see how pissed off I was and how I couldn't do anything about it. He wouldn't be smiling if he was in my shoes. Not with the Parker cops and Billy's friends on their way to Los Angeles and after him.

Fifteen minutes later we had moved just a few feet. There seemed to be even more people in the waiting room, and the more people that came in, the less the line moved. I turned to the man behind me, forgetting my resentment, and said, "Why are there so many people in here?"

"It's always like this, except maybe around midnight to six in the morning. But it's worse in the big cities where it gets real cold or real hot. The weather here in Los Angeles is pretty mild, never really too cold or too hot. But you take a place like Chicago where it gets real cold or a place like Phoenix where it gets real hot, then things can get really cramped up. Worse than this. In those places street people be looking to get out of the cold or heat and they sneak into these waiting rooms and things can get pretty bad. In those places, Greyhound has hired police to come in and stay in those waiting rooms they say to keep order. But it's really to keep street people out."

He was a handsome man, and the white hair that had taken over the sides of his head along with his white mustache gave him a dignified look.

"Yeah, but like you just said, if it's not real cold or real hot in Los Angeles, why are there so many people in here?"

"Like I said before, for most of these folks it's their only way to travel. Moneywise, planes, trains, and even cars are out of the question for these folks."

It was 12:03. Back in Malaga, the well-dressed man had told his people that I wasn't there, and the money wasn't there.

My part of the line could now see the ticket man and the person wanting to buy a ticket talking. There always seemed to be a problem with the luggage. Suitcases were put on and then taken off a lower counter. Sometimes the suitcases were opened and things were taken out that were either put back in or kept out. Whatever they were doing up there, it was taking a long time, and the well-dressed man in Malaga knew by now that he had to find me. I turned again. "So what's going on with those suitcases and backpacks up there at the counter? Why are they taking things out and putting some back in?"

"It used to be that you could take however much luggage you

could carry out to the loading dock and have it checked there and put in the baggage section of the bus. But when Greyhound saw how much money the airlines were making for luggage over fifty pounds, they decided to join the club. So they put a scale down on the side of the counter, and now when you buy a ticket, you have to put your things on that scale to be weighed. Anything that weighs more than fifty pounds you're charged extra for. That becomes a problem for the folks that don't have the money for the extra weight. And there are quite a few of those. So then they have to open their suitcases while they're on the scale, while the ticket man watches, and figure out what's best to leave behind until they get down to fifty pounds. And what they leave behind, they leave behind right there on the floor. And probably will never see again. That always causes a lot of commotion and even tears. But it's either get those things out of their suitcases or not get on the bus. And that too explains why a lot of times the line's not moving very fast."

It was 12:07, and the well-dressed man in Malaga had to know by now that the only way I could get out of Parker or Malaga was by bus. Billy's friends had to be checking with all the buses.

Then I noticed that the ticket man was making some of the people open their suitcases and backpacks, but not others. The ones that were opened he looked in, and in some, he even felt inside. I had my traveling bag inside my suitcase. There was no way he was going to make me open my suitcase, and I'd never open my traveling bag for him or anybody.

"What's that all about?" I asked the man behind me.

"What do you mean?"

"How come he's making some people open their bags and inspecting them?"

"That's because they're over fifty pounds or real close to it."

"And if I tell him he's not opening my bag?"

"Well then, you don't get a ticket. Simple as that and he'll just say, 'Step aside. Next.' And since I'm next, that means that I'll get through this line faster."

I didn't think my suitcase weighed over fifty pounds, but I wasn't sure. If he told me to open my suitcase, I'd have to say no and walk away. But where would I go? I didn't know anyone or any place in Los Angeles, and it was so close to Parker that the cops or Billy's friends were sure to find me.

It was 12:12. I was next. The man with all his kids and wife and mother-in-law was at the counter, and all his things including the cardboard boxes were on the scale. And the man was nodding yes, yes, yes to everything and his kids were all excited as he took out his wallet and took out a bunch of bills and paid for everything. And his wife and mother-in-law were smiling and then they all hugged and laughed.

The ticket man said, "Next," and I stepped to the counter with my black suitcase.

"Where you headed, young man?"

"I'd like to go to Dallas and then Laredo, Texas."

"I can sell you a ticket to Dallas, but not to Laredo. The bus to Laredo from Dallas is called the Americano. It's still owned by Greyhound, but it's like a shuttle service to Laredo and back with a lot of departures during the day. So you have to buy your ticket to Laredo in Dallas.... Now you want to go to Dallas?"

"Yes, sir."

"Just you?"

"Yes, sir."

"One way or round-trip? Cheaper round-trip."

"Just one way."

"OK, let's see what I got for Dallas. Meantime, why don't you go 'head and put your suitcase on the scale down there next to you.... Is that the only luggage you have?"

"Yes, sir."

"Go 'head, put it on there."

I put my suitcase on the scale. I was breathing hard. I was ready for anything. I was watching him. He was looking at his computer screen and then over at the pounds on the scale that I couldn't see.

Then he said, "I've got a bus leaving for Dallas through Phoenix and Albuquerque this evening at six o'clock."

"Six o'clock?" What would I do until six o'clock? Where would I go? How would I hide?

"Next one doesn't leave 'til tomorrow morning and goes through Reno first. Takes longer to get to Dallas and it's a lot colder that way."

My mind scuttled back to my suitcase and his opening it. "And what about my suitcase?"

"What about it?"

"How much is that gonna be?"

"Nothing. It's only thirty-two pounds and I'll write you two tickets, one for you and one for your bag. They'll start boarding out here at gate number one about 5:40. You want the six o'clock bus then?"

It seemed like I had no other choice. But there was still one more problem. "One last thing. I have a small traveling bag in my suitcase with a lot of personal things in it. Am I gonna be able to take that out of the suitcase and keep it with me on the bus before I check the suitcase?"

"Well, let's have a look."

I unzipped the suitcase and held up the traveling bag.

"Oh sure, that's not a problem. That'll fit in the overhead bin. You won't have to keep that in the suitcase. You can carry it with you on the bus."

"OK, give me a ticket to Dallas then."

"Alright, that'll be $98.58."

I took a loose hundred-dollar bill out of my pocket, and he took it and gave me change without a blink.

It was 12:19. I backed away from the window and scanned the wall-to-wall crowd of people. I looked more closely. No cops and no well-dressed man. I had five and a half hours to wait. I couldn't stay in the waiting room. That would be the first place they'd come to, the first place they'd look.

"What's up, son? You look like you're lost or something."

It was the man behind me. He had a ticket. I must have been standing there for a while. "Huh? No, just trying to figure out what to do. My bus doesn't leave until six o'clock."

"Where you headed?"

"Dallas."

"That's a long haul. A day and a half to two days, isn't it?"

"I guess."

"The weather could start getting cold there and be a problem."

"I guess."

"Well, I better get going. They're going to start loading my bus pretty soon. Good luck."

"Thank you."

I watched him make his way through the crowd to the boarding doors. Then I looked at the ticket line. It wound around the side doors way past where I had started and wasn't moving. Suddenly I felt very tired, exhausted. I hadn't slept very much the night before, waking every few minutes it seemed, thinking that the cops or the well-dressed man were at the door. Then it occurred to me. The hotel. Of course. I could stay there. But I had spent fifty dollars on a room last night and I couldn't... I was looking down at my suitcase. Hell, I probably had more money there than I could ever spend.

The hotel lobby looked as empty and dark as the night before except that the front door wasn't locked. A bell rang when I opened the door. But everything remained as still and empty as the night before until I was almost at the front counter. Then a man who had been sitting reading a newspaper saw me and my suitcase and said, "Sorry, but check-in time isn't until three o'clock and you're quite a bit early."

He was younger than the clerk the night before and started to go back to his newspaper when I said, "But I need a room now."

Irritated, he stood up and pointed to a sign on the wall behind him that said. CHECK IN 3:00 P.M.—CHECK OUT 11:00 A.M. "Those are the rules of the house, sir. They were set by management long before I started working here, and I don't intend to violate them and maybe even lose my job if I do."

"But I was here last night."

"So?"

"Why can't I stay in that room again?"

"Because it's not ready, sir."

"What do you mean it's not ready? I stayed in it last night and it was ready when I left."

"No, sir. Every room occupied yesterday has to be cleaned before it's rented again."

"I'll take it the way it is. I don't need it cleaned. There's nothing to clean and I'll only be there for about five hours. I just need to take a nap, and I have a bus to catch at six."

"Well, if I did that, I'd still have to charge you for the full day. I couldn't give you a cut rate."

"I'm not asking you to do that. I'll pay full rate."

"Hmmm... What room was that?"

"Room 303."

He pulled out a card, read it, and said, "OK, thirty-five dollars was what you paid last night. And you say you're going to pay me thirty-five dollars right now?"

"Yeah."

"OK, I think we can work something out."

"There's one more thing."

"I'm going to need someone to wake me at five fifteen."

"I'm sorry, sir, but we don't have room service here. Besides the maids, I'm the only one on duty now, and I can't be running up to the third floor and leave the front desk here unattended."

"What if I paid you a little extra?"

"How much?"

"Ten dollars."

"Well, I guess I could run up to the third floor real quick and knock and then run back down. I don't think anyone will be bothered by that. Alright, that will be forty-five dollars then."

I PUT the chain on the metal slot behind the door and then rolled the suitcase to the bed, opened it, and took out the traveling bag. For a moment, I thought of counting all the money I had, but thought better of it. How could I be sure that no one would see me with all that money? I laid down on the bed with my bag and all my clothes and shoes on, thinking I might have to make a fast exit. But how? They'd be coming through the door. I got up with my bag and went to the window at the back of the room that had looked out into darkness the night before. Now I could see that it was a shaft between four buildings, big enough for me and my bag. Once they started pounding on the door, I'd throw out my bag first, if I had to, and then go out the window and hang on to the ledge so that my drop would only be a little more than two floors. I might get hurt falling, but if I stayed in the room I might never have to worry about getting hurt again.

I was so tired I thought I'd collapse before I got back to the bed. Step by step I made my way back and then plopped down on the bed with my bag. I got into my favorite sleeping position with my bag between me and the wall, and I closed my eyes hoping that stupid clerk wouldn't forget to wake me. But try as I might, I couldn't sleep. I was so tense that I was having trouble breathing. Every muscle in my arms, legs, hands, and fingers was tight. And my mind wouldn't stop. It kept reminding me that they were on their way, that they were getting closer.

I rolled over like one big plank and reached into my suitcase with one stiff arm and four joined fingers and found the vial. Using my thumb and my palm, I brought the vial to my eyes. It read what I was afraid it would read: Zyprexa 10 mg., take one pill at bedtime. Could I make this bedtime? No, it wasn't even one o'clock yet and the doctors had warned me: one pill per day and one pill only. I never asked what would happen if I took more than one pill, and they never told me. But what they said sounded very bad. Worse than what Billy's friends were bringing? I let the vial drop back into the suitcase. If I could only sleep...

There was a pounding at the door. "Mr. Ramirez! Mr. Ramirez! It's five fifteen! It's five fifteen, Mr. Ramirez!"

Mr. Ramirez? Who the hell is Mr. Ramirez? Oh, that's right. It was the clerk. But I couldn't remember sleeping. The last thing I remembered was that I couldn't sleep. I looked at my watch: 5:16.

I had to get up. I had to catch that Dallas bus. I got up and put my bag in the suitcase and went out the door. As I hurried down the stairs, I kept thinking over and over again that once I was on that Dallas bus they would never find me. My name on the ticket was Jimmy Ramirez and with that horde of people in the waiting room and in the ticket line, they'd never be able to trace me. But what if they were in the waiting room? They had had enough time to fly to Los Angeles once they knew I had taken the bus.

In the lobby I asked the clerk, "Can I leave my suitcase here for a couple of minutes while I go across the street to make sure that my bus is still leaving at six?"

"Of course, Mr. Ramirez."

I took my bag out of the suitcase and carried it with me around the block to the loading dock. From those windows I looked into the waiting room for cops or well-dressed gringos who might be waiting for me. None. I looked again. Still none. I breathed long and softly. Another half hour and they would never find me.

It was 5:29. I went back to the hotel. The clerk was talking to another customer. The suitcase was exactly where I had left it. I put my bag back in the suitcase and was about to leave when I had a better idea. I waved to the clerk.

He turned, "Yes, Mr. Ramirez?"

"My bus doesn't leave for more than half an hour. Would it be OK with you if I just sat here in the lobby for just a few more minutes rather than go over there and stand in line with a mob of people?"

"Of course, Mr. Ramirez. You didn't even have to ask. Sit wherever you like."

I went to the couch on the far side of the lobby and sat where I could see everyone entering and leaving the depot through the main doors, but where it was almost impossible for any of them to see me. I watched thinking, *If they're gonna come, they'd better come soon or they'll never find me.*

It was 5:41. They were loading now. I had a few more minutes. I could wait. Better to sit here where I could see everyone coming and going, rather than standing over there in line on the loading docks where I couldn't.

It was 5:46. I better get going. I hadn't seen any cops or well-dressed gringos come or go. I stood and waved to the clerk who was alone again, sitting and reading a newspaper again, and left.

I went around the block again rather than through the waiting room even though I had only thirteen minutes. I entered the loading area from the street. The driver was standing next to the bus door taking tickets from people in line who then climbed up onto the bus.

"This bus going to Dallas?" I asked, standing to one side of him.

"Yes," he said turning, "but you're going to need a ticket for that suitcase too."

"I already got one earlier today," showing him the two tickets.

"Well, you better get in line then."

I went to the end of the line and didn't look into the waiting room through the loading dock windows and chance that they might see me looking. If they were in the waiting room they had only ten more minutes to find me. And they were never going to find me in Dallas, and even less so in Laredo.

A young Mexican came up to me and said, "You got a ticket?"

He scared me. "Sure I got a ticket," I answered, showing him my Dallas ticket, annoyed.

"No, for your suitcase."

"Oh." I handed him that ticket and he put it in his shirt pocket and tore a ticket he had in his hand in half and gave me half. He tied the other half around my suitcase handle and picked up the suitcase and started for the bus.

"Hey!" I jumped out after him.

"What's the matter?"

"I need to get my traveling bag out of there."

He stopped. "Why didn't you tell me?"

I unzipped the suitcase and took out my bag and went back to the line thinking that I was going to have to be two steps ahead of everyone from now on.

There were several people in front of me, but the ones I paid attention to were a young couple. They were holding hands and he had a small bag on the ground next to him that he would move forward with his foot every time the line moved. So that their hand-holding wouldn't be interrupted, I thought. Every now and then she would look up to him and smile, and he would look down at her in turn and smile. I had never had a girlfriend, but in those moments watching them, there was nothing I wanted more. Once they boarded the bus, I stopped watching people ahead of me.

When I reached the driver, he took my ticket and tore it in two and gave part of it back to me. "Played it kind of casual, didn't you, son," he said with a smirk. "Waited 'til the last minute to show up even though you got your ticket a lot earlier," he nodded with squinty eyes. "You're lucky we have a full bus this evening and a long line, otherwise we might have left you behind. Reminds me of the time in San Antonio. A young fella did what you did, waiting for the last minute. But I didn't have the line I had this evening. So when the time came that I was scheduled to leave, I left and left him behind. Oh, he raised hell. I think he even got back to my headquarters. When they asked me what happened I said, 'It was six o'clock. He wasn't there. I was supposed to leave at six o'clock and that's what I did, and not a minute sooner.' It's five past six now," he grinned, but there was nothing friendly in that grin. "So hop on. We got a long trek ahead of us."

I was the last one on the bus and as I took my first step up, I felt a great relief, as if a huge load had been taken off my shoulders. Neither the cops nor Billy's friends would ever find me now. And again as I reached the aisle, I remembered the huge amount of money I was carrying and I gripped my bag with both hands and took note of who was on the bus. More whites and blacks than Mexicans. Where did all those Mexicans in the waiting room go? Far more men than women. A woman with a baby. A woman with two small children. And three couples. The only empty seat was an aisle seat in the row next to the toilet near the back of the bus. Remembering yesterday, I was thankful to be next to the toilet.

It was only as I got closer to that empty seat that I saw why it was still empty.

There was a big man, a Mexican man no less, sound asleep next to the window who was spread out onto half of the empty seat. I stood in the aisle with my bag in my hands looking down at him, knowing I had to wake him but not sure what the best way was to do it, when the bus jerked forward, sending me up the aisle almost making me fall before I got my balance back. I moved to the empty seat again when the bus shot forward, pushing me back almost onto the hand-holding couple who were sitting in the last row near the back of the bus. I lost my balance, dropped my bag, and grabbed onto the toilet door to keep from falling. The bus's motion steadied, and I straightened myself and picked up my bag and stepped back to the half-empty seat. I squeezed myself into it setting my bag on my lap so that one end was pressed against my stomach and the other was resting on my knees.

Squeezed I was. His big bare arm was twice the size of mine and now was covering part of mine. Some of his big thigh flapped over mine. I tried wiggling in my portion of the seat to wake him, but I was so squeezed that I couldn't wiggle and after several tries I stopped. His breathing was loud and deep. He wasn't snoring but sometime during the night he sounded like wind blowing through a tunnel. I said, "Hey! Hey!" to him as loudly as I could without disturbing the others, but his closed eyelids didn't even wrinkle. I shook his shoulder with my left hand, but nothing, not even a break in his breathing.

I pinched his bare arm as deep and as hard as I could, and after several tries his eyes did flutter. I pinched again. More fluttering and a sputtering in his breathing. On the third try he opened his eyes, raised his head, and looked over at me.

"Hey! Hey!" I said again in English. "Move over, you're sitting in my seat."

He nodded several times, keeping his eyes open and looking at me. But he didn't move.

"*Órale!*" I said in Spanish. "*Muévete! Estás en mi asiento!*"

He nodded again and this time he did move, inches, but he was still in my seat.

"*Muévete! Todavía estás en mi asiento!*"

He moved his upper body a few more inches and went back to sleep. His lower body, the part that was still on my seat, didn't budge this time. I looked down and around him and saw that his huge, right thigh was pressed flat against the bus wall. This was the best I was going to get. I thought of putting my bag in the upper bin to get it off my lap, but decided against it, thinking that the minute I stood up from my seat his spreading would begin again. And the bag had a lot of money in it. It could easily slide down the bin and be picked up by somebody else, or maybe in an emergency I wouldn't be able to get to it.

It was going to be a long night. But I reminded myself how lucky I was to be scrunched in half a bus seat on my way to Dallas, rather than riding in the whole back seat of a cop car or in the back seat of one of Billy's friend's car. The day had darkened, and outside the window next to the sleeping man I could see house lights and streetlights and traffic lights everywhere. It seemed like we would never get out of Los Angeles. And as long as we were in Los Angeles, it wouldn't take much for the Parker police to contact the Los Angeles police and have them stop the bus. The fear I thought would be gone once I got on the bus wasn't really gone. Finally, the bus left all the houses and businesses and seemed to be on a highway. Until it stopped completely. My first reaction was that the cops had stopped the bus for sure and I was trying to think of what to say to the cops when they got on the bus. And what would I do with my traveling bag? But the bus started up again, slowly, and I could see that we were in a sea of cars, trucks, and buses. The stops and goes seemed endless until one of the goes went on and on and faster and faster into the increasing darkness and I thought for sure that we had left Los Angeles.

Finally, there were no lights and the bus was going very fast and I thought, *They won't find me now.* I felt exhausted. I didn't know how much I had slept the night before, but it wasn't much. I didn't want to try to sleep then because if I did, I would probably wake up in the middle of the night and not be able to go back to sleep. For the first time in a while I thought of how scrunched I was and about the hulk of a man who had half of my seat. I couldn't see him in the darkness, but his deep, heavy breathing told me he was still there. This time I consoled myself by thinking that he was just part of my journey, a journey that could be saving my life.

I had to have been sitting over the bus's rear tires, because in that darkness I thought I could hear and feel their hum: round and round and round. It would be a good rhythm to sleep by, but later. Later came when someone opened the toilet door with the light on. The light jolted me and I looked at my watch: 10:40. I had been sleeping. But for how long I wasn't sure. In the day and a half that was to come, there were times when I didn't know or couldn't tell if I had been asleep or awake. Sometimes, one seemed the same as the other. It was 10:40. Late enough for a pill. I reached in my pocket for my vial and only then did I remember that it was in my suitcase and my suitcase was now locked somewhere below me.

"Oh, shit!" I yelled and then quieted myself. But I needed that pill, I needed those pills. Or the voices would come. *Oh, God! No! Not the voices, please not the voices!*

I jumped out of my seat and started down the aisle with my bag in my hands repeating in a frantic voice, "Stop the bus! Stop the bus!" When I reached the driver's compartment, I pulled on the door but it was locked.

"Open this door! Open this door!" I shouted. And when the door wasn't opened, I pounded on it and yelled, "Stop the bus! Open this door! Stop the bus!"

Behind me people were stirring and waking, saying things to me that I couldn't hear. Until someone yelled, "Hey man! Go sit down before I sit you down! He can't stop this bus! You're gonna get us all killed!"

The driver's door opened. He was in his seat and he yelled back over his shoulder, "What the hell is going on back there?"

"Stop the bus! Stop the bus!"

"What's going on back there?"

"Stop the bus! You have my pills and I need my pills!"

"I don't have your pills or anybody's pills!"

"Yes, you do! They're in my suitcase locked under the bus!"

"I'm not stopping this bus! We're in the middle of the desert and there's no place to pull off and stop, and I sure as hell am not going to stop on the road."

"You have to!"

"I don't have to do anything! Now go sit down and be quiet!" And he shut his door.

I started pounding on the door again when someone much bigger than me grabbed me from behind. "I'm gonna sit you down, you crazy little fuck. And if you don't shut up and stay put, I'll see that you do!" He dragged me back down the aisle. "Where was this little fuck sitting?"

"Next to the toilet in the aisle seat," someone answered.

When we reached the toilet, he felt around for my seat. Finding it, he stuffed me in it. "You stay in your goddamn seat and I don't want to hear a peep out of you. And if you don't stay put, you'll be sorry as hell that you ever saw this bus!"

That woke the sleeping hulk next to me. "What's going on? What's going on?"

I waited until I was sure that whoever had sat me down had left. "I need my pills and they're in my suitcase down below and the driver won't stop for them."

"How's he gonna stop? Look outside. There's nowhere to stop. We're in the desert. He couldn't stop if he wanted to."

"Yeah, but those pills are my medication. And I'm supposed to take them before I go to sleep. If I don't take them, I'm gonna be real sick."

"There's no way the man can stop now. Besides, we get to Phoenix around five. It'll still be dark and you can take them then. Just go to sleep 'til we get there. Go to sleep, man." And he turned his head and went to sleep.

Could I wait until we got to Phoenix? I tried to remember how the voices came the first time, how they got started. First it was one. But that one had always been there. I had always talked to somebody in my mind. I still talk to somebody in my mind. That somebody has to be me, part of me, even though a lot of times he gives me answers I don't like. No, it didn't start then. Then I was just talking to myself. It started with the staring. I wasn't staring yet. I didn't think I could see and know everything just by staring.

The bus's jerking motions got my attention. We had slowed way down and were off the highway. Maybe he was stopping for my pills after all. I saw a lot of bright lights and more buses parked around a building that was all lit up. We stopped. Were we in Phoenix? The lights inside the bus went on and the driver's door opened and he said loud and clear, "Rest stop! Rest stop! Twenty minutes! You have twenty minutes and then we'll be on the road again!"

This wasn't Phoenix. I must have fallen asleep. I could see nothing but darkness beyond the other parked buses. But no cops or well-dressed man. Then everyone was standing. Even the hulk next to me was trying to stand.

"Move over, bud," he said to me, "I need to use the john."

"What's this?"

"It's just a restaurant out here in the desert that all the buses use as a rest stop. Are you gonna get out or are you just gonna sit there? I gotta use the john."

"I'm gonna get up," I said, clutching my traveling bag.

I stood up then, and he got up and shuffled behind our seats to the toilet. I started following people down the aisle. Stepping out of the bus, I felt a blast of bitterly cold wind. "Whoa!" I said aloud to myself. "I thought it was supposed to be hot in the desert."

Someone behind me said, "It's always like this at night in the desert at this time of year."

I ran for the door. It was a big, clean, well-lighted place. There was a long counter with stools that ran against one wall with a kitchen behind it. Fifteen tables or so were spread out on the floor with two waitresses moving around them. I wasn't interested in eating. What I was interested in was finding the driver. I found him sitting at the counter with other gray-suited drivers.

I started toward the driver when someone at a table said, "Hey boy, this ain't quite Phoenix yet. You better put that bag back on the bus." There was laughter from the tables and I saw for the first time that I was carrying my bag in front of me, holding onto it with both hands.

"Looks to me like he's got his 'jamas in there and's planning to spend the night in here," someone else said, adding to the laughter.

"Nobody's thinking of taking your precious bag from you, little man." More laughter. But I wanted to get to the driver so bad that none of that mattered.

The driver had seen me coming and shifted in his seat when I reached him and said, "Let me tell you right now, mister, before you open your big mouth. I'm not going out there in that freezing wind and darkness and start unloading every piece of luggage on my bus to find your suitcase and your pills just because you say you need them right now. That can wait 'til Phoenix. You look fine to me except a little ridiculous with that bag and the way you're carrying it. A person might think that you have a million dollars tucked away in it and you're afraid of everybody on my bus. Well, let me tell you that in all the years I've been driving, I've never had a single thing taken off my bus or stolen while we were at a bus stop. So I suggest that you stop all your foolishness and take your bag back to the bus. And then come back in here and sit down and relax. You'll get your pills soon enough when we get to Phoenix."

There was a lot of snickering and some more laughter. And I turned and walked away as quick as I could out of that dining room on my way to the bus, but I stopped in the lobby because I could see from there that the bus doors were closed.

"Where you headed?"

It was the white guy who had been holding hands with his girlfriend in the Los Angeles line. He was sitting alone on a bench in the lobby.

"I was heading out to the bus but the doors are closed."

"It's locked. No one gets in until the driver comes back out. So where you headed?"

"To Dallas and then down to Laredo."

"That's a good haul."

"Yeah, how about you?"

"We're going to New York City."

"New York City! Wow! That's a real big haul."

"Yeah. Three and a half days."

"What're you doing that for?"

"We're getting married, and Mandy says she can't do that until her folks meet me first. Her mom's pretty sick and they're both pretty old."

"But three and a half days on the bus? I'm hoping I can make it to Dallas and we just got started."

"Yeah, but there's no other way. I mean it'd cost us three thousand dollars to fly when you figure everything up. We can't handle that. I work at 7-Eleven and she works at Walmart. And nothing's cheap these days. Did you see the prices in there? Seven-fifty for a hamburger, and three-fifty for a Coke, and more than a dollar for tax, although it's hard to figure who's getting that tax out here in the middle of nowhere. And that's more than twelve dollars for just a snack."

"Yeah, but you gotta eat something."

"We're lucky. Mandy did this trip once before when her mother almost died. She got us ready. We've got a big bag and a little kind of refrigerated box on the bus full of sandwiches and drinks and snacks and all kinds of things. Enough to get us by for three and a half days. She says the prices in all the depots are outta sight. She thinks it's because usually there's nowhere else to go or you can't get back in time on the bus if you go too far from the stops."

When I got on the bus again, I saw that a few people had stayed on the bus, which made me glad I had taken my bag with me even though they had laughed at me inside. The hulk hadn't gone into the restaurant. He was still sitting in his seat and part of mine with his eyes closed as if he was asleep. I didn't believe that he could have fallen asleep so easily, and this time as I stood next to my seat I said real loud, "Hey, move over! You're in my seat!" He did go through the motions of wiggling and shifting but that only gave me an inch or two more. I could still see that he was pressed tight against the bus wall. I thought of putting my bag up in the bin mainly because of what they had said in the restaurant, but I knew I'd feel safer with it on my lap. Besides, once the bus started up all the lights would be turned off and no one could see the bag on my lap then. I scrunched my way into my seat again. Then I thought that it might better if the lights were kept on all the way to Phoenix. That would make it easier for me to stay awake and move my bedtime to five o'clock in the morning. No, I wasn't staring or hadn't been staring at anything yet. I probably could make it to Phoenix without my pills.

THE NEXT thing I knew, the lights came on and the driver was standing at his door repeating, "This is Phoenix. You have thirty minutes here. This is Phoenix."

Everybody seemed to be getting off the bus and that made my movement down the aisle a torture. I was now so close to my pills and so far away from them. What made it worse was that two old people were insisting they could get out of their seats without any help, but they couldn't. When they finally got into the aisle, people had to help them shuffle their withered old legs down the aisle, inches at a time. At last I got off the bus. But before I did, I looked outside in every direction from the driver's seat. No cops. No well-dressed man. Now for sure they weren't going to find me.

As soon as I stepped off the bus, I was met by that brutal, cold desert wind that was blowing even harder now than it had at the restaurant stop. I had left Los Angeles in shirtsleeves and was freezing. But I had to get my pills before I could run to the waiting room. I joined the crowd that had formed on the side of the bus around three open baggage doors. There was a mountain of suitcases and bags and backpacks and cardboard boxes stuffed five deep into the side of the bus. Standing next to those openings was a brown man in a khaki uniform with a baggage ticket in his hand, and he was trying to match that ticket to something in that mountain of luggage. I was stepping in place as I waited like so many others who somehow believed that movement would fend off the icy wind.

When the baggageman started another round of searching at the open doors with the ticket in his hand, the crowd got unruly. Someone yelled, "Hey, you're never gonna find the bag you're looking for in there. It's probably stacked way in the back somewhere. Take some other tickets and search for those!"

"I can see my bag from here. The tan suitcase in the second door. Here! Here's my ticket! Give me my suitcase!"

The baggageman wasn't hearing them or answering them or stopping his ticket-by-ticket search for the mate to the ticket he had in his hand. When he started his search at the third door a second time, someone yelled, "Hey, just take out all the suitcases and put them on the ground and we can tell you which ones are or aren't ours! It's freaking cold out here!"

This time the baggageman answered. "I can't do that. It's against regulations. I have to get out only the Phoenix luggage. There's a lot of other luggage that's going on to Albuquerque and Dallas."

"I don't give one goddamn good shit about regulations. We're freezing out here."

But the baggageman went on with his regulation search as more and more people protested. Then someone or something must have gotten to him because he stopped and turned around and looked at us, looked at the people who were yelling, then turned back and started taking out suitcases and bags and everything and putting them on the ground around him. The woman with the baby went to the first stack and started rolling her suitcase out.

"Hey, where you going lady? I need a ticket."

"I don't need to show you anything. My baby's gonna catch pneumonia because of your silly rules. Just try to stop me, mister." And she left with her suitcase.

Two men ran up to the bus, one went to the first open door and the other went to the second open door. They began unloading luggage from both doors.

"Hey!" the baggageman yelled. "You can't do that! Stop it!" He went over to them but they paid him no attention. They were bigger than him.

At the same time, the woman with the two small kids had put a tiny backpack on each of her kids and one on her back and was rolling her suitcase and kids away from the crowd.

"Hey, lady!" the baggageman shouted. She and the kids just kept moving.

There were several black suitcases with rollers that were now out of the side of the bus. I stayed back to make sure that anyone leaving the loading area with a black suitcase was not walking away with my pills. None were. As the crowd thinned out, bags and suitcases and boxes and backpacks were still lying around on the ground at the side of the bus. I started going through them to find my pills. There were only three black suitcases with rollers left and I found mine right away. I unzipped it and was taking my vial out when the baggageman approached and said, "What do you think you're doing?"

"I know what I'm doing. I'm taking out my pills and my jacket. Here's my ticket stub and it matches the one on the suitcase. Take a look."

"This suitcase is going to Dallas, and even if it's yours, you're not allowed to take anything out of it until the bus gets to Dallas."

"That's what you think. Let's go inside and take this up with your boss. These pills are medication prescribed by my doctor. If I don't take them pretty soon, I'm gonna be real sick."

He stared at me and looked like he was going to cry. He turned in every direction. When he turned back to me he said, "And where's your ticket for the bag you're already carrying?"

"Look! There's no ticket on this bag, so how could I be carrying a ticket for it? How could I need one?"

"Did you take the ticket off?"

"It's never had a ticket. I've had it on the bus with me ever since

I left Los Angeles. So nobody's ever given me a ticket for it."

"What's it doing out here then?"

"I brought it out here with me."

"Why?"

"Because I wanted to. That's why."

"Why don't you get in the waiting room where you belong."

"I will once I take my pills and jacket out of my suitcase."

He walked away.

I put the vial in my pocket, took out the jacket and put it on, zipped up the suitcase, left it where I found it, and looked up at the sky. It was still dark. I hurried into the waiting room. There was a smell of food. I hadn't eaten since yesterday morning, but I needed to take my pill. I went to the men's room. There was no one in it and it was clean. *It's too early yet to take the pill,* I thought. I went to a washbasin, put the pill in my mouth, cupped water in my hand, and swallowed. I sighed a big relief. I had six left.

I went back to the waiting room and the area where the smell of food was coming from. A crowd of people were standing around a corner in which there was some sort of cafeteria. I wondered how much of the thirty minutes was left and if I could wait. A minute later, a man came out of the crowd holding a white Styrofoam plate with food on it. When he saw my curious look he said, "Don't waste your money or time. Look at this crap. I ordered scrambled eggs and potatoes. Can you find any scrambled eggs in that grease? And those potatoes look raw. And when the toast came out of the toaster, it had shrunk to half its size. He charged me nine bucks for this. I tried to order some coffee, but he said I'd have to get it out of one of the machines out here. Do you know what machine coffee tastes like? That machine will probably want two dollars for its brown water. Eleven bucks, imagine that. If I wasn't so damn hungry, I wouldn't even *try* to eat this crap."

I went to the vending machines, of which there were plenty, and bought two candy bars and a Coke, which cost me six dollars. I was hungry but these would have to do.

There was a new driver standing at the bus door taking tickets.

"Same seats?" I asked him, hoping to get a full-size, regular seat.

"We'll probably have a few empty seats on our way to Albuquerque, but it could fill up at the last minute. Take the seat you had, and once we get started, you can switch to a better one if you like."

I got on the bus looking at seats that might become available. But when I got halfway down the aisle I saw that the hulk wasn't there. I looked in the toilet and checked the overhead bin. No sign of him. Nor had I seen him in the waiting room. Gone! A whole seat to myself leaped through my mind!

I took the window seat and spread out kind of like the way the hulk had, hoping to discourage anyone from sitting with me. No one did. The bus eased out of the yard at 5:05. It was still dark and I felt exhausted and sleepier than I could ever remember. I hadn't slept much, it seemed, for two nights. When I had finally gotten to sleep in the hotel, it was a fearful, uneasy sleep, as if I was expecting the cops or the well-dressed man to come crashing through the flimsy door. Then on the bus out of Los Angeles, I tried again and again to sleep but couldn't until I woke up at that restaurant in the desert. It was weird. So many times I couldn't tell if I had slept or hadn't slept. But pulling out of the Phoenix bus yard, I desperately wanted to sleep.

I closed my eyes and told myself that now I would sleep, but I couldn't sleep. I kept thinking of the cops and the well-dressed man and Billy, too. Of Billy telling them where they could find me. All those years of growing up with Billy, of being so close to Billy, and it had come to this. I opened my eyes and looked out into the darkness as the bus tires churned. I closed my eyes and opened them again and again and again until I finally saw the black rim of faraway mountains against a blue-black sky.

Then I woke with the sun beating down on me, and my face, shirt, and neck soaked with sweat. I moved to the aisle seat and wiped my face and neck dry with the bottom of my shirt. I must have slept around three hours. I tried going back to sleep in the aisle seat. But I couldn't. The churning feel and sound of the tires below me were keeping me awake.

It was then that I started to make some sense of those skinny white markers with black numbers and lettering that popped up along the roadside every minute or so. There was a mile between two markers and ten miles between road signs that gave the distances to oncoming cities. For many miles, I kept track of ten passing markers to tell me when the next road sign would arrive. I did this until the driver slowed and we pulled in alongside two parked buses and stopped, and he opened his door and said, "Rest stop! You have twenty minutes! Twenty minutes!"

I looked out the window, and the countryside was the same that I had seen for miles and miles: flat, dry, white earth with scrubby, green-black bushes and an occasional cactus plant. It seemed like everyone was getting off the bus, but I took my bag with me anyway. The sky was a bright blue and the air was warm, but it had a crisp, cool breeze in it. If this was November daytime in the desert, I liked it. I was almost to the general store when it occurred to me that until then I hadn't thought of the cops or the well-dressed man or even Billy. They would never find me here.

The truck stop was huge. It had several islands of gas and diesel pumps under a high metal roof. Next to the pumps was a big building that had a general store in which you could buy all the same things sold in the Parker supermarket. It also had restrooms and showers and locker rooms and a food counter that specialized in selling hot, prepared dishes. The smell of food reminded me how hungry I was. I bought six pieces of fried chicken and a big bag of french fries, both of which were kept hot and attractive in a glass case with a heat lamp. And I bought a big Coke to wash them down outside on benches alongside the store. I sat there until the driver opened the bus door and said loudly, "Albuquerque! Al-bu-quer-que! Let's go!"

The food probably put me to sleep. I slept at least two hours. It was afternoon when I woke up, and I watched for the next highway road sign to Albuquerque, which said 123 miles. I was pretty sure the next one would say 113. And it did.

I watched the flat, dry, barren land passing for a while. Bored, I started to use the second hand on my watch to gauge the coming of the next road marker, seeing if it would appear exactly sixty seconds from my last count. They usually arrived a few seconds before or after they should have. Then I started gauging the road signs with my watch: ten minutes meant a new road sign. The timing of the road signs was far less accurate than for the road markers. After many miles of gauging road marker and road sign appearances based on road markers, the whole process suddenly seemed dull, pointless, and stupid, so I stopped.

But now I was very much aware of the passing miles. I could see road markers coming and going out of the corner of my eye. Soon the road markers seemed to be taking longer and longer to arrive. I had to stop noticing. The trip was getting longer and longer. I moved to the aisle seat and kept my eyes on the aisle even if there was nothing to see in the aisle except the aisle. But then I could hear the bus wheels churning and churning under me and going nowhere. Or if I had to admit that they were going somewhere, then that was ever so slowly, so tortuously slowly, that it was better not to listen to them. I covered my ears but I could *feel* the wheels churning endlessly under me and Albuquerque was getting farther and farther away. Would this bus ride ever end? Maybe not. And after Albuquerque there was Dallas. If I couldn't handle this, how was I going to handle that? I had to stop thinking of distances and time, and it was far too early to take another pill. It hadn't even been six hours since I took the last one. I had to stop thinking, period. But the more I said I had to stop thinking, the more I thought. I reminded myself that everything had to end. Everything. This bus ride had to end, end, end. Never mind how much longer it would take or how much farther we had to go. This bus ride had to end. Then sometime after I was able to stop thinking about distances and time, I began seeing lights and houses. The closer we got, the greater the number of lights and houses and buildings. Albuquerque.

As we neared the bus depot somebody said loudly, "For those

of you who don't know there's a Burger King a block away from the station. We'll have thirty minutes and you have plenty of time to go there and eat! Whatever you do, don't buy the crap they're selling here in the station. It sucks and it's not cheap."

I was one of the last ones off the bus but the first to reach the Burger King. I had my bag with me so I ran all the way, not stopping in the waiting room like most of them did. I knew sooner or later, if they weren't already, that people on the bus were going to start wondering why I always took my bag with me wherever I went. I didn't care. At least that's what I sometimes told myself. But I did care. I worried that some would think, like the man on the bus from Bakersfield, that I had something very valuable in the bag to always be carrying it with me or always have it sitting next to me on the bus. Was I making my bag or myself a target? Maybe.

So after ordering a Whopper and two bags of fries and a Coke, I left that Burger King and took a long way around back to the depot. I ate my dinner in the loading area and then thought I might have to go into the waiting room to use the men's room. But how ridiculous or suspicious would I look with my bag in the men's room? I decided to wait in the loading area until the driver unlocked the bus and then use the toilet on the bus.

He was a new driver and seemed nice enough at the bus door.

"Did you get something to eat?"

"Yeah, I went to Burger King."

"I didn't see you there."

"I was there. I just didn't eat inside, I ate outside. I just felt too cooped up to eat inside. I've been on this bus for a day now and on two others before that for another day."

"How far you going?"

"After Dallas to Laredo and then down to Mexico."

"Sounds like you've got a big chunk of traveling to do yet."

"Yeah."

I was the first one on the bus and thought of changing my seat, but decided against it. In the back of the bus where I was sitting, I could see everything that was happening, and if the cops or one of those other guys ever got on the bus, I'd have just that much more time to react. I watched a lot of new people get on the bus, faces I didn't know, and then it occurred to me that the farther east we were going, the fewer Mexicans there were on the bus. There were a good number of them when we left Los Angeles, but some got off in Phoenix. More must have gotten off here in Albuquerque, because now we were just a few. The rest of the passengers were now pretty much evenly divided between white and black.

As we made our way out of Albuquerque, it was going to be my third night on a bus and I seemed to be getting less and less sleep. Once on the highway I was careful to take a pill with some of the Coke I had saved. I had five left and thought I could get a refill in Dallas. Sometime after that I fell into a deep sleep until I was awakened by the young guy on his way to New York with his girlfriend. He was standing in the aisle screaming, "Hey, goddamn it! Can't you close the fucking door after you've taken a shit!" I didn't know who he was yelling at because it was dark and no one, except him, seemed to be in the aisle.

The toilet was in the walled-off space behind me that would have otherwise been used for the last seat on my side of the bus. Sheet metal had been wrapped around that space, and a narrow, sheet-metal door had been installed on the aisle side across from the last row of seats on the other side of the bus where the young guy and his girlfriend were sitting. Behind the door was a toilet and a tiny washbasin. After a full night and day and part of another night, the inside of the toilet space stunk when I last used it. But now, whenever anyone opened the door I could smell the stench where I was sitting. It must have been stronger where the young couple was sitting.

"What's the matter?" I said to the young guy.

"Some son of a bitch took a crap and left the door wide open when he left. The stink woke us both up, and I had to jump up and close it before we both puked. Some people are worse than pigs."

Later, someone else used the toilet and the young guy was up again, screaming in the aisle. "Get your filthy ass back here and close this fucking door, you fucking pig!"

This time there was someone standing in the aisle but I didn't want him coming back. "You better watch who you're calling a pig, punk. I closed your mother-fucking door."

"Then you better get your ass back here again and close it so it stays shut!"

"And you'd better shut your mouth and sit down, punk, before I come back there and stuff your head in that toilet."

I leaned over and said softly, "Hey man, cool it. That sounds like one of those big black dudes sitting up front. Just close the door. You don't need to be messing with those guys. Close that door, man, it's really starting to stink back here."

"You outta be sitting where we're sitting. It's dead-on stinking."

"Close the door, man."

He closed it and sat down.

We were both awake when the next guy came. The young guy greeted him with, "Close the door, man."

"I was fully intending to, man. I don't especially like pissing in public."

"I was talking about when you come out. Please close the door."

"That's what people usually do, ain't it?"

"You'd be surprised."

When he came out, I heard the door close and the young guy said, "Thank you, man." But the visitor had just stepped past me when the door opened. "Oh, shit! Oh, shit!" the young guy said. "It's the fucking door! It's the fucking door! The fucking door won't stay closed!" He rushed down the aisle to the driver's door and I got up and leaned against the door.

When he came back he said, "The driver can't do anything now, but he said that he'd take care of it during the rest stop in about half an hour."

Then for the first time the girl said something. "Why don't we stick a piece of folded-up paper between the door and the door lip? That ought to hold it until we get to the rest stop."

"Okay, but I think most people will hold themselves until we get to the stop. I was loud as hell up there with the driver about the problem back here."

The driver spent most of his thirty-minute rest stop working on the toilet door, but he couldn't fix it. He said that a part had broken and he couldn't make the door work without that part. He said that he couldn't move the guy and his girl to another seat because the bus was full except for the seat next to me. The girl shook her head no, that she didn't wanted to be separated from her husband-to-be. I kept my mouth shut about trading seats with them. The smell was bad enough around me but a lot worse around them. Then when everybody was on board again, the driver told everyone about the problem and asked us to hold off using the toilet as best we could until we got to Dallas, which was just a little more than four hours away. "That shouldn't be so hard to do," he said, "because most of you will be sleeping during those hours anyway."

But later, I woke to a woman near me in the aisle in the dark saying, "I can't help it, I have to go."

The young guy said, "Lady, if you open that door, me and my woman here won't be able to sleep the rest of the night. It really stinks bad in there, and it's getting worse and worse here, too."

"I can't help it. I've been trying to hold it, but I can't hold it anymore."

"You heard what the driver said. It's only a little while more 'til we get to Dallas."

"That was almost three hours ago and I've been holding it most of that time. But I just can't hold it anymore. You want me to pee here in the aisle?"

"The driver said everybody had to hold it 'til we got to Dallas."

"He said no such thing. And I'll be damned if I'll pee all over myself."

"Let her go, Timmy, let her go," the girl said.

"But we won't sleep the rest of the night. You said that yourself."

"Yeah, Timmy, but it'll be worse for everybody if she pees right here."

"Go 'head in there and piss, lady. Go on in and piss your heart out. Maybe some day we'll get to trade places and then we'll see how *you* like it."

I could hear the woman feeling and feeling in the dark for the folded piece of paper that was jamming the door shut. For a minute I thought she was going to piss all over everybody. Then she found it and pulled and pulled on it, and me thinking that she couldn't hold it any more, but the door opened and she stepped into the toilet.

"Close that goddamn door behind you!"

"Timmy, please."

"Yeah, it's easy for you to say, Mandy, but I'm the closest one to the toilet and I don't need any more fresh smells."

I could hear the woman struggling to close the door and at the same time take care of herself. Then there was silence and after a few moments, the flush of the toilet, and the door creaked open.

"Close the door, lady."

"I'm trying to but I can't."

"What do you mean you can't? It's closed isn't it?"

"I'm holding it closed, but I can't find the paper in the dark that was keeping it shut."

"What do you mean you can't find the paper? Where did you put it?"

"I don't know. I can't remember. I'm feeling around for it out here but it's too dark and I can't find it. And if I open the door and feel around for it inside, you'll just start screaming again."

"Lady, why don't you just get the fuck out of here!"

"Timmy, please. Timmy, stop."

"But I'm trying to tell you that if I get up and go, the door's going to open and you're going to start yelling again."

"Lady!" he shouted. But then his girlfriend started crying and he stopped and for several moments said nothing. Then he said very calmly, very quietly, "Lady, please go. You've caused enough problems. Please go. I'll take care of the door."

The lady left and it took Timmy a while but he found the folded paper jam on the floor in the toilet and closed the door shut. The stench was more than awful and no one came back to use the toilet again before we got to Dallas.

It was 4:47 when I knew for sure that we were in Dallas. It had been a dark night and for miles and miles we had been on a big freeway with lights and more lights around it and beyond, which, every time I was jarred out of a sleep, made it hard to know where we were. But then I woke and could see lights high, high above me, and pressing myself against the window, I saw that they were lights on skyscrapers. I had never seen buildings that high, not even in Los Angeles. And rather than drive around them, the bus seemed to be driving right into them. I was happy to see Dallas, not because I knew there wouldn't be any cops or Billy's friends waiting for me there, but just because I would finally be getting off that bus.

As I waited for my suitcase at the loading dock, I was very cold and worried that my jacket wouldn't keep me warm for the rest of my trip. In Phoenix and Albuquerque the wind had seemed to sweep the cold off the desert. There was no wind in Dallas that morning. The cold just seemed to be part of the air, and part of that part was falling down heavily on me.

I went to the waiting room with my suitcase and a giant of a man opened the door for me and nodded. It was a big, warm, well-lit waiting room. I looked for the men's room, found it, and hurried to it with my suitcase and bag as best I could, moving around people, men mostly, who were sitting and lying on the floor everywhere. There was no one in the restroom and both the urinals and the washbasins worked. In fact, it looked like they had been working nonstop for a while because there was water splashed everywhere.

I came out of the restroom thinking I had to find out when the next Laredo bus left and buy myself a ticket. The ticket counter was at the opposite end of the room. It had three ticket windows, but only one was open and there was a line from it clear to the street doors. Seeing the line slowed me down and I looked around the room more closely. The first thing that caught my attention was the tall man who had let me into the waiting room. He was moving slowly about the room. He was a handsome, light-skinned, black man who had to be at least six feet four inches tall and muscular. He looked like many of the star athletes I'd seen on television. He wore a neatly pressed, khaki-colored, short-sleeve uniform with patches high up on both sleeves that said SECURITY in red. A polished, brown baton hung from his belt on his right. As he moved slowly around the room, he looked at all the people, most of who were sleeping. He talked to some, shook others, and tapped some of the bags on the floor with his baton. He was heading my way and I waited for him, wanting to be sure that neither the Parker cops or Billy's friends had been asking about me.

"Where you headed?"

"Laredo."

"Is that your bag?"

I had put my traveling bag in my suitcase. "Yeah."

"That's all you got?"

"Yeah."

"You got your ticket?"

"No."

He looked me up and down and when he came back to my eyes he said, "Well, you better get over there in line then."

"Yes, sir." Not a hint of the cops or Billy's friends. I was home free.

The waiting room was a big rectangle. At the top were the ticket windows and office spaces. At the bottom were the openings to the men's and women's restrooms. Along the right side facing the ticket windows were doors to the street. Along the left side were doors to the loading area and a small, short-order cafeteria. In the center were benches and chairs for people waiting for buses. Those benches and chairs were bordered by six- and ten-foot walkways. From where I was standing outside the men's room, the benches and chairs were full, occupied mostly by women. As I wound my way through the bodies toward the ticket line on the right, I noticed for the first time that the top two-thirds of the sitting area had been roped off and that only half of the seats were taken. When I got in line, I asked the red-faced, grizzled-haired man in front of me, "What's that all 'bout?" pointing to the half-filled sitting area.

"What's what?"

"How come that section's roped off and only half-filled?"

"That's reserved seating."

"Reserved? Reserved for who?"

"Reserved for anyone who wants to pay five dollars."

"Five dollars to get a chair or a seat on a bench? When did that start?"

"I don't know when it started, but it's not just five dollars. It's five dollars an hour."

"Who do you pay the five dollars to, the ticket man?"

"No, no, you pay it to the big black dude in the brown uniform. Hasn't he asked to see your ticket yet?"

"No, he just asked if I had a ticket and I said no that I just got here and was on my way to Laredo. And he said to get in line."

"Don't worry that's not the last time he'll ask you. You know, the asshole thinks the whole waiting room is his. I'm sure he was put in here to keep the street people out because it's colder than shit outside, and those street people would be in here top to bottom if he wasn't here. But he's gone way beyond that."

"What's he doing poking at that guy sleeping over there? Did he just sneak in here?"

"Oh, no. Believe me he knows everybody's status in here. That's part of his business. He knows the guy he's poking has a ticket. But see, he's probably got a hard-on for that guy. I saw him poke the guy awake the last time he was around. The guy must have given him lip or something and he doesn't forget. He's forever showing who's boss in here. Every now and then some guy'll have a go at him. Believe me, that's something you should never do. Besides beating the shit out of those stupid idiots, I've actually seen him pick up grown men and carry them to the doors and throw, and I mean throw, throw them out on that sidewalk, and that's concrete out there. He's nobody to fuck with. They say that he used to play for the Cowboys until he got injured."

The man he was poking was lying on the floor, and after several pokes, he just held up an arm with a ticket in his fingers without even looking at the security man.

"So people pay him five dollars for those seats? Do you think those five dollars are all his or does he split that with someone?"

"I don't know nothin' about him splitting with nobody. My guess is that he gets it all. Because he's so damn greedy about it. Say you give him five dollars for a seat, first thing he does is ask to see your ticket. No ticket, no seat. When you give him your five dollars, you give him your ticket too. Then he checks the ticket to see what time your bus leaves. If it's more than an hour, the seat costs you ten dollars. More than two hours, you're talking fifteen dollars for that seat, and so on right up the line."

The security guard came closer and the red-faced man stopped talking and turned from me. For a while the security guard stood close by us watching over his kingdom. The only other conversation we had was when the security guard moved away. Then the red-faced man asked, "What time does your bus leave for Laredo?"

"I don't know."

"Well, no matter what time it leaves, get your ticket now. Those buses tend to fill up and you could find yourself waiting for the next one if you don't get your ticket now."

The line moved slowly, although not nearly as slowly as it had in Los Angeles. And every once in a while I would look around the waiting room and tell myself that I was home free. No cops, no Billy's friends. It was 5:27 when I got to the ticket counter.

"Where to, young man?"

He was a white man with slicked-down, black hair with a big part on the left side and wire-rimmed glasses that sat halfway down his nose, but he seemed okay.

"Laredo."

"One way or round-trip?"

"One way."

"Cheaper, if you buy a round-trip now."

"I might not be coming back."

"OK then, when do you want to go?"

"When's the next bus?"

"The next bus is the first bus out today and it's at 7:45."

"It's not full, is it?"

"Oh no, not yet. There's plenty of seats available now."

"I'd like a ticket."

"You gonna have any luggage?"

"Yes, sir, this black suitcase right here, and I'll probably take out the traveling bag and carry it with me."

"Well, I can sell you a ticket now, but you'll have to come back an hour before 7:45 and get a ticket for your suitcase then."

"Why? Why can't I buy it now?"

"Because the bus doesn't load until 7:45, and I don't have any place to put your suitcase now."

"Am I gonna have to get in line for that suitcase ticket even though I already have my ticket?"

"Yes."

"Why can't you just sell me a ticket for my suitcase now and I'll keep the suitcase with me until 7:45? I'll take it outside with me and check it in then when we load."

"I can't do that."

"Why?"

"Because if we weigh your suitcase now and it's under fifty pounds and I don't charge you extra for the suitcase, what's to keep you from adding more weight to it before you take it out to the loading dock without paying for that extra weight?"

"Why would I want to do that?"

"Because a lot of people would do just that."

"But I don't have anything more with me to add to my suitcase."

"I'm sorry, the rules are the rules."

"Okay, give me a ticket. And I have to come back at 6:45 and get in line again to get my suitcase's ticket?"

"Yes, sir."

1 5 7

I turned to go but stopped. "Oh, I have another question."

"Yes?"

"This seat you sold me, is it for the front or the back of the bus?"

"It's not for any particular seat. It's for whatever seat's available when you get on the bus."

"And if I don't want to sit in the back of the bus?"

"Well, just be here early and get on the bus as quick as you can, and there shouldn't be a problem."

I had more than two hours before I could get in line again and that big security asshole was watching me, probably waiting for me to buy one of his seats. That would have cost me fifteen dollars then. I had enough money in my bag to buy out his whole damn section for the rest of his life, but I'd be damned if I'd give the punk fifteen cents.

I was hungry and the little cafeteria was closed. I decided to go out on the street to see if anything was open nearby. I took the long way around to the street doors, away from that asshole guard so that he'd get the message that I wasn't interested in any of his slimy seats. When I stepped out onto the sidewalk it felt like I had stepped into a dark freezer. It was cold as hell. I would have gone right back into the depot except that I had never seen anything like I was seeing out there. Everywhere I turned there were skyscrapers and they went up and up. Except for two cabs across the street, the streets were empty. Nothing was open. Everything was closed. Everything, the sidewalk, the streets, the buildings, had the same color: a dark gray, shiny iron. There was so much of nothing there then, where there had to be so much of everything later. I looked and looked until from opposite street corners two people were walking toward me. As they came closer, I could tell from their walk and clothes that they were street people, and I went back inside.

I still had more than two hours before I could go back to the ticket counter, and from what I had just seen, it looked like I was going be spending that time in here. I stood at the doorway looking for a place to sit. Because of the watch caps and hats that the men lying down and sitting wore, and the way they used their clothes to cover themselves it was hard to tell anything about them other than that they were older and mostly white. Across the room near the loading-dock doors, three men were sitting on the floor with their backs against the walls. It looked like there was space for me. I went over there and sat, and as I was taking my other shirt out of my suitcase for more cover, the man sitting next to me said, "What's up, *Ese?*"

He surprised me. Not only was he awake but also he was a young Chicano. "Not much. Just trying to get a little warmer."

"Where you headed?"

"Laredo."

"Got people there?"

"No, just kind of checking it out, you know.... And you?"

"I'm going back to Los. You know, L.A."

"Is that where you're from?"

"Yeah... As a matter of fact, I'm just coming back from Laredo. I got a real sick grandpa I went to visit. Probably the last time I'll see him."

"What's it like?"

"It's not a little border town like it used to be anymore. They got more than 250,000 people living there now. When you drive into town on Highway 35 you'd think you were on Main Street in any-town America. They got Walmart and Target and McDonald's and Burger King. And there's Pizza Hut and Kentucky Fried Chicken and Dunkin' Donuts and Starbucks. And if you need a place to stay there's a chunk of 'em on Highway 35. Motel Six and Red Roof Inn and Days Inn and you name it."

"Any drugstores?"

"Oh yeah, there's plenty of those too. Funny thing, a lot of those people along Highway 35 don't know what they are: Mexican or American or a little of both or wanna-be-whites. It's not like being in L.A., East L.A., or South Central. Everybody there knows who they are. We're Mexicans, *Ese, raza,* pure and simple."

"So what time does your bus leave?"

"It left yesterday at two o'clock."

"What? Then what are you doing sitting here?"

"I'll tell you why I'm here. I'm here because of that big fuckin' nigger over there. That overgrown monkey with his stupid baton over there. Fuckin' niggers always bitching about how they're still being treated like slaves. Then you give one of them, like that big asshole over there, a little power, and they treat people worse than they ever got treated."

"I don't get it."

"I don't either. I got here yesterday about noon. I got in line and got my ticket and the ticket man said I had to come back an hour later to get a ticket for my bags. They told you the same thing, didn't they?"

"Yeah."

"So I'm getting hungry and I see this black dude eating outta a McDonald's bag and he tells me there's one a couple of blocks from here. I be damned if I buy anything outta this punky cafeteria. Yesterday they wanted three dollars for a bottle of water. They're always talking about us being criminals, but who's the criminal here? Anyway, so I headed down the way he told me and after a while I could see a McDonald's a block away. They call that place where McDonald's is the West End. I guess because it seems like the end of downtown. But let me tell you, there's a bunch of angry niggers down there. Some bad dudes who got no use for white people. And cops galore walking around trying to keep a lid on everything. I kinda stopped when I saw that crowd. But then I told myself 'Shit I ain't white. I never done nothing to them, and besides, I'm darker than some of those niggers they call high yellow. They can see that. We get into a lot of hassles with them in South Central, but they know we got it just as bad as them.' That little pep talk kept me going. And nobody bothered me, *Ese,* they could see I wasn't white. There was a whole lot of black people in that McDonald's. McDonald's always been their favorite restaurant. So it took an extra long time to get my burger and fries, and I wasn't about to push my weight around in there. Then I took a few minutes to eat down there because I wasn't going to make it back here with my bags and that giant Coke and my fries and burger.

"So I got back here at twenty to two, and of course there was a huge line and only one ticket window open. I get in and naturally it's not moving very fast, and without a ticket for my bags, they're staying here and I can't get on that bus without them. Well, it gets to be ten minutes to two and there's still seven people in front of me, and I'm gonna miss that bus for sure. So I jumped the line and I go up to the counter beside the guy he's waiting on, and I tell that old white dude that he needs to give me a ticket for my bags or I'm gonna miss my bus. And he starts giving me a lecture about what he told me earlier and I'm being as polite and desperate as I can be, telling him that I'm outta money and don't have no place to stay in Dallas. And he's starting to bend a little when from behind me, that big nigger says, 'This boy's jumped the line.'

"And I get all desperate and beggin' to that old white dude, 'I'm gonna miss that bus. Please, sir, I need to get on that bus.'

"From behind me comes, 'Rules are rules, Mr. Ticket Man. If any order is going to be maintained here with these people, remember, we long ago decided that rules have to be followed.'

"I looked back at that big nigger but he wasn't looking at me. He was staring hard at that old white dude like he owned him. And the old white dude was squirming.

"And I said, 'I know you said to be back here an hour before two. And I got here fifty minutes ago but the line wouldn't move. And now with eight minutes to two, that would make it fifty-eight minutes that I've been here. And for two minutes, please don't make me miss my bus.'

"'He's lying, Mister Ticket Man, this boy got here at twenty to two. I know that for a fact. I saw him come in and I timed him. So he's lying and you can't reward lies with gifts. Or how else am I going to keep order in here?'

"I looked at the ticket man, real sorry like, but he wouldn't look at me. He was leaning as far back as he could away from me.

"'Get back in line, boy!' And he grabbed me by my shirt and

pulled me. Imagine that big nigger calling me 'boy.' All them niggers always be bitchin' about being called boy, and the first chance
they get, I'm a boy."

"So what did you do?"

"I got back in line. That's why I'm still here, sitting next to you,
sitting on the floor staring at all them empty seats in front of me.
Because that fucking nigger has roped them off and I would have
had to pay him a hundred dollars since yesterday to sit in one of
them."

I looked at the security guard. He was looking at us. "Hey man,
I think we better cool it about him. I don't wanna be put on his
shit list. Look at him. He's giving us the evil eye. He knows we've
been talking about him."

"Damn straight!"

"I'm gonna move, man. I don't have that long to wait for my bus
and I don't want him calling my number. I'm sorry, man, but I
gotta be on that Laredo bus."

"I understand, *Ese.* Do what you gotta do."

I went to the other side of the room and sat between two sleeping men. The security guard was watching me, and I raised my
arm and pulled back my jacket sleeve and pointed to the time on
my watch, and he nodded.

I looked over at L.A. *Ese* and he was shaking his head in disbelief. I didn't care what he thought, I had to be on the 7:45 bus to
Laredo. I sat and thought about Billy and what he had done, and
what he had done to me. I thought about the two cops that missed
me in Malaga and about the well-dressed man and his new car,
and other well-dressed men that might be looking for me. Now I
knew that none of them would ever find me and they would have
even less of a chance when I got to Laredo. I only had five pills
left. I had thought of getting a refill in Dallas but everything was
closed. I wasn't worried because L.A. *Ese* said there were plenty
of drugstores in Laredo, and I'd get a refill later that afternoon.

At 6:40, I looked at the line and was tempted to get in it then,
but thought better of it, afraid of what the big nigger might do if

he thought I cheated. At 6:44, I pulled back my jacket sleeve again and as soon as the security guard looked in my direction, I raised my arm and pointed to my watch, and he nodded and motioned for me to get in line. I did and then I looked over at my L.A. *Ese* friend and he was just shaking his head in disgust again.

The first ten minutes the line moved pretty quickly and there were only six people in front of me. I was sure I'd be on that 7:45 Laredo bus. But then there was a lot of screaming at the ticket counter and we weren't moving. I stepped out of line to see what was going on. There was a skinny little blonde woman standing next to the scale shaking her head no. On the scale was a huge cardboard box that was open. The rope that was supposed to keep it shut was lying on both sides of the box. The woman was shaking her head at two skinny little blonde girls who were standing next to her crying. The girls looked to be about five and six years old. Then the woman bent over the box and picked something out of it and tossed it to the other side of the box where some clothes and things were lying on the floor. The girls screamed and ran to the pile and brought back what looked like a small blanket and tried to put it back in the box. The woman yanked the blanket away from them and threw it again, this time beyond the pile. Both girls screamed, but just as they were about to start to move toward the pile, the woman grabbed each of them and sat them down on the floor in the same motion. Then there were screams and tears and gagging and choking as the girls tried to let out louder protests.

The security guard stepped in and hung his big body over the two tots and said something to them that made them stop crying and screaming, and they jumped up to their mother and wrapped themselves around her in silence, terrified. Then he went over to the box and took out an item at a time and looked at the mother who either nodded yes or shook her head no. The yeses he tossed to the pile, and the noes he dropped back into the box. After several tosses, the ticket man said, "Okay, it's under fifty." And the security guard retied the box, and the woman dragged it out to the loading area, with the girls hanging onto her dress, sniffling.

I WAS the first one on the 7:45 bus to Laredo. I looked around to see where the toilet was in the bus. I saw it in the back and then took a seat just behind the driver with my traveling bag on my lap. The bus was smaller and older than the one that had brought me to Dallas, but it didn't quite fill up. All the passengers were Mexicans. I had no idea where they had come from because I hadn't seen that many in the waiting room. The driver was a pudgy, older Mexican who spoke enough heavily accented English to make himself understood while he was taking our tickets. But then on the bus as we were about to leave, he told us in Spanish that we would arrive in Laredo about 3:15 in the afternoon. He said that we would be taking Highway 35 to get there, stopping in San Antonio just long enough to let people off and pick up new passengers. A half hour later there would be a fifteen-minute rest stop. There was no one sitting next to me and before we were out of Dallas I fell asleep, not waking until we came to the stops and goes in San Antonio.

At the San Antonio depot, I was at the driver's door as he opened it to announce San Antonio and I asked him if I could use the restroom inside the waiting room. "Only if you hurry. I don't wait for anyone." I wanted no part of the toilet at the back of the bus. I found the men's restroom in a glance and was in and out of it in a minute and back in my seat before the new passengers boarded.

This time the bus filled up with older Mexican men and women who seemed to be day-trippers who had come to San Antonio from Laredo for doctors' appointments or shopping or visiting family and friends. A nice old man with a sparkle still in his eyes stood at the empty seat next to me and said, *"Buenas tardes,"* and then smiled at himself and said, *"mejor, buenos dias."* It wasn't afternoon yet. "Can I put your bag in the bin while I'm still standing?"

"No, thank you. I'd rather have it here with me."

"I don't have any bags and I'm sure there's plenty of room up there for your bag. You'll be a lot more comfortable. It's three and a half hours to Laredo and that bag's going to get pretty heavy after a while."

"No, no. I want it here."

That made him uncomfortable and he sat down without another word. He probably wouldn't speak to me again the rest of the way, I thought, but that was okay.

In less than ten minutes we were on Highway 35 and I was dreading the monotony of the next three and a half hours. I tried to sleep but couldn't. I didn't want to talk to the old man next to me. He'd probably start again about my bag again. And I didn't want to get into the craziness of timing the road markers and road signs again. Somehow, the three and a half hours would pass. And before I knew it, we were at the rest stop.

It was a truck stop, a small version of the one between Phoenix and Albuquerque. There were trucks with trailers parked everywhere. Where they were headed, only they knew. There were truckers of all shapes and sizes and colors at the cash register stocking up for what was to come. I didn't envy them.

There was a smell of food and I looked in the direction I thought it was coming from. On a wall halfway down the aisle was a long list of sandwiches, soups, hot plates, pizzas, fried chicken, fries, and baked potatoes. I looked for a kitchen but saw none. A trucker was at a counter looking at the list, or so I thought. I stood next to him and saw that he was actually looking at a woman on the other side of the counter who was watching a microwave oven tick down. Below him in an open refrigerated case were the prewrapped listed items waiting for their eventual turns in the microwave.

There was a closed case with a heat lamp that had fried chicken and fries in it, which looked better than all that prewrapped stuff. But I was wondering how long that chicken and fries had been in there. It was weird. In a way I was hungry, and in a way I wasn't. It had been at least twelve hours since I had eaten anything, but I was finding that the less I ate, the less I wanted to eat. I knew I had to eat, but that prewrapped stuff waiting for its turn in the microwave didn't look very appealing. I wanted something hot, something that looked like a meal. I kept wondering how long the fried chicken and those fries had been in there with that heat lamp.

"Can I help you, sir?" she said.

"How long's that chicken and them fries been in there?" I said, pointing.

She looked at me as if she had never been asked anything so ridiculous. "Oh...it's today's."

I looked at the chicken's breaded coating and it told me nothing. And she was looking at me as if I was weird. Maybe because I was carrying my bag... But she hadn't answered my question, not really. Still, I knew I had to have something to eat. And the way she was looking at me told me that I didn't need to draw any more attention to me and my bag. "I'll take some chicken and fries."

"How many pieces?"

"Four."

"Hungry, huh?"

"Yeah." I wanted to say more, like it wasn't any of her damn business how hungry I was. But I didn't dare create a commotion.

"Any fries?"

"Yeah."

"One bag?"

"No, two."

"Hungry, huh?"

I wished she'd stop that. "Yeah."

"Anything to drink?"

"Coke."

"What size?"

"Big."

"Thirsty, huh?"

I nodded.

I took my lunch or breakfast or whatever it was outside. There was nothing to sit on. So I leaned against the building where I could keep an eye on the bus, as I ate, for whenever it would be getting ready to leave.

Once we left the truck stop, it didn't take me long to realize that the scenery I had seen before the stop was continuing, going on and on, not changing. It was kind of like when we were crossing the desert: flat, dry, land drained of color by the sun, with nothing growing on it anywhere, going on and on. This scenery was going on and on too, but it was totally different. On either side of the road were thick, green, bush-like trees or treelike bushes, I couldn't tell which, eight-foot high at most, with smaller bushes and grasses growing all around them so there was no way anyone could ever get through them. At times when the road went up a bit, that dark, dense, green growth seemed to go on forever behind what was facing the highway.

And yet, every now and then there would be small green signs with white letters and white arrows pointing to towns or villages with names like Lytle and Devine and Derby and Dilley and Millett and Cotulla, towns or villages carved out of that thick, evergreen tangle. Sometimes after the signs, I would see a water tower or a gas station, but usually only a road that went into that dense green. Who lived there and why I wondered? And then there was another one of those signs.

For the first hour or two, I thought the old man next to me was sleeping. But every time I turned to look, he was wide awake, looking straight ahead, and not once did he so much as blink at my turning. Well, I thought, old people are easily offended, especially by the young. And they hold grudges. That's how my grandmother and her friends used to be in Malaga. But when we were about an hour and a half out of Laredo, he turned to me and said, "You got people in Laredo?"

"No."

That wasn't much of answer. Not what he wanted. I thought he'd take the hint and leave it there. He did for a while, but then he asked, "Where you from?"

"California."

"Los Angeles?"

"Yeah."

I didn't know what he was going to ask next, but I had already let him get too close. I should never have said California. Arizona or Phoenix would have been good enough. There was no telling who he was or who he might be connected to. The next time he opened his mouth, I was going to tell him that I wanted to get some sleep. But he didn't open it again, not for a while anyway. He just kept looking straight ahead, and I leaned my head against the window and closed my eyes.

"You're going to do just fine in Laredo. People like you, young people, Laredo's your town now. You know, I was born and raised in Laredo, grew up there, went to school there, had kids there, kids who grew up and moved away. And now when they come back to visit, they say they should have stayed, they should have stayed and taken advantage of what's happening here."

I might have been sleeping and I didn't know who he was talking to. I opened my eyes and looked over at him. He was talking straight ahead just like he was looking. I sat up and turned to him, which was a mistake, because then he turned to me and said, "I don't live in Laredo anymore. Do you know why?"

I was sorry I sat up. I shook my head no.

"Do you know where I live now?"

I shook my head again. I was between being annoyed and feeling sorry for the old geezer.

"I live in Mexico. I live across the bridge in Neuvo Laredo, Mexico. I've been living there going on five years now. Do you know why I left, why I had to leave Laredo?"

I shook my head again. He had my attention.

"I couldn't take it any more. I couldn't take walking down to what used to be my downtown anymore and seeing everything closed, boarded up, dead. It's like a ghost town down there now. There's only two stores still open and only the old folks, the real old folks like myself, go there. Sometimes I think those old folks still go to those two stores to make believe the place is still alive. I don't know how they can keep fooling themselves with everything else boarded up, blocks and blocks of deadness. My house was only a block away, and I used to go down there just about every day. But all that boarding up just seemed to bring death a little closer. Don't get me wrong, I know I'm going to die. We're all going to die. Nobody escapes it. But going down there, looking at it all boarded up, even from where I used to live, just kept telling me that part of me was already dead. So I left."

"Why is everything boarded up?"

"I'll tell you that in about half an hour. I want to wait that long because then I can not only tell you, I can show you too."

"So where's this Nuevo Laredo?"

"On the other side of the bridge in Mexico."

"Why do they call it Nuevo Laredo?"

"That's just it! That's what's so stupid, so crazy about the whole thing. Most everything on this side of the bridge is new and most everything on the other side of the bridge is old. This is Nuevo Laredo and everything over there is just old Laredo like it's always been."

The old man turned from me and stopped talking. Outside my window that dense green kept peeling past. I shut my eyes and tried to sleep. Sleep wasn't there. I opened my eyes. I was numb. For days now the bus's constant movement and its sounds were parts of my life, big parts. It was like breathing. It was happening and kept happening without me thinking about it. I had been going to Laredo for days now and it was the going that existed, not Laredo. Sometime maybe the going would stop and I would be in Laredo. Until then, the word Laredo had no meaning. The going did. And then, like out of a deep sleep, I saw a clearing. The green was gone and there was a big clearing with a cyclone fence around it and big trucks and trailers parked everywhere. In the center was a big aluminum shed with windows. Over that clearing was a high, huge, concrete ramp with trucks and cars moving in one direction and then next to it another high, huge ramp with trucks and cars moving in the opposite direction. Then in the distance, on the side of the road, I saw a big, red Target sign, but not the store until we got closer, the store was behind a giant parking lot.

The old man turned and leaned toward me and said, "That's Target in that big building and those are all small stores in the little buildings on both sides of it. Coming up is Penney's in the next block with parking for hundreds of cars in front of it and small stores all around it and..."

He kept naming the stores, those that were there and those that were coming. They were all huge and new, like the new stores out in north Parker, except that they went on and on. "This goes on for more than two miles on both sides of the road almost to the bridge. And behind all those big stores and restaurants and motels are rows and rows of new houses and new streets and new schools and new churches. This has to be Nuevo Laredo and the old town across the bridge is really Laredo. That's why I live there."

I was surprised when the bus pulled into a big, tan, two-story, stone building across from a park, and the driver said, "Laredo! Laredo! This is Laredo!" It didn't look like a depot to me. There were several other big, tan, two-story, stone buildings around the park and they all looked like offices. When the bus stopped in the loading area, the old man stood and turned and said, "This is it, son. Good luck." And he left. I let others go out after him, separating us. When the bus was nearly empty, I stood and went out and claimed my suitcase and put my bag in it before I went in the waiting room. I was hungry and I needed a refill of my pills.

ANOTHER surprise: two young guys, Mexicans, not much older than me, behind the ticket counter, wearing jeans and sport shirts and no ties. I asked the one closest to me where I could get something to eat. He pointed to a set of doors across from us and I was relieved.

I went through those doors and felt myself sink. It was another Burger King. It was full of people and smoke and noise and a bad smell. I didn't like any of it. All I could hear was Spanish being spoken and I knew we were still in America. There wasn't the usual line to the counter. I didn't care. I wasn't going to have another burger, fries, and Coke. I went back through the double doors and back to the ticket counter.

"Is there some other place around here where I can get something to eat besides a burger and fries?"

The young guy I asked turned to the other young guy. "Hey, Luis, he wants to know if there's another place to eat around here?"

"Maybe Eddie's."

"There's another place three or four blocks down the street," he said, pointing away from the park. "It's a little early, but they should be open. You can get a regular meal there, nothing fancy but not too expensive either. It's OK. There's not much of anything around here anymore. All this used to be the Civic Center, but that's changed."

I pointed to the street he'd pointed to and he nodded. I started to leave, but remembered, "Is there a drugstore around here?"

"Oh yeah, right across the park, just about kitty-corner from here. You can almost see it from here."

"Is it open now? What time does it close?"

"It's open now, and I'm pretty sure it doesn't close until eight. You've got plenty of time. It's not even three thirty yet."

"Thank you."

I crossed the street with my suitcase rolling loudly behind me.

At the corner the young guy had pointed to, I raised it up onto the sidewalk. The street was wide enough for two cars and some parking but the sidewalk was very narrow and uneven; there were some cement squares rising over others as if they had been uprooted, but there were no trees in sight. At the corner was a small, single, gray-stucco building with two big windows on either side of a glass door. There was nothing in the windows or as far back as I could see. The whole block was a series of small, boarded-up or empty buildings that had once been stores. There was no way of knowing what kind of stores any of them had been. There was no one on the street or the sidewalk except me. And I thought of the old man on the bus who was now living in his "old Laredo." The cracked and uneven sidewalk was hell on my suitcase so I carried it and watched where I stepped.

The next block was more of the same, but as I neared the end of it, across from me on the sidewalk, I saw a woman sitting on a folding chair at the corner behind what looked like a card table. She was facing the street that ended our block. There still were no cars and no people anywhere. Everything around her was as empty as it was around me. She had to be looking at the side of the building across from her. I reached for the vial in my pocket and shook it, feeling the rattle of the five pills that were still in it. I wasn't hallucinating. The voices weren't telling me that there was a woman on that empty corner, when there was nothing there. There was a woman there. A breeze shifted the streaked, white hair on her shoulders. I remembered for sure taking a pill last night on the bus before all that rumbling began about the toilet.

I was standing across the street from her. I moved a few steps closer. She didn't notice, or if she did, I wasn't important enough for her to turn. She was just as she was when I first saw her, sitting, staring out at a wall or an empty space. Zyprexa had kept me sane. There was no way I wanted to go back to that hell. I could sense the voices somewhere in the corner of my mind wanting to get at me. But as long as I had my pills, they couldn't. That woman wasn't part of them. And yet, she was so familiar to me.

I thought I should just get the hell out of there. I didn't know her, she didn't know me. There was no reason for me to get involved in her hell. But I remembered my hells and what a hell this had to be for her, sitting on the corner of a deserted neighborhood staring into space. The old *curandero* crept into my mind, and I remembered him saying that in the old days before they had medication for crazy people, how people brought their crazies down from the mountains to him, so that he could talk to them because somehow that seemed to help. People had helped me: Padre, the *curandero,* the doctors. Lots of people had helped me.

I walked across the street. I stopped a foot from her on her left. She didn't turn, she didn't look up. She had to have heard me, she had to have seen my shadow. She was talking to someone, was deep in a conversation with someone. I didn't hear her, I couldn't hear her, but I could see her mouth moving rapidly and then stopping. I saw her brow gather and release itself. And I remembered. Oh, how I remembered what it had been like for me. And I could feel the voices in me straining, wanting so much to bust free. Whoever she was talking to was giving her a bad time because she began shaking her head no and shutting her eyes tight, not wanting to give in.

I nudged her gently. She didn't turn. "What's up?" I said. She kept shaking her head "no" to him or them or to whomever she was talking to, and then began talking again, moving her lips again. I put my hand on her bony shoulder and shook her gently and said loudly, "Hey! What's going on?" That startled her and she turned and looked at me. If I had had any doubt about what she was or where she was, it disappeared in that second. Her eyes were jolted wide open as if I had suddenly yanked her from another place and another time and she was trying to make some sense of it. She was thin, skin and bones. Her brown skin was stretched tight across every bone in her face and yet there were deep creases in her brow. Too deep for someone I thought couldn't be much older than me.

"Who are you?" she said, both threatening me and frightened by me.

"Who am I?"

"Yes, and who sent you?"

"No one sent me. I just got off the bus. See my suitcase. And I'm looking for a place to eat called Eddie's."

"Eddie sent you?"

"No one sent me. I was looking for a restaurant called Eddie's."

"Eddie's is a restaurant? How could Eddie be a restaurant?"

"No, no! Listen to me," tightening my hand on her shoulder. "I'm looking for a restaurant. I'm hungry."

"Then what's all this about Eddie. I used to know an Eddie but I don't anymore. Who are you?"

Her eyes didn't trust me. I was an intruder. I had no right to be in her world. I knew that look and I knew that fear.

"Nobody sent me and I'm just a guy looking for a place to eat and I saw you sitting here and I was wondering what you were doing here. That's all."

She looked at me for a long time, her eyes measuring me, weighing how much trust she could give me. The longer she looked at me, the more her eyes narrowed, and the more, I thought, I was fitting into her world.

"What are you doing here?" I said breaking the silence, thinking I'd better rely on what trust I had before it faded.

"What am I doing?" she said puzzled. "Can't you see I'm selling handkerchiefs. I sell handkerchiefs here every Sunday. A person can't be supported all her life by her parents. She has to come out here and earn her living too."

She did have a stack of white handkerchiefs under a big rock on the right edge of the table that I hadn't noticed.

"You do this every Sunday?"

"Every Sunday," she said proudly.

"How much do you charge for your handkerchiefs?"

"Well, this Sunday they're on special. It's one dollar for the handkerchief and one dollar for embroidering your initials on it."

"I've never had a handkerchief."

"You've never had a handkerchief?"

"No, I just use toilet paper."

"That's not very clean."

"Why isn't it?"

"Because it's toilet paper. You use that for the toilet."

"You can use it for anything you want."

"I wouldn't. It's not clean."

"You come out here *every* Sunday?"

"Yeah."

"There don't seem to be too many people that pass through here."

"There's more than you think."

"Is that who you were talking to when I came over here?"

"No. I was talking to myself. I always talk to myself. Don't you talk to yourself?"

"Yeah, but not back and forth like you were doing."

"You mean you say something and then another part of you waits for a few minutes and then he talks and then you talk and wait again? Like that you mean? I think that's pretty ridiculous, stupid if you ask me."

"You live here in Laredo?"

"All my life... Hey, you gonna buy a handkerchief or aren't you? I'm not out here to have conversations. I'm out here so I can sell handkerchiefs, so I can hold up my end at my parents' house."

"What colors are they?"

"They're all white. Except I can use any color thread you want to embroider your initials on it." She had about ten handkerchiefs and she spread them all out on the table for me to examine. "See, they're all white."

I pretended to look at them but I was thinking, *This is insanity, I should walk away from this now while I still can.* But even as I thought that, I knew I couldn't.

"Which one do you like?"

"They're all the same, aren't they?"

"To the untrained eye they might all look the same. But I work with them all the time and there are big, big differences there."

"I'll take the one at the top."

"Good choice, but which one are you gonna take for your wife?"

"I'm not married."

"You're not married! A good-looking, young guy like you and you're not married. Don't you like girls?"

"I love girls but I'm not married yet."

"Well then, take one for your girlfriend. She'll love you for it."

"I don't have a girlfriend."

"You *are* strange. When I was your age..."

"What makes you think you're that much older than me?"

"When I was your age, I had lots of boyfriends. I never got married. Turned them all down because I knew the first thing they'd try to do is coop me up, change me, and I wasn't going for that.... But you're not lying to me, are you? You're really not married and you don't have a girlfriend? Or are you just telling me that to beat me out of another two dollars. Because if you are, I won't sell you a handkerchief. I don't do business with liars and thieves. Are you lying to me?"

"No, I'm not lying."

She looked at me again, studied me again for several more moments as her eyes narrowed even more, and I tried not to blink or look away.

"OK, I don't think you're lying." She pulled out several small spools of different colored threads from a pocket and laid them on the table. "Pick your color."

I had to see this through no matter where it ended. "Green."

"Green it is. It's a good color. It'll go good with your complexion."

She put all the spools, except the green one, back in her pocket and brought out a needle from the same pocket. "What are your initials?"

"J and R."

"OK, but before I get started, I want you to understand a couple of things."

"What's that?"

"I don't like anybody watching me when I work, and I don't want anybody talking to me when I work. So you can take a walk and come back in ten minutes. You can stay if you want, but you have to turn and stay turned until I'm finished and you can't talk."

"I don't like walking around with my suitcase. What if I just close my eyes?"

"No, that's not gonna get it. Turn around or go."

I turned and stayed turned for however long it took her to sew those initials on the handkerchief. While I was turned my mind became flooded with all those days at the Alvarezes'. That was painful.

"OK, you can turn now."

I turned. She was holding the handkerchief up with the fingers of both her hands. The green initials at the bottom edge of the handkerchief were actually very nice. They changed the whole handkerchief. J.R., that was me now. I liked it and reached for it. But she pulled back the handkerchief and shook her head. "That's two dollars." I gave her two dollars and she gave me the handkerchief and I held it and admired it.

"You like it?"

"Yeah."

"I thought you would."

I put the handkerchief in my back pocket and looked at her. We were both pleased. There was almost a smile on her face and I thought this would be a good time to talk to her.

"Have you ever tried medication?"

"Medication! What are you talking about?" The smile vanished and a frown was back. But somebody had to talk to her.

"Well, you know, like medicine. Like aspirin for a headache."

"Yeah, I've had aspirin. But that's not what you're talking about, is it! You're trying to fuck me over, aren't you!"

She was angry now.

"No, no, I'm just trying to help you."

"Help me! Who in the fuck do you think you are! You don't know the first fucking thing about those medications! Who sent you here? Was it my father or that silly-ass priest friend of his?"

"Nobody sent me here. I'm just trying to help you."

"Help me! You don't know the first fucking thing about those medications! I do! I took them! I know how all that shit in them can fuck a person up! How it fucked me up! People have died behind those pills! People have committed suicide behind those pills! Who sent you? You came over here to spy on me, didn't you? You're part of their conspiracy, aren't you? This is my workplace, my shop. You better get your ass outta here before I call the police. Go! Move!"

She began screaming, "Police! Police!"

I couldn't get out of there fast enough with my suitcase and my bag full of money. I walked as fast as I could with my suitcase. I picked it up and ran faster. At the end of the block I turned right and was out of her sight. But I could still hear her. She was still yelling, "Police! Police!"

I turned again at the next block and couldn't hear her anymore. I kept walking, it seemed endlessly, through that abandoned neighborhood not knowing where I was. Finally, at the end of another block I saw an old man walking toward me. I met him and asked him, "Where's Eddie's Restaurant?"

"Eddie's? Eddie's?" he said confused, until I said, "Where's the Greyhound Depot?"

Then he turned and pointed and said, "One block down and two blocks over."

I found my way back to the Greyhound Depot walking past empty little store after empty little store.

"How was Eddie's?" the young guy with all the phony information asked me with a big smile.

I thought the guy was laughing at me. "I didn't find no Eddie's. Nobody even knew where it was. People that live here have never even heard of it. I don't know why you sent me there."

The other youngster behind the counter came over. He must have heard how pissed off I was. "No, there's an Eddie's. I've been there. I've eaten there. But you have to be right on top of it to see where it's at... Which reminds me, you asked about a drugstore. And Chuey here told you there's one right across the park from here. I heard him tell you the hours, and those are the right hours because my girlfriend used to work there. But I forgot, and he must have forgotten too, that today it's Sunday and the drugstore over there is closed."

"Closed! Jesus!" I only had five pills left and tomorrow it'll be four. I had to get a refill.

"You need something real bad now?"

"Yeah. I've got some heavy medication. Pills. I'll get real sick if I don't have them."

"There's a lot of pharmacies open right now on Highway 35. All the big stores, like Walmart and Target, have one, and they're always open."

"Yeah, but I don't have a car."

"We can call you a taxi."

"I'll get lost out there."

"No, the taxi will wait for you and bring you back here if you want."

I thought about it for a moment. It might work. But I had my suitcase with me and I'd be dragging that around with me, drawing attention to myself. Not a good idea.

"Should we call you a taxi?"

"No, I have my suitcase that I'd be dragging around with me."

"Leave your suitcase here with us. We can take care of it."

That was even worse. "No, no. It's OK. I still have enough pills to get me through tomorrow. You're sure the drugstore here will be open tomorrow?"

"No question. It'll be open tomorrow morning at nine o'clock."

As much as I needed a refill, I was still hungry. "I know I've asked you guys already, but is there someplace close by that's open where I can get something to eat?"

"There's nothing around here, but there's plenty of places open on 35."

"No, I'm not going up there, not with this suitcase."

"You can leave it here and we can…"

"No, I don't want to do that…. I guess it's Burger King."

I WENT into Burger King again and stood at the doors with my suitcase at my side. The late afternoon sun was blazing through the side windows showing the smoke and the grime in the air real good. The room was filled mostly with older, unshaven, dark-skinned men who were still wearing winter jackets even though the afternoon had been warm. There was a lot of loud animated laughing and talking in Spanish. There didn't seem to be much eating going on, but there were plenty of dirty plates and cups laying around everywhere. I saw two empty tables at the back of the room and I knew I had to stay.

I went up to the counter with my suitcase and waited. A tired, middle-aged woman finally came up front. *"Bueno, joven, que te gustaria?"*

"What'd you say?"

"Ño hablas español?"

"Yeah I do, but this is still America, ain't it?"

"Don't give me no grief, boy," she said in a heavily accented English. "I've had enough of that today. So don't come in here getting smart with me. Now what do you want?"

I wanted to say, "Fuck you," and leave but I was so hungry that I had to eat something, anything. The best comeback I could think of was to look up at all those Technicolor pictures of burgers and fries behind her and act like I couldn't decide, while she tsked two or three times and shifted her weight from one foot to the other and finally said, "Come on, boy. I got a lot of work waiting for me back there without much help. What are you going to have?"

"OK, I'll take two Whoppers, three orders of fries, and a jumbo Coke. And please don't ask me if I'm hungry again."

"What?" she said looking at me as if I had something wrong with me. "You're not here with somebody, are you?"

"No, it's just me."

"That's a lot of food."

"Look, that's what I ordered, that's what I'll pay for, and that's what I'll eat, OK?"

She sighed. "You sure are a smart one for your size. You better watch who you talk to like that around here.... Have a seat at one of those tables back there and I'll call you when it's ready."

When the order was ready, I went up to the counter with my suitcase. She had a full tray in front of her. She looked at the tray and then at me. "This is what you ordered, right?"

"Yeah."

"Good, because I'm not taking any of it back. That'll be $19.37."

Try as I did, I could only eat two-thirds of one Whopper, one order of fries, and I drank only half of the jumbo Coke. I left everything else on the table and went back to the Greyhound waiting room with my suitcase.

"I'M GOING to need a place to stay near here for tonight, so I can get my medication refilled first thing in the morning at that drugstore you told me about."

Luis thought for a moment and then said, "They got some really nice rooms at the Posada Hotel just a block and a half from here. But their cheapest room is $119 a night plus tax. So you're looking at $133 a night."

He looked at me and waited. When was I ever going to be able to spend some of that money in my bag? He was thinking I was too embarrassed to say that I couldn't afford $133 a night. Hell, I could probably buy the damn place. But there was no way I could spend that kind of money for a room and not draw attention to myself. I shook my head. "I can't pay that kind of money just to sleep for one night."

"There's a lot of motels out on 35 that are cheaper, but you've been saying that you don't want to go out there."

"Isn't there any place around here besides that $133 room?"

For several moments they were silent, taking turns looking at each other. Then Chuey, the stocky one said, "What about old man Sanchez's place. They say the old lady still rents but is pretty fussy about who she rents to. But it might be a good place for him, at least for tonight. Then tomorrow, after he gets his medications, he might want to look around."

"But there's no plumbing in the rooms," Luis added, "and he'll have to use the showers and toilets outside. Still, she's only charging thirty dollars a night. The rooms are pretty bare, but they're very, very clean."

"So what do you think?" Chuey asked. "You think you could stay in a place like that?"

"Yeah." It was getting dark and the temperature outside seemed to be dropping fast. "But how do I get there?"

"Luis, you better go with him. Old lady Sanchez might not rent to him if he shows up alone with a suitcase and it's getting dark. Besides, she likes you."

Luis nodded.

It was cold and dark when we left the depot. Yet, as cold as it was, I waited until we were alongside a very dark part of the park before I unzipped my suitcase and took out my jacket and put it on. Then Luis led me to an old house on a big lot a block and half past the park. We went around to the back side of the house and he knocked hard on the back porch screen door and said loudly, "Señora, it's me Luis Cruz. I have a guest for you." A kitchen light went on and an old woman came out to the dark back porch. He told her that I was a friend of his family who had just come into town and needed a room for the night.

"Is he trustworthy?"

"Absolutely."

"Just one night?"

"Yes."

"Wait, I'll get a key."

She left the porch and came back with a key saying it was for room three and asked for the thirty dollars.

We started toward the back of the lot. "Where's the room?"

"Right here," he said, "just follow me."

A few steps later we came to some sort of a structure, and Luis turned on an overhead light that showed a long, narrow, plywood building on stilts, with five doors and five windows and a block of wood under each door for a step up.

"Where's my room?"

"Right there, the middle one, number three. Come on, let's go in. I've got to get back to the depot."

The room was just wide enough for a double bed with a small bureau on one side. I was disappointed. Luis must have seen the look on my face because he said, "What'd you expect for thirty dollars? It's clean and the bed's fine. What more do you need for a good night's sleep?"

It wasn't the room that was disappointing me, it was the gauzy, wine-colored curtain that was hanging over part of the window. I had planned to finally count all my money that night and now I wasn't sure. "It's OK, it'll do," I said. It was dark and I couldn't go running around looking for another place with my suitcase full of money. "But where's the toilet?"

"Turn around. There are two toilets under the tree and a shower right behind them."

"Outhouses. That's what we used to have when I was a kid."

"Those aren't outhouses. They're plumbed. You can flush them."

"Why are they under a tree?"

"You wouldn't want to be sitting in one of them during the summer here without any shade. And next to the shower is a washbasin. I've got to go. Maybe we'll see you tomorrow, huh?"

As soon as Luis was gone, I pulled the curtain all the way across the window and then went outside to see what I could see. Everything. I could see everything. That curtain might be keeping the sun out during the day, but it wasn't keeping the light in during the night. I went back into the room, sat on the bed, and thought. I came up with the idea of hanging all of my clothes over the curtain rod. Then maybe I could count my money.

I sat under the window taking off my clothes. When I was taking everything out of my jeans' pockets. I saw RAYMOND LOPEZ typed onto the information label pasted on the vial. Also on it were VESEY DRUGS IN PARKER, CALIFORNIA. Billy had probably told the cops that I had a prescription with refills for Zyprexa, and they were just waiting for my name to pop up in the system for a refill to tell them where I was. And what about Billy's friends? With all their money in my bag, they had to be watching the Internet, too. If they ever found me, I wouldn't have to be worrying about refills.

I had been using the name Jimmy Ramirez from Los Angeles and had planned to use it for the refill. But with Raymond Lopez plastered all over that label, how could I do that now? I sat on the floor under the window with the vial in my hand for a long time trying to think of another way, but I couldn't. Then I noticed that at the bottom of the vial some of the letters had been rubbed off the label. I rubbed at a letter with my thumb and after a minute or two it came off, but it left a smudge. I rubbed on LOPEZ. It came off but left a dirty smudge and tiny uneven paper rolls where the letters had been. I rubbed off RAYMOND and then PARKER, leaving the same dirty smudges and rolls. I didn't like the way it looked. It was pretty easy to see what someone was trying to do. So I rubbed off everything else except ZYPREXA 10MG and the label was one whole dirty unreadable mess.

How was I going to explain the condition of the label at the drugstore? The best I could come up with was that I had been traveling by bus for days. And each time I took a pill, it had been in the men's restroom where first, I would wash my hands and then, use them as a cup for the water I needed to swallow a pill, which meant that I handled the vial and label with wet hands twice each time I took a pill. And then I would stick the wet vial back in one of my dirty pockets.

I was feeling good about what I had just worked out, when it occurred to me that each time I had gone into the Parker pharmacy for a refill they had checked for it first on the computer. If they did that here, there would be no trace of a Jimmy Ramirez and Zyprexa. Then too, Medicaid always paid for the refill there and there would be nothing tying "Jimmy Ramirez" to Medicaid on the computer here. Maybe I couldn't get a refill at all. What then? It was late and I was too tired to think beyond that. I turned off the light and got into bed. Then I remembered that once the Parker computer couldn't call up my case and they had refilled the Zyprexa anyway without charging me the three-hundred-and-something dollars because they knew I was on Medicaid. I got out of bed and took out five more loose hundred-dollar bills from my traveling bag and put them in my pants pocket just in case. I got back into bed but remembered that I hadn't taken my pill. I got up, put on my pants and jacket, and went out to the washbasin and swallowed a pill. I had only four left and that kept repeating and repeating itself as I went back to the room and got into bed again.

The doors to the drugstore were open and the rollers on my suitcase announced my coming long before I reached them at five minutes past nine. There was a loud clacking as they passed over the threshold, and a young kid in a white T-shirt who was sweeping the floor near the door looked up at me and then at my suitcase, annoyed.

It was a small store. Just a few steps put me at the counter. Through a doorway on the other side of the counter, I could see shelves and shelves of drugs that went much farther back than the space I had passed through. A man in a white coat came through that doorway and said with a friendly smile, "Good morning. How may I help you?" He was soft-spoken, wore glasses, and was getting gray on the sides.

"I need a refill."

"A refill for what?"

I handed him the vial.

"Zyprexa. Is this for you?"

I nodded.

"Ten milligrams." He looked at me again, but gently, I thought.

I nodded again.

"How long have you been taking it?"

"About six months."

"And before that?"

"I was pretty sick."

He nodded. "What happened to the vial?"

"I've been traveling. On the bus. On my way to Mexico. I've been taking my pills in the restrooms. I'd wash my hands as I got started, but there's usually no paper towels in those restrooms. Then I'd take out one of my pills, usually with my hands still wet, and I had to use my hands to cup some water and swallow. Then I'd put the wet vial back in my dirty pants pockets with wet hands. And I think that's what happened to the label."

"Have you had refills before?"

"Yeah. Five or six. No, just five."

"Where?"

"In Los Angeles."

"You're from Los Angeles?"

"Yeah."

"And your name is?"

"Jimmy Ramirez."

"Jimmy or James?"

"Jimmy."

"And each refill has been for thirty pills?"

"Yeah."

"And where were you getting your refills?"

"At Long's Drugs."

"In Los Angeles?"

"Yeah."

"OK. Let's see what the system says." He stepped to his computer and typed into it and waited. He tried it again and waited.

"Are you sure you used Jimmy Ramirez as your name? And for thirty Zyprexa pills? Ten milligrams?"

"Sure I'm sure."

"Well, nothing's coming up."

"This happened once before and the people in Los Angeles let me have it anyway because they knew me. You don't know me, I know that. And if you're worried about how I'm going to pay for them, don't worry. I can pay you in cash. I need those pills because I don't want to cross over into Mexico with only four Zyprexas on me. And I can't stick around here. I've got to get going because I've got a very sick grandmother over there who could die any day now."

"I'm not worried about payment. I just need a little more information. Would you happen to have a copy of your doctor's prescription and what he said about refills on there?"

"That was more than six months ago and I was in pretty bad shape then and I don't even know which of the doctors made the prescription.... Look, are you gonna give me a refill or not?"

"Well, I'm just a little concerned that..."

The vial was on the counter and this whole thing was starting to worry me. The more answers I gave him, the more suspicious he seemed to be becoming. I didn't need the Laredo cops down there. I grabbed my vial and said, "Look, if you don't want my business, I don't need to give you my business. There's plenty of drugstores on Highway 35 that would be only too happy to have my business," and I walked myself and my suitcase out of his store as slowly as I could, but in a hurry.

I had gone about a half a block when I heard someone yelling behind me, "Hey man! Hey man! Hold it! Stop!" I panicked. It was the cops. I wanted to run but I couldn't, not with all that money in the suitcase. I didn't know what to tell them. That I had found the vial? That it wasn't really mine? "Hold it, man. Hold it!" I slowed and turned and saw that it was that little guy in the white T-shirt who had been sweeping the floor when I went into the drugstore. I didn't know what he wanted, but for a minute I thought that maybe the drugstore man had changed his mind and had sent that guy after me to give me a refill. So I stopped.

When he came up to me I said, "Yeah?"

"Hey man, we need to talk."

"Talk about what?"

"About that little scam you were trying to pull off back at the store. I've seen a lot of scammers come in there. Druggies come into the store all the time with a scam, but yours was one of the sorriest ones I've ever heard. You're lucky you got out of there when you did or you might have had a cop asking you some questions instead of that man."

"I don't know what you're talking about but you better get out of my way. I gotta get going. I gotta get a refill."

"Where you headed? To Highway 35? Man, those people out there in those drugstores are nobody to fool with. You start giving them that sorry-ass line you were giving Ben, and they'll put you in one of their holding rooms and call the cops on you before you can lay down even half the shit you were giving Ben. Besides, which one of them folks out there is gonna want to have anything to do with a guy who comes off the street rolling a suitcase behind him? First thing that tells them is that you can't afford a car, a jalopy even, or pay for a taxi. You need me man, you need me."

He was looking at me with a cocky grin. I didn't know who he was or what he was. His pomaded, slicked-back, black hair and his greasy face and the way he stood and slouched could have made him a Mexican, but his white skin and his little, beady black eyes and his long, skinny face could have made him white. He worried me and I didn't like or trust him.

"Need you? What would I ever need you for?"

"Oh, come on, man. You come in that store with a vial that no one can read anything on it, except that it's for a drug, the drug you just happen to want. That vial could be yours or mine or the cop's down the street. You don't have a prescription or a refill order. You give him a name and a drugstore that you know the computer's not going to be able to find. And then you act surprised when the computer can't find anything. Then you come up with the lame excuse that all the junkies use, that computers have been having trouble locating your prescription. You're just lucky it was Ben you tried to sell that shit to. Ben's way smart about books and computers and medications, but he's dumb as hell about people. I've seen so many junkies come in that store it makes me think that he's either stupid or a kindhearted fool. The word's out on him and I bet every junkie in town's been in our store. If they've got any kind of story at all, one that will hold up with the cops, he'll prescribe. But I have to admit, he doesn't just do it for the money. The damn fool actually feels for a lot of those people. And you take the cake. You come in there with absolutely nothing. Hell, that could be Mother Teresa's vial, and you think old Ben's gonna buy it, and you know he can't. That's why you need me, mister."

"Need you for what?"

"Need me for getting the drug you say you have to have but don't have the slightest clue how to get it…. But look, I don't want to argue with you. I don't have the time to argue with you. I say you need me, you say you don't. So I'm not gonna keep standing here wasting my time because I don't work for free. And even if you said you needed me, we're still a long way from the bottom line, which is how much you need to pay me? Sweeping and mopping Ben's floors, putting in a couple hours a day doing that just keeps the cops off my butt. Because I hustle. That's how I make my real money and there's a lot of hustle in this here border town…. Let me see that vial."

I handed him the vial. I must have bought into him by then.

He looked at it and nodded to himself. "You know what? The only thing this crappy little container is going to get you is a visit to the county jail."

"Why?"

"Because everything's been scratched out except the name of the drug and the quantity. It's pretty obvious that you're using somebody else's vial to get these drugs."

"That's my vial and the pills in there are my pills. Why would I be trying to get somebody else's Zyprexa. Those pills in there don't get you high or loaded. They just keep you from getting sick."

"What is Zy… How do you say it?"

"Zy like 'sigh' and prexa."

"What you're saying's no different than what a junkie says who's strung out on heroin. He needs the smack just to keep from getting sick."

"Yeah, but he still wants to get high. Those pills have never been there to get me high. They're there to keep me from losing it, from cracking up."

"You mean crazy like?"

"Yeah."

"Hmph. Well, whatever they're there for, I can tell you right now that no drugstore on this side of the river is going to give you those pills in the shape that vial's in. You're asking for trouble if you try to pass that vial again in Laredo, especially out on 35. With what I see here, you can't pay me enough to try to get you those pills on this side of the river."

"So what are you saying?"

"I'm saying that I've got a doctor friend on the other side of the river that I can get those pills from, for a price."

"What kind of price?"

"The doc's gonna want whatever the pills cost him plus payment for the time and trouble it took him to get the pills."

"How much is that?"

"It usually runs around two hundred dollars."

"I can do that."

"But then there's me too. I don't work for nothing. I'm gonna want a hundred dollars to get you to the doctor, and once he turns the pills over to me, then another hundred dollars before I turn them over to you."

"What if he can't get them?"

"Then you're out a hundred dollars. I don't work for free."

"I don't even know you and we're talking four hundred dollars."

"Wait a minute! Wait a minute! Don't play that poor mouth on me. I heard you telling Ben not to worry, that you could pay for the pills. Remember? Yeah, you remember alright. Do you have drug insurance?"

"No."

"Well then, you have to know that without insurance those pills are gonna cost you between three and four hundred dollars. So don't play that song with me. You've got to have at least that kind of money on you."

"I'm suppose to give you a hundred dollars now and three hundred dollars more when your doctor comes up with the pills. That's four hundred dollars and I don't even know you."

"You don't know me, huh? That's easy to take care of. My name is Joey Reyes. Which is easy to remember. *'Rey'* of course is 'king.' *'Reyes'* are 'kings.' So I'm Joey of the kings. Easy enough, right? I've lived here all my life. Everybody knows me because I'm a Mexican citizen and an American citizen. Some times I live on that side of the river and sometimes I live on this side of the river. You see, my mother was an American hippie who came down to Laredo and fell in love with my Mexican father who's an artist. They had me and for ten years she sold jewelry and paintings to the gringos to support us. Then one day she took me down to the post office and applied for an American passport for me. When it came she gave it to me and said she wanted me to have it so I could visit her wherever she went with her new Mexican boyfriend. He was an artist too. Then she left. The problem was she never told me where she was going or where she's at. So I moved across the bridge to my grandma's house with my father who's still painting. Sometimes I stay over there and sometimes I stay over here. There, now you know who I am. So what are you gonna do? Either way, I gotta get back to Ben's. I just dropped my broom and ran out of his store chasing you."

"I don't know. I just met you and we're talking four hundred dollars."

"Look, if you don't trust me, don't hire me. I don't care who you hire, but you're going to have to hire somebody to get you out of your mess."

I was in a mess, one I had made. I could almost hear the voices then. I had to do something. "OK, here," I said, handing him a hundred-dollar bill. "I guess I'm gonna have to trust you."

He took the bill and stretched it and held it up to the light in the sky before he put it in his pocket. "Now, do you want to try to see my friend the doctor today or wait until tomorrow?"

"Why do I want to wait 'til tomorrow?"

"I don't know. Some people don't like going to doctors. So you want to do it today?"

"Yes, the sooner the better."

"OK, we'll go as soon as I finish sweeping and mopping at Ben's. That won't take more than another hour. But do me a favor."

"What's that?"

"Don't stick around here."

"Why not?"

"Ben doesn't like to see me talking to junkies after they leave the store."

"Why not?"

"You come into the store with that lame story. Hell, it was worse than the scams most junkies use. Maybe that proves you're not a junkie because a righteous junkie would have never used that approach. Listen, go down to the bridge and wait for me. I should be there in about half an hour. We should cross together."

"How do I get to the bridge?"

"Simple. Go to the corner and turn right and go straight down that street, not quite three blocks, 'til it ends. You'll see a tan, two-story building there. Go into the building to one of the windows and pay a fee to go across the bridge."

"Whose bridge is it?"

"How in the hell do I know. Who cares whose bridge it is. It's there. That's all that counts."

"I was just wondering who gets the money they're collecting?"

"Look, I've got a lot bigger things than that to worry about. Right now I gotta go. You'd better get going too."

The tan, two-story building looked a lot like some of the buildings around the park. Over the front doorway a sign said CITY OF LAREDO. The fee turned out to be seventy-five cents.

"Who's bridge is this?" I asked the woman behind the window.

"Well, I've always assumed that half of it belongs to the United States and half of it belongs to Mexico."

"To the governments you mean?"

"Yes."

"So you're collecting this money for the governments?"

"No, this fee has nothing to do with the bridge and the governments."

"Then what's it for?"

"You've been using the city of Laredo's streets and sidewalks to get here, haven't you?"

"Yeah."

"That's what it's for."

"And everybody pays it?"

"They sure do."

Behind the building was a fenced-off area with a gate, and a guard standing next to it. That gate put you on the bridge. I sat on one of the benches to wait for Joey. The bridge seemed to be between two and three blocks long and about a hundred feet above the river. Looking at it from Laredo, there was a caged, covered walkway for pedestrians on the right. Next to that were four lanes of road: two for leaving the United States and two for entering the United States. To the left of the road was another caged and covered walkway for pedestrians entering the United States.

After a while, I went over to the bridge to look down at the river. It was wider, deeper, and swifter that I had ever imagined. Steep cliffs on either side of it seemed to make it impossible to get to it from where I was standing. All the stories I had heard about people crossing it in the middle of the night with the few things they could carry didn't make sense. They would have drowned. But I couldn't believe that my people had been lying about their crossing. And I had heard those same stories from strangers too, at fiestas and after baptisms when the men started drinking, and others always had something to add.

I went back to the benches and waited for someone I didn't like or trust. What had I gotten myself into? But there was no other way. When the man in the drugstore said he had some concerns, I panicked and grabbed the vial and left. When Joey yelled at me to wait, I thought it was the cops and I started getting ready to deny that the vial was mine. Those reactions told me what I knew deep down. The rubbed-out vial would only get me in trouble. I jiggled the vial in my pocket. Four. Liking or trusting that little worm didn't matter. I didn't have a choice.

When Joey finally showed up, his first words were, "Let's go."

"Where we going?"

"To the doctor's office."

We got on the bridge. For about the first block, there was a steady stream of Mexicans in front of and behind us returning to Mexico. We didn't speak. The only sound that came from us was the clacking of the rollers on my suitcase. When we neared what I thought was the halfway mark I said, "Where's Mexico?"

"About ten yards from here."

A few steps later a plaque said we were in Mexico. A few steps after that, he stopped and said, "You know, I never bothered to ask you how you planned to get back in the States."

"What do you mean?"

"You see that line of people over on the other side of the bridge? Those are people waiting to cross into the States. And unless you buy a car in Mexico, you'll be in one of those lines when you go back to the States. But you'd better have a passport or a visa with you or you're not gonna get back in."

"What are you talking about? I'm an American citizen."

"OK, OK, we'll see."

We started walking again and he said, "What do you have in that suitcase?"

"My stuff."

"It used to be until a couple of years ago, you could just walk into Mexico whenever and wherever you pleased bringing anything you wanted with you. But ever since that War on Drugs and that 9/11 bullshit, you're gonna have to put your bags through one of those detector machines."

"What?"

"Yeah, now they've got two armed guards from the army on the Mexico side standing next to the machine, making sure you put your bag through it and aren't bringing any contraband into the country."

"Wait a minute! Wait a minute! I can't do that!"

Joey stopped and said, "What's the problem?"

"I can't do that!"

"What do you mean? You can't do what?"

"I can't put my suitcase through that machine."

"Why not?"

"They won't let it pass. They'll want to keep it."

"They won't let it pass only if a red light comes on as your suitcase goes through it. And the red light will come on only if you have guns or drugs in your suitcase."

"I don't want to do it."

"Oh, ho, ho! Now we get to reality. Since the War on Drugs, I thought all the contraband, all the drugs went that way," pointing back toward Laredo, *"from* Mexico, not *to* Mexico. My, my, my."

"I don't have any drugs or guns in my suitcase, but they won't let it pass. Red light or no red light they're gonna wanna keep my suitcase for themselves. I gotta go back! I can't put my suitcase through that machine!"

"Go back where?"

"The way we came, back to Laredo, that's where."

"You can't go back the way we came. You're in Mexico now and to get back to the States, you have to get in that line across the road. And if this little detector machine scares you, wait 'til you see all the machines and guards they have over there on the American side. They don't mess around over there. They'll open up your suitcase, and from what I think you might have in there, you're on your way to prison."

"I'll just go back the way we came."

"And I keep telling you that you can't enter the States from this side of the bridge. No one can. Everybody knows that. You come up to the guard at the gate back there and he's going to ask you, 'Where do you think you're going?' Meanwhile, he's seen you coming and he's already called for backup help. They're all gonna be suspicious of you and your suitcase. And my guess is that you're going nowhere then except to jail."

I didn't like him or trust him, but he was making sense. I didn't know what to do. I was stuck, suspended a hundred feet over the

Rio Grande, halfway between Mexico and the United States. And as long as I had the traveling bag with me, I couldn't go backward or forward. And even if I wanted to, which I didn't, I couldn't throw my bag into the river because the walkway had cyclone fencing on both sides and a roof overhead.

Then Joey said, "Look, the only way you're gonna get off this bridge with that suitcase is by paying your way off."

"Pay? Pay who?"

"Pay the guards. Give them enough money so that they'll agree to let the suitcase pass, red light or no red light. I know most of the guards on both sides of the bridge and they know me. I usually cross it once a day and sometimes two or three times a day. Let me see who's at the detector today and maybe you can pay your suitcase's way past that machine. But before I start talking to the guards, I want to know if you have enough money to pay them."

"How much is it going to be?"

"Maybe a couple hundred. I don't know. But you don't have much of a choice. If you don't get off the bridge yourself, sooner or later guards will come and take you off, suitcase and all. And don't think for a minute they won't want to know what's in the suitcase…. But we gotta be talking money now. A couple hundred for the guards, two for the doctor, and you still owe me a hundred. Can you do that?"

I hesitated but I had no choice. "Yeah, I can do that."

"Wait here," he said leaving, "I don't want the guards to see you. I'll be back." And off he went to the guards at the detector.

I stood to one side for about ten to fifteen minutes with a stream of people passing me, looking at me wondering what I was doing standing there. A few stopped and asked if I was OK. I nodded hoping that they wouldn't report me to the guards before Joey got back. A little old lady who still had her work apron on stopped and said, "What's the matter, son. You look so sad?" Somehow I felt that I had to convince her that I wasn't sad. "I'm fine. I'm fine," I said and then smiled. She shook her head and walked on. She didn't believe me.

Joey came back smiling. "OK, let's go. It's all set. We pay them a little American money and the suitcase goes through."

"How much do they want?"

"Now don't ever go around saying that I've never done anything for you. There's two of them, and I got them to take fifty dollars each. One hundred bucks total and your suitcase passes any and all red lights. You better give me that before we start."

I felt in my pocket and then gave him another hundred.

"Good. But there is one problem."

"What's that?"

"Guns aren't legal in Mexico. Only the police and the military can have them. I had to swear up and down that there were no guns in your suitcase."

"There's none."

"But I want to see for myself."

"What?"

"Yeah. I want to see for myself to make sure. Because if there are guns in there and they can feel them when they handle your suitcase, then I'm in big trouble and so are you. I might as well leave the country then. That's too big a risk for me to take. So just casually open the suitcase for me without making it a big deal in front of all these people passing by."

"Open it? Are you kidding? I can't open that for you or anybody."

"Well, you better open it, 'cause we're not moving 'til you do."

He was staring at me. Those beady little black eyes were intense, hostile. I didn't look away, but I couldn't look at him. Finally, shaking my head a little I said, "I can't open it for anyone."

"You'd better make me an exception, because I can't and I won't take that risk. I've got to be sure there's no guns in there."

I didn't answer. I didn't know what more I could answer.

"Here's the hundred back you just gave me for the guards." He was standing with the hundred-dollar bill in his hand and his arm held out to me. People were looking at us as they passed.

"But you're not getting the first hundred back, 'cause that was supposed to be for me trying to get you your pills and you're not letting me try. So here," he said, dropping the bill on my shoe, "I can't wait around here all day. I've got things to do. And don't worry about the guards. They'll be here pretty soon to take you off the bridge. Nice knowing you." He turned and walked back in the direction of the guards.

I panicked. "Joey! Joey! Come back!"

People stopped and stared at me and looked in Joey's direction. Joey came back and shooed people away. "Go on! Go on! Move it! This is between him and me." The people moved on.

"Look, I really don't have time to be fooling around like this. All I wanna be sure of is that there aren't any guns in there. The guards are gonna be handling your suitcase and if they feel any guns in there, we're both in deep shit. Are you gonna open that suitcase or not?"

I nodded.

"Well open it!"

Two more people had stopped, watching us. I looked at them and Joey told them, "Go on! This is not your business. Go on!"

I opened the suitcase. He looked and then looked at me and said, "There's nothing in it except that bag."

"There's clothes in there."

"Yeah, a few. It's the bag you're hiding. What's in the bag?"

"Not guns."

"How do I know that?"

I picked up the bag and said, "Here feel it. There's no guns in there."

He took the bag and felt it, shook it, and slapped it. "What the hell do you have in there? It's not even powder."

"It's not guns and all I can tell you, and will tell you, is that what I've got in there means a lot to me."

I gave him back the hundred-dollar bill and we started toward the detector. But as we got close enough to see the detector and the guards, I stopped. What went flashing through my mind was the first time I had seen one of those metal detectors at the Parker courthouse.

THAT DAY I was late for court and there was a line outside the courthouse door. The line wasn't moving and I asked the guy in front of me, "What's holding everything up?"

"It's the metal detector, man."

"The what?"

"The metal detector. Ain't you ever seen one of them?"

"No."

"Well, step aside, boy, and look through the glass next to the doors.... See the machine?"

"Yeah."

"And the guard standing over it?"

"Yeah."

"When you get inside, you're gonna have to take off your shoes and put those and anything you have with metal on it in a tray. Then you're gonna put that tray and your backpack on a conveyor belt. The guard standing next to the machine runs that belt and watches everything passing through that machine, looking for weapons or contraband."

"Can he see what's in my backpack?"

"Oh yeah. Not only can he see what's in your bag, he can also take a picture of it that they can use in court against you."

JOEY HAD kept walking. "Joey! Joey!"

He came back. "What the fuck's the matter now?"

"Are they gonna put my suitcase on and through the machine?"

"Yeah, why?"

"I can't let them do that."

"Why?"

"He'll see what's in my bag in the suitcase."

"So what? They already said that even if the red light goes off, they won't hold up the suitcase. They'll let it pass,"

"I can't put it through the machine."

"Look, I don't want to spend the rest of my fucking life on this fucking bridge. I'm gonna walk over there and give those two guys their hundred bucks like I told them, and I'm gonna keep walking and probably never see you again because if whatever's in that bag is as heavy as you're making it out to be, your ass will be in prison. All I know is that I've kept my part of the bargain, so I'm leaving. Like I said a while ago, it's been nice knowing you."

"Wait, Joey, please. Give me a minute to think about this. There's gotta be a way out of this."

"Think all you want, but I'm not hanging out on this bridge much longer."

There was a way. "Joey, what if I give you another hundred to give to them if they'll let my suitcase pass without it going through the machine?"

"Look, I've already got a deal with them. I'm not gonna back out on my word and start negotiating again. 'A deal's a deal,' they're gonna say."

"What if I give you another hundred for yourself plus the hundred for them. And this other hundred is yours, no matter what the doctor says, if you can get them to let the suitcase go around the machine and not through it."

"Let me get this straight. Another hundred for me, right now, if the guards let your suitcase go around the machine and not through it. And if the doctor gets pills for you, still another two hundred for me, right?"

"Yeah."

"Boy, you must have a lot of money."

I didn't answer. I gave him another bill.

He unfolded it, looked at it, held it up to the sky, and said, "I'll be right back."

I watched as Joey went back to the machine and started talking to the closest guard, watched as that guard motioned for the other guard at the end of the machine to join them, watched as Joey talked to them...hoping I wouldn't see any shaking of heads. Instead I saw them nod and Joey handed them what had to be the two bills.

Joey came back smiling. "They went for it. But they want us to wait here 'til they're sure no one will see the suitcase go around the machine. Where's my hundred?"

I handed him another bill.

With the first break in the people crossing, the guard at the machine motioned for us to come. The guards were young boys, Indians, out of a jungle somewhere dressed in light-green, camouflage fatigues. They watched me wide-eyed as I went around them and their machine, submachine guns in their hands at the ready.

WE WALKED several blocks through crowded downtown streets of Nuevo Laredo with the rollers on my suitcase clacking loudly on the uneven sidewalks, turning heads.

"How much longer you gonna keep dragging that thing around with you? People can hear you coming a block away. And the way you've been acting, I don't think you want people looking at that precious suitcase of yours."

"As soon as I get my pills, I'm outta here. I'm on the other side. This doesn't look like any place I wanna be."

"A lot of these people know me. They know I've got a little side business 'cause I've been bringing gringos over here to the doctor for a couple of years now, and it doesn't take much for them to figure that one out. And they know I don't work for free. So some of them might be wondering right now what you've got in that suitcase."

"I wouldn't be over here if that boss of yours in that drugstore over there had just given me a refill."

"Hey, wait a minute. Let's not get into that. The truth is you ran out of that store because you knew you had a phony vial and you were afraid he was gonna call the heat. Let's just keep the facts straight, OK?"

I didn't have to like him, I just had to use him.

The doctor's office was in a small, cinder-block building on the edge of downtown Nuevo Laredo. "Step inside, my friend," Joey said opening the front door. What I stepped into was a dark, narrow hall that ran the length of the building. Metal chairs lined both sides of the hall whose only light came from slits of glass on either side of the front door. What I didn't see until my eyes adjusted to the darkness were the people sitting in some of those chairs. After a while I counted nine people.

"Where's the doctor's office?" I whispered.

"This is it."

"Where?"

"Here."

"What are these people doing here?"

"What else would they be doing here? They're waiting to see the doctor."

"All nine of them?"

"Yeah."

"They're ahead of us?"

"Yeah."

"Why didn't you call and make an appointment?" I wasn't whispering anymore, but then I didn't think that any of these folks could understand English.

"Because this doctor doesn't take appointments. He says that Mexicans are never on time, and after a few years of that, he decided on first come, first served."

"So I have to wait 'til he sees all of them?"

"Yeah. I can't help that. You're the one who said you wanted to come right now. If we had waited 'til tomorrow morning, like I thought we should, we could have come a few minutes before he opened and been the first ones in."

The guy never loses, I thought. But I didn't have to like him. I didn't say much for a while, until none of this made any sense. "So where's his office? I mean, where does he see me?"

"On the other side of the door on the left, the only door in this hall."

"Where does his receptionist or nurse sit?"

"He doesn't have a receptionist or a nurse."

"How does he run a business without a nurse or a receptionist?"

"He does it all by himself. He's in there with a patient right now. When he's finished with that patient, he'll open the door and let that patient out and then ask who's next."

"Yeah, but there's nine people in front of us. We're gonna be here a long time. Can't we go to another doctor?"

"Look, you can go to any doctor you want. But this is the only doctor I know that's gonna see your phony vial and still get you the drugs you need. So if you know of another doctor that won't make you wait so long, then go. But I'm not going with you. I've been doing this for a couple of years now. I know what I'm doing."

I didn't like him, but I couldn't say that I didn't trust him anymore. He got me over that bridge, and to do that, he had worked those guards pretty good the first time and the second time, too.

"I just know we're gonna be here a while."

"It may be even longer than you think. Because here in Nuevo Laredo, a lot of the doctors follow the old practice of being open from eleven to two, then they close from two to five for *comida*, and open again from five to eight. It's after twelve now and we may not get in to see him before two. We may be looking at some time after five."

"I hope not.... Are all these people druggies?"

"No, they're just ordinary people who've got health problems."

"Why so many?"

"Because he's good and cheap and today's Monday. He doesn't work on the weekend. Look at these folks. He's not getting rich treating them."

"If he's so good, what's he doing taking your strung-out clients?"

"He only sees my clients once. The fact that I come with them, and they're usually gringos, automatically tells him that they're probably strung-out. He talks to them first to see how strung-out they are. If he thinks they're really strung-out, he tells them that this it, that he hopes that they've seen enough misery because he won't help them again and they'd better start helping themselves and straightening out. And he means it. He won't let me bring the same person over here twice."

"Why does he do it at all?"

"Maybe for the money, but I think he also feels for them. I sit in there with them and I get that impression."

"Yeah, but you said your boss over there at the drugstore feels for these people too. I sure didn't think he was feeling for me and about to help me, and you're probably bringing people over here that he's turned down."

"There's a difference. My boss is afraid of the police and losing his license and his business. This doctor's not worried about the police. He's not gonna get arrested for writing a prescription or getting some drugs for a junkie. The police here could care less."

About then, the door midway down the hall opened and a woman holding a baby came out saying, *"Gracias,* Doctor, *gracias,"* over and over again. A small, bald man in a white coat nodded and said, *"Quien siga?"* A middle-aged man who was sitting closest to the door stood and limped to the doctor. They stepped into the office and he closed the door.

"Why can't we go to a doctor in the States?"

"Are you kidding me? Those guys are so afraid of losing their license and business that they'd probably have me arrested for just approaching them. No, I've heard too many stories about them. They're paranoid. Ask any junkie."

Eight people shuffled closer to the door. So did I once Joey said, "Move over." As the woman with the baby was leaving, a woman with a boy who had his arm in a sling came in the front door and they took the seats behind me. I looked at my watch: 12:20. And there were eight ahead of me and one behind me. I didn't think I'd get to the doctor before 2:00.

"If that doctor is so good and so cheap, why is he charging me two hundred dollars?"

"That was me talking, not the doctor. I wanted to make sure you could cover whatever he charged. I didn't want to get here and you not have enough money to pay him. I've never had anyone before that uses Zy...or whatever you call it. I put it on the high end, like I said, just to be sure. He'll talk to you first and then set a price. I've seen him go as low as thirty dollars and as high as a hundred and fifty dollars. With one sorry son of a bitch, he just shook his head and said, 'No charge.'"

I looked at the people ahead of me. The women looked distressed and the men were stone-faced. What was I doing in this dingy hall with these people? "Why are these people so tense, so uptight?"

"Most of them don't have a lot of money. They've been taking care of themselves at home with home medicines. That hasn't worked. So now they're here. This has to work. If it doesn't, then they've got some big problems."

I didn't feel one bit sorry for them. I had four pills left, and the voices were ready and waiting. Whatever these people had couldn't begin to compare with the voices. There were times I could feel those voices watching and waiting.

The line moved faster than I had expected. Most people were in and out with that so-called doctor in about ten minutes. At a quarter to two, there was only an old man in front of me. A woman had gone in five minutes before and should have been coming out soon.

"Joey, if we get into his office a minute or two before two, will he still take care of me?"

"Yeah, as long as we get past his door before two, he'll take care of you no matter how long it takes."

People kept coming in and now there were four people waiting behind me. "These people behind me have to know they're not going to get into his office before two. Why are they sticking around?"

"They're reserving their places for the five o'clock session. Because at two, he'll come out and say that's it for the morning, but that people returning at five can come back to the places they had in the morning."

I started watching the second hand on my watch, as if somehow that would make the woman in the doctor's office come out sooner. It didn't, and at two o'clock the doctor came out and said we would have to come back at five and we could keep our places in line. I cursed him under my breath, but Joey said, "It's not the end of the world. You'll probably have your pills by six."

We were at the far end of the hall, and as we were leaving, the people who had been behind us were now in front of us, and each one at different times turned to see what was causing the clacking on the tiles. Outside Joey said, "You're gonna have to do something about that suitcase and those rollers."

"Like what?"

"Like stop dragging that thing around with you. It gives you the attention you don't seem to want. People are really gonna start wondering what's up with you, and now you've got three more hours to let them see you dragging that thing around."

"What do you want me to do with it?"

"It's *your* suitcase. Do what you want with it. But if you were willing to pay some punky-ass guards two hundred dollars so they wouldn't look at it, I would think that you'd want to get off the streets with it, so that people don't keep looking at it and looking at it and wondering about it."

"So how do I do that?"

"There's a little hotel around the corner about a block from here that's…"

"What do I want a hotel for? I'm not staying here tonight. Once he gives me my pills I'm outta here."

"I'm not talking about staying here tonight. I'm talking about people staring at you and your suitcase for the next three hours."

"I can't be paying for a hotel room for three hours."

"Don't poor-mouth me. You just gave away three hundred dollars so that the guards wouldn't take thirty seconds to look at your suitcase….

"But seriously, listen to me for a minute. I got some business to tend to on this side of the bridge right now. I've got to get to that right away, but I'll be back by five. So what're you gonna do for three hours? Where you gonna hide with that big thing and those noisy rollers? This is a small town. People have already noticed you. You kept stopping on that bridge and waiting. Nobody stops on the bridge and waits, especially nobody with a suitcase. You were arguing with me about that suitcase on the bridge and you finally opened it on the bridge. People saw all that. There's already enough people wondering about you and that suitcase, and you're gonna give them three more hours of it by hanging out on the street 'til we go back to the doctor?

"A lot of people saw you with me when we walked through the downtown earlier. They know I don't bring law-abiding U.S. citizens over to Mexico so they can go to church. And then they're gonna see you, a stranger, walking around the streets with your suitcase for three hours like a lost soul. Some of them are gonna be convinced you'd be an easy take. Get the picture? Look, I don't care what you do. I've already earned two hundred dollars. But for your own good, you oughta get a room and get off the street, at least until I get back."

I didn't have to like the guy, but I was starting to dislike him less. And I was even starting to trust him more. He made a lotta sense.

"So how much is this room gonna cost me?"

"I'm not even gonna talk to that, Mr. Big Spender. Twenty dollars."

"OK, OK, where is this place?"

"It's right around the corner, a block down. I'll even walk you down there. Those people know me. I'll tell them you're a friend of mine that's gonna be here for a few days."

"A few days!"

"No, no, that's just what I'll tell them. You'll get a better room that way."

The hotel turned out to look like the small motels I had seen in Parker. It was a two-story, L-shaped structure that overlooked a large parking lot. There was a row of rooms on the second floor stacked exactly on top of a row of first-floor rooms. Joey did know the people at the motel, and the wife said she was giving me a very nice room on the second floor, even though from the office all the rooms looked to be exactly the same. Joey said he'd come to my room when he was finished with his business so that we could walk back to the doctor's office together. As I was climbing the open stairs to my room, I thought that at last I'd have a place to count my money. But once I was in the room, I could hear every sound the maid was making in the next room. The walls were paper-thin, and the room's big aluminum sash window felt like it could be forced out with a push of my hand. I decided not to count my money after all. I lay on the bed and before I knew it, I was asleep.

I WAS awake when Joey knocked. In fact, I had been awake a long time before he knocked, lying there, looking up at the ceiling, thinking, and worrying about what to do with the bag now that Joey had convinced me that I couldn't keep walking around with the suitcase. I had gotten out of bed once and taken the bag into the bathroom, where the window was frosted, and closed the door and set the bag on the floor. Then I made sure there were no cracks or holes in the walls or the ceiling. I knelt over the bag not wanting to open it, but knowing that I would probably need more money in the morning.

The bag was the type used by athletes to carry their equipment. It was canvas with two leather handles and was about three feet long, a foot wide, and a foot deep. In the fitting room of the sporting goods store in Merced, I had carefully transferred the half-inch packets of hundred-dollar bills from the duffel bag to the sports bag. I had stacked the packets of bills in layers from bottom to top and from side to side. I had rewrapped the loose bills from the one packet I had opened and set it on top of the other packets where I could easily reach it. I took five bills from the rewrapped packet and zipped the bag up again.

When Joey knocked, the only thing I had decided was that I was taking the bag with me wherever I went until I got my pills. Then I'd go back across the bridge and head for Florida. They said it was warm there in the winter.

"You better get dressed. We only got eighteen minutes, and I want to make sure we get there a few minutes before five so that I don't have to start arguing with anybody about our reserved, second place in line."

I put on my pants, shoes, and shirt. I combed my hair, put on my jacket, picked up my bag, and started for the door.

"Where you going with that thing?"

"I'm taking it with me. I'm not leaving it here."

"First, it's that suitcase. Now, it's that fucking bag. People are really gonna think you're weird."

"I don't care what they think. As soon as I get my pills, I'm outta this place and you'll never see me again."

WE WERE back at the doctor's office at 5:00, second in line. At 5:12 the door opened and the little doctor said, "Who's next?"

As we stood and moved the few steps toward the door, the doctor's eyes were on me. From the door, he looked briefly at Joey and then back at me, studying me for several moments before he said, "Come in, gentlemen."

It was a big room, maybe the only other room in that small building. To our left was a big, old, dark wooden desk with a wooden swivel chair behind it and two old, wooden chairs in front. At the opposite end of the room was an examination table with a footstool next to it and a small writing table and stool across from it. Across from us were several shelves of books that covered most of the wall. Next to the books near the examination table was an old scale with a height-measuring pole attached to it. Metal filing cabinets were set against the remaining wall. The room was well-lit. Panes of glass had been inset at the roofline in the walls behind the doctor's desk and the bookshelves. Rows of fluorescent lights hung on the other side of the room. Big slabs of dark tiles covered the floor.

"What can I do for you, Jose?"

"Doctor, this is Jimmy Ramirez, a friend of mine who..."

"A friend of yours?" interrupted the little man with a cynical grin. He was sitting in his big chair behind his huge desk. His words and his look made Joey stumble, which amused the little man even more, his big brown eyes lighting up behind his rimless glasses.

"Well maybe not exactly a friend, but someone I met on the other side in the pharmacy where I work and..."

"You meet quite a few people there, don't you, Jose?"

"Doctor, the man's got a problem, I think a real problem. So I've brought him here for your help."

"Can't he get help for his problem in the United States?"

"He can't and that makes his problem even bigger."

The little man pursed his lips, nodding, and asked, "What exactly is his problem?"

"He's taking Zy...Zy...you'd better tell him, Jimmy."

The little man turned an iron look on me. "Yes, you'd better tell me, Jimmy. But before you do, Jimmy, are you under the influence of any drug or alcohol right now?"

"Like what?"

"He wants to know if you're loaded on anything."

"I'm not loaded on anything right now."

"Jimmy, there's no need to try to sugarcoat anything in here. Jose will tell you that. Correct, Jose?"

"Yes."

"Your problem then is?"

Behind that desk and with that look and tone of voice, the little man seemed two or three times bigger.

"My problem is that I take Zyprexa and the people in the States won't give me a refill. Tomorrow morning I'll be down to three pills."

"You take what?"

"Zyprexa," I said, handing the little man the vial.

The doctor looked at the vial. "Zyprexa, Zyprexa. I've heard of it, but I've never had an occasion to prescribe it to any of my patients. Excuse me," he said standing, "I'll be right back."

He went to his bookshelves and took out a book and read from it. Then he read from another book and came back to us.

"Why won't they give you a refill in the United States?"

"I think it's because they think I've tampered with the vial. The truth is that I've been traveling on the bus for a few days, and in the restrooms water got all over the vial and..."

"No, no, I don't want to hear any more of that. The label has been tampered with. Who did it or why, I'm not concerned with. Among the individuals that Jose brings me, you are unique. He usually brings me people who are badly addicted to a controlled substance. They are very sick and about to be sicker. All I can do for them is provide temporary relief from their pain and hope that in the interim they will take steps to effectively deal with their addiction. You're not addicted to a controlled substance. Zyprexa does not provide the euphoria of narcotics. It's a medication that treats an existing illness rather than creating one. I'll try to help you if you can tell me why you need Zyprexa."

He kept his eyes on me. It was a kind look, as if he were trying to understand me. He asked, "How long have you been using Zyprexa?"

"A little more than six months."

"Why did you start using Zyprexa?"

"Because without it, my mind has no borders. When I was sick, mentally ill as they call it, the voices took complete control of me and my mind. I lived in constant fear of them. They dictated what I had to do, things that I would never do or want to do. Tomorrow morning, I will have only three pills left, and I can feel the voices waiting, ready to drive me completely crazy like they did the last time."

"How did you overcome that bout of insanity?"

"The police arrested me. I had been running through my little village screaming and yelling and terrifying people in the middle of the night. The police took me to a hospital where I refused to take medication. The voices were telling me, ordering me, not to take it. The doctors injected me with Zyprexa. Gradually the medication beat the voices back and gave me back my mind. Or at least put some borders on it."

He looked at me for a while...a bland look.

"Will you help me? Will you help me get Zyprexa?"

"I'll try. As I said earlier, I haven't had an occasion to prescribe Zyprexa or see how people are treated with it here in Nuevo Laredo. Unfortunately, there's a scarcity of funds and treatment for the mentally ill who are poor in Mexico. On the other hand, I'm sure that Zyprexa is no stranger to the wealthy here. And not having ever prescribed it, I have no idea where it's available. I don't have much time to check on its availability here tonight, but I'll have some time in the morning. Why don't you and Jose return tomorrow morning at 11:00. I should have something for you then."

"You'll help me then, Doctor?"

"We'll see."

"Thank you."

As we were leaving, the doctor said, "Jose, you'd better help him get a place to stay tonight."

"I already got him a room at Beto's hotel."

He looked at me again and said, "Then why are you carrying that bag around with you? This morning you had a suitcase, now it's a bag. Why?"

I searched for an answer but only stumbled for words.

Joey said, "It's complicated, Doctor, but it's not a big deal. He's going to take care of it in a few minutes."

"Good."

As the doctor opened the door and we stepped out into the hallway, Joey asked the doctor about another of his "friends," and I stood there waiting as they talked. All of the chairs in the hallway were taken. I recognized a few of the people from the morning and then I saw that everyone seemed to be looking at my bag. As we started down the hallway, I carried the bag on my right side away from their stares. But the bag was too big to hide. All eyes were on me and the bag, more on the bag than me.

Once outside, I felt a wave of relief. But Joey wouldn't have it. "Why did you bring that goddamn bag with you? Can't you see how weird it makes you look? Even the doctor asked about it."

"I know, Joey, but I can't leave it in that room at the hotel."

"Why not?"

"Joey, that room is so flimsy. All anyone would have to do is lean against the window and it would cave in. This afternoon I heard every noise, every move the maid made in the room next to mine.

And every time I moved an inch, I was sure the people below me heard and felt me."

"You're the one that doesn't want anyone looking at that precious bag of yours, and here you are showing it to anyone on the street who even glances at it."

"I know, Joey, but I'm not leaving my bag in that room when I'm not there. In fact I'm gonna have a hell of a time tonight, wondering who's gonna kick the door in."

"You want to get a room in a different hotel?"

"I don't know. I don't know what to do."

"I can show you other hotels. There are two big, new, expensive ones here. I don't think their prices are going to be a problem for you, not the way you've been throwing money around. The real problem is that the *narcotraficantes* stay in them. Some people say they own them. When you show up with your suitcase and bag, they're gonna wanna know who you are and what you want and where your money is coming from. They'll put someone on you real fast to get some answers. And if they don't like what they hear, there's no telling what they'll do. I wouldn't go near those two hotels if I were you.

"There's a ton of third-class, filthy, seedy hotels on this side of the bridge. You'd be red meat in any one of those. And there are two other hotels like the one you're in now. I really don't know much about them, but I know the hotel you're staying in inside out. Our family and friends stay there when they come to visit my grandma and dad. No one's ever had a problem there and they always have good things to say about it. In my opinion, Jimmy, you're in the best place possible."

I was scared. I didn't know what to think.

"Come on. Let's go get something to eat. You like *mariscos?*"

"Yeah."

"There's a real good place a couple of blocks from here. Come on. You don't have to decide anything this minute. Let's go have a couple of drinks and relax. I'm sure you could use some of that."

We hadn't been walking more than half a block when Joey said,

"You know, Jimmy, you better get used to the idea that even if the doctor comes up with the pills for you tomorrow morning, you may be on this side of the bridge for a couple more days."

I didn't want to hear that. "You gotta be kidding me. Why?"

"There's hundreds of Mexicans that cross that bridge every day to go to work over there. And crossing into the States is nothing like crossing into Mexico. The Border Patrol checks everyone and everything entering at the bridge, and then later, twenty miles down the road, they pull everybody over and check again. The first checkpoint after the bridge is mainly for Mexican workers. All the people crossing to go to work have been issued a worker's visa they show the guards there. I don't show anything because they all know me and know that I'm a U.S. citizen. You shouldn't have any problem with that either. Your problem's gonna be your suitcase and that bag. Because after that first checkpoint, there's a second checkpoint a few yards away with guards at tables where everything you're carrying is opened and inspected. There's no way you're gonna buy your way past that inspection. There's too many guards there. And there's no way you're gonna get past that checkpoint without the guards opening and inspecting your precious bag. Believe me, your bag's gonna get opened and inspected."

I stopped and looked at Joey, shaking my head. He stopped too.

"Look, I'm not making anything up. I'm telling you like it is. And you should be damn glad I'm telling you like it is."

This was becoming a nightmare. "So what do I do?"

"There are things you can do, but it'll take a few days and some money to get them ready."

"Things like what?"

"You can have suitcases and bags made with false bottoms and sides that aren't easily detected. And they don't usually pat search you when you're crossing, so some people paste things to their bodies. Or if worse comes to worse, you can contract with some folks to put you and your suitcase and bag on one of their home-made wooden rafts and push you across the river at night."

"If the doctor's got the pills for me tomorrow morning, why

couldn't you help me get on one of those rafts tomorrow night?"

"That's a lot tougher than it sounds."

"Why?"

"Because that's become such a booming business, that some of the *narcotraficantes* have taken it over, or most of it over. And more and more people who thought they had bought tickets to cross end up being raped, robbed, and even murdered on this side. So you wanna make sure you know who you're buying a safe ticket from to the other side. And that could take some time, some doing."

"So what do I do in the meantime?"

"You stop carrying that bag around with you."

"I'm not leaving it in that room."

"Fine. We've talked about that enough. Let's go, I'm hungry."

At the end of the block, there was a big, new, deep-red building.

"What's that?"

"It's the new supermarket here. Big, modern, not even a year old. They've never had anything like it on this side before."

As we started across the street Joey said, "Hey, wait a minute, Jimmy. I want to show you something."

"What?"

"I thought of something. I want to show you something in that new supermarket. It'll just take a minute. Let's see what you think."

"I don't need anything. I don't wanna buy anything."

"I'm not asking you to. Just take a look."

It was a huge, bare, boxlike store with lights hanging from the ceiling. A wide aisle ran across the front of the store. Behind it were the checkout stands. We were a few feet from the closest checkout stand when Joey said, "Turn around. Look."

A big part of the front wall was gray metal. But it wasn't until Joey said, "Those are lockers," that I knew what they were. We watched as a woman went to one of the open ones and put a bag in it, closed the door, and took something from it.

"I know what you're thinking, Joey, but they're too small."

"Not the ones on the left end. There's a bunch of big ones that you can put your bag in."

"Joey, I'm not putting my bag in one of those things."

"Why not? The open ones have a key in the door. You put a five-peso coin in the door, then close it, and take the key out and your bag is automatically locked. Those lockers are supposed to be just for people shopping here, but there's no one here to stop anyone from using them. And there's no way to tell which locker that woman just put her bag in unless you have the key. There's a little number on the key and a matching number on the locker door that will open when the key is used. The store's open seven days a week from six in the morning to ten at night. Those are much better hours than you could get at any bank. And let's face it, you wouldn't be able to get a safety deposit box in any bank unless you first let them see what you're depositing. So here's five pesos, try it."

I took the coin and thought for a moment and then said again, "I'm not putting my bag in one of those things."

"Why not?"

"'Cause I don't trust it, that's why. Let's get out of here."

As we neared the intersection, someone from a side street shouted, "Stop! Hold it right there! I mean it! Hold it right there!"

It was a cop coming toward us. It was too dark to see if he had a gun, but I didn't want to run and test it. I stopped and Joey stopped too.

"What the fuck, Joey. What's this all about?"

"I don't know, man, but don't do anything stupid. He's calling for backup. Let me do the talking. And don't start protesting or protecting that fucking bag of yours."

"Where you boys headed?"

He was still a few feet away, but I could see a gun in his hip holster.

"We're just going to get something to eat."

"Is that right?" he said, stepping up to us and looking us over. "So where you coming from?"

"From the doctor's office."

He nodded several times and seemed to be almost smiling until his nostrils flared and his eyes bulged and he said, "Look, you little punk, I asked you an honest question and I want an honest answer. Where the fuck *are* you coming from?"

Joey looked flustered, which made me nervous. If we got arrested, not only would I go to jail, but I'd lose everything, every single penny.

"I thought I told you the truth, Officer. I've got no reason to lie to you."

"Except I saw you come out of the store with that bag chockfull of stuff. What's in that bag?"

Joey hesitated and then said, "I don't know. You're going to have to ask the other guy. It's his bag."

The cop turned his angry look on me. "What's in the bag?"

I didn't know what to answer or how to answer. All I could think was that I was about to lose everything.

"I'm not gonna ask you again. What's in the bag?"

"My clothes and some things," I managed.

"Show me your receipt."

"Receipt?"

"Yeah, your receipt for those things. You didn't even bother to use one of the store's bags. You just went wild in there filling that bag with everything and anything you wanted, didn't you?"

I shook my head.

"Alright, I'm gonna need some light. Let's go back up to the store. And don't get cute or you'll hear from my gun."

As we walked back to the store, I knew that this was the way my life was going to end. Once they opened the bag and they saw all that money, I would either be on my way to a Mexican prison or have a bullet in my head.

Inside the store, the cop took us to the first checkout stand. "Señorita, I'm going to need a pen and paper to itemize all the things these two *ladrones* have taken from your store."

"What did they steal, Officer?"

"Everything that's in that bag. And they don't have a single receipt for any of it."

"Things in the bag?"

"Yes."

"They didn't steal anything, Officer. I saw them come in with the bag just the way it is now. One of them was explaining to the other one with the bag about how our lockers worked. He said a lot about the lockers but the other one just kept shaking his head no. Finally, they left with the bag just like it was when they came in. They never went into the store. They never went past these registers. They were never close enough to anything they could steal."

The cop was confused and upset. "Are you sure, señorita," he kept asking. And she kept answering, "Yes." A backup came and the cop told him that there had been a mistake, that the dispatcher had made a mistake, and that he would tell him more about it outside. Then he turned to us and said, "If I ever see you two again on my beat, you won't be so lucky." Then they took off, leaving us with the checker.

Joey hugged and kissed her. I was in shock. I had been through enough to go to a locker as we started out and put my bag in a big one. Then I put Joey's coin in the slot, took out the key, and closed the door. Joey stood watching and nodding.

All the way to the restaurant I shuddered and shook. I kept thinking about how close I had come to the end of everything. The waitress was the first person I said anything to, after she asked three times, *"Y usted, señor?"* I ordered *sopa de mariscos* and stared off into space again.

"I think you made a good impression on the doctor," Joey said.

I couldn't have cared less right then what the doctor thought. I didn't even blink. But he wouldn't stop.

"Damn sure he's gonna have pills for you, and we better talk about how you're gonna get that fucking bag of yours and those pills over on the other side."

That fucking bag! What a relief it was not to have it with me. I didn't care if I ever saw it again. No, that wasn't true. All that money would buy me anything and everything I ever wanted. It would make me the happiest guy in the world.

"You hearing me, Mr. Big Spender? I don't have all night and I'm gonna do my best to be back over here tomorrow morning by eleven o'clock to collect that other hundred you're gonna owe me."

I looked at him. I hated him. Did he ever stop conniving?

The waitress brought our food, set the plates on the table, said something to Joey that I didn't hear, and then left.

"Look, I don't need your silence or your misery. I'll take a couple of bites of this and be on my way. And I'll see you tomorrow at eleven o'clock."

He was staring at me and I said, "What do you want?"

"What do I want? Are you kidding me, man? I'm trying to help you. That's what I want. I'm not a complete asshole that's gonna leave you hanging high and dry with that fucking bag and your pills. You don't know the first thing about getting back across that river with those things. It's not like I'm trying to be a Good Samaritan. It's more like you're gonna have paid me three hundred dollars, and the least I can do for you is show you how to do what I do every day."

"What's so hard about crossing?"

"Nothing except that you're taking a bag with you that you don't want anybody looking at and a bunch of pills that you couldn't get in the States."

He had a point. "So what are you saying?"

"I'm saying that before you cross back over tomorrow, you ought to at least know what the process is like, especially with that fucking bag you'll be carrying."

"So how do I learn that process before tomorrow?"

"I don't have the time to show you now but maybe I can show you in the morning. Early, like at six or seven when the bridge will be packed with people crossing to go to work. That's probably the best time for you to cross when you're ready, because the guards can't be that finicky then."

"Six in the morning?"

"Yeah, what else are you doing then?"

"Nothing."

"Then I'll meet you here at six thirty tomorrow morning. Then we can go with the flow over the bridge so you can see what you're going to need to do to get across with that bag and those pills. Once we're past all those guard stations, you can come back here and I can go to the drugstore and do what I have to do there, and we'll meet again at the doctor's office at a quarter to eleven."

"OK."

"Do yourself a favor, will you?"

"What?"

"Don't start going to that store every fifteen minutes checking on your bag. It's there now and it'll be there first thing tomorrow morning."

"Hey, don't start telling me when I can check on my bag. I'll check on it whenever I goddamn please."

"Go 'head. I don't care. It's your bag. But if you start checking on it every fifteen minutes, those checkers are gonna get suspicious seeing you coming and going like that. And you not being a customer, they're gonna tell the manager. That's the problem. Because the manager's got a master key that can open every one of those lockers."

"Master key! Shit! Why didn't you tell me? I would never have put my bag in one of those lockers if I had known that the manager has a master key."

"Go get it out then. And keep it with you all night long and tomorrow too. If you really think that's safer, then go get it out. No one's stopping you."

"You shoulda told me about that master key."

"Listen to me. That master key's not a big problem unless you make it one.... There's more than a hundred lockers on that wall. Right now that manager doesn't have the slightest fucking idea that your bag is in one of his lockers. He wasn't around when you put it in the locker. The checker was busy with people that had backed up in her line when the cops showed up. She doesn't know you put your bag in one of those lockers. And the manager doesn't go around opening more than a hundred lockers a day just to see what's in them. He'll only use that master key if there's a problem. And you're the only one who can make it a problem by going in and out of that store every fifteen minutes to open and close that locker."

"Who said that I was gonna go down to that store every fifteen minutes to check on my bag?"

"Nobody. But going down there a few times tonight before they close would be enough to make those people suspicious."

"Are you trying to tell me that I can't check on my bag whenever I want to?"

"Check on it all you want. Check on it now. I don't give a rat's ass when you check on it. Makes no never mind to me. You heard what I said, and I'm not going to say any more."

Joey raised another forkful from his plate, chewed, and then stood and said, "I'll see you here tomorrow morning at 6:30," and left, leaving me with a plateful of food and people staring at me. Their looks made me glad that I hadn't brought my bag with me. Still, I hadn't decided whether to leave the bag overnight in the locker or take it back to the room with me.

The supermarket was three blocks from the motel, which meant I would be carrying it through a rough, busy neighborhood in the dark. And once in that flimsy room, any one of Billy's friends could bust the door down with half a kick. On the other hand, with the exception of the checker who had talked to the police, no one from the store had seen me put my bag in one of the lockers. And Joey was sure that she hadn't seen me do that either, that she was way too busy with customers who had waited while she was busy with the police. So the manager had no reason to go around checking on my locker, unless, like Joey kept harping, I made it his business by checking on it every fifteen minutes, which I didn't plan to do. And the store would be closed from ten to six. So, as much as I didn't want to admit it, it seemed safer to leave the bag in the locker overnight. But now I began wondering if I had closed the locker door hard enough to lock it. I wasn't sure.

I sat chewing and chewing tasteless food now trying to decide whether I should go back to the store, not to check on my bag, but rather to be sure that the locker door was actually locked. I could feel people watching me from every corner of the restaurant. This was a neighborhood restaurant and they had to be wondering who I was and what I was doing sitting alone in their restaurant on a Monday night chewing on food that I wasn't really eating. Especially after the person I had come with had all of a sudden taken off. I stopped chewing and began rubbing my forehead and the sides of my face.

The waitress came and asked, "Are you OK, sir?" which heaped more attention on me.

"Give me the check. I want the check."

She put a check down in front of me, and I reached in my pocket and brought out a hundred-dollar bill and placed it in on the check.

The waitress jumped back, as if she was scared. "*Ai,* señor, I'm sorry but we don't take American money here. And even if we did, we probably wouldn't have enough change."

I didn't know how to get out of there fast enough. Now everyone knew for sure that I was an American with a lot of money, and I was going to have to walk down those dark streets with everyone knowing. I grabbed the hundred and stuffed it in my pocket and reached into another pocket and pulled out Mexican bills and laid those on the check.

"I'll be back with your change," she said as she picked up the money and the check.

"I don't need any change. You keep it. I have to leave. I have some people to meet."

I stood and started to leave and she looked at me startled and said again, "*Ai,* señor, gracias."

Outside the restaurant, I walked to the corner, crossed the street, and quickly turned and looked. There was no one behind me; no one had come out of the restaurant. I walked down the block looking over my shoulder several times; no one behind me other than a man who was more than a block away. I saw the supermarket in the next block, but I still hadn't decided if I was going to check out the locker door.

I thought several times that it would better to walk past the supermarket without stopping. But when I reached it, I stopped. I went to the front doors and looked in to see if the checker who had helped us was still working. There were two check stands open with a checker at each. I looked and looked at the closest checker but couldn't tell if she had been there earlier.

"Can I help you, sir?" It was a man in a tan uniform with *Seguridad* written all over it. "You've been looking in the store for quite a while now."

"I was just trying to see what your store hours are."

"They're right there on the front doors just below your chest."

"That might be. But just because I speak Spanish doesn't mean I can read it."

"We're open until ten at night seven days a week, and we open at six in the morning seven days a week. Does that help?"

"Yeah."

"If you need to buy something, I suggest that you go inside now and buy it now. If you don't need to buy anything, then I suggest that you just keep moving on. Otherwise people, including me, will start getting the wrong impression."

I went in knowing he was still outside the doors watching my every move. I slipped past the closest checker when she had her back to me. I went to the bread aisle and stepped back and forth along the different kinds of breads until I could turn enough to look at the doors to see if he was still watching me. He was. I took a loaf of bread and went to the back of the store where the milk was. I took a carton of milk and as I turned, I looked again. There was no one at the front doors. He wasn't watching me. Just to be sure, I walked a few aisles down the back of the store, stopping at one to pick up a box of cereal.

I went to the farthest check stand. I was sure that the checker there hadn't talked to the police earlier. She waited on me with an easy smile. She asked if I had been able to find everything I needed. I nodded. She put my things in a plastic bag and quickly made change for the bill I handed her. She didn't know me. Our hands briefly slid across one another as she gave me the change. And I wished I did know her.

It was the other checker, the one closest to the exit aisle that was worrying me. I still didn't know if she was the one who had talked to the police. Luckily she was busy with customers as I walked past her and started up the exit aisle. The lockers were on the front wall just a couple of steps to my right. I stepped over the low brick divider intending to give the locker door one hard yank. But when I was in front of the locker, I started feeling in my pockets with my free hand for the key. Finding it, pulling on it, the grocery bag slipped out of my other hand and fell hard on the concrete. Milk squirted straight up in the air. I did everything I could to stop it, finally flipping the carton upside down so the milk was filling the bottom of the grocery bag. I didn't know if anyone had seen me at the lockers, but I got out of the store as quickly as I could, without checking the lock, and threw the grocery bag into the first garbage can I saw. All the way to the hotel, I wondered if I had done anything at the lockers to tie me to locker number six, if anyone had seen me at locker number six.

It was just after seven when I got back to my room. I could hear the people in the room next to mine arguing. I could hear every angry word, every accusation, and every reply accusation, and I was glad I had put my bag in locker number six. But when they finally quieted down, the worry returned, taunting me: Had I really locked the locker door?

I thought several times of going back to the store before ten to make sure that the locker door was locked. But each time I decided that would create more problems than it was worth. I came so close to going one time that I took the locker key, a little metal tube with the number six engraved on the flat head, and put it in a dresser drawer so that I wouldn't be reaching for it again when I told myself again that I was just going to go there to check on the door. At five minutes to ten I reminded myself again that the locker door had been closed when I was near it and that would have to be good enough until morning when I could check it before meeting Joey.

At 10:02, I went into the bathroom and took one of the four pills I had left. Then I rubbed and rubbed the vial, hoping that tomorrow morning, once we saw the doctor, the vial would be full again. I had never been through a more terrifying night than my last one at the Alvarezes' and later in Malaga. I looked at the vial. Three left. I moved the pills up and down in the vial. Those three pills were all that were left of my sanity. Only three days more. Without them, I didn't think I could withstand the voices. And I knew the voices were watching, waiting.

I didn't sleep much that night. The locker door kept finding a way into my mind whether I was asleep or not. I was up at five, showered and dressed, and I sat on the edge of the bed waiting for six. I was sure that anyone who had been working at the store the night before wouldn't be working at the store that morning at six. I had the locker key with me because I had decided, this being another day, that whether the locker door was locked or not, I was going to open the locker door and check on the bag myself.

The doors to the store were open and all the lights were on at 6:05, but I couldn't see a single worker anywhere. I could hear workers in the aisles but no one was at the check stands. The door to locker number six was locked tight and I opened it and saw my bag sitting there exactly where I had left it. I looked around. Still no one in sight. I unzipped the bag and felt inside. All the packets were there, including the rewrapped one on top. I zipped up the bag, deposited a coin, took out the key, and shut the door hard, yanking on it a few times. It was locked. I was relieved and happy as I walked out of the store on my way to the restaurant to wait for Joey.

THE DARK street was filled with people walking fast toward the bridge. At the restaurant I ordered a cup of coffee and sat by a window so Joey would see me. A few minutes later, Joey rapped on the window and mouthed, "Let's go!" motioning toward the bridge.

"It's not 6:30 yet."

Whether he heard me or not, his second "Let's go!" was stronger and his pointing toward the bridge was frantic.

I left my coffee and went outside. "What's up?"

"The line to the bridge is getting longer and longer, and every minute we wait to get in that line means at least another five- or ten-minute wait when we get to the U.S. side. And I've got work waiting for me on the other side that I have to do before I can come back to the doctor's office and collect my other hundred dollars."

We walked a little more than a block and then stopped.

"What are we stopping for?"

"This is the line to the bridge."

"Yeah, but this isn't the bridge."

"Good guess, genius. This is the line that will put us on the bridge."

"What?" The line was five to six across and stacked back to back in front of us for as far as I could see. "Where are all these people going?"

"To work on the other side."

"Work? Where? Doing what?"

"A lot of them will do the dirty work at all those stores on Highway 35 and get paid a fifth of what white people would get if they would lower themselves to do that kind of work. Others will do all kinds of work in and around Laredo for underpaid wages too. It's cheap brown labor, and it's not just here at the border, but all over the States.

"You're lucky my mom's not here. Sometimes standing in these long lines, she'd start screaming about how the politicians in the States are always making illegal immigrants a big deal when in fact illegals are a big part of the economy, breaking their backs for peanuts, especially on the ranches and farms in the States.

"My dad could be worse. Sometimes the long waits or the way the guards were treating lesser Mexicans would get to him, and he'd start yelling about what hypocrites the Americans were. He'd always start talking about the 1920s when the Americans decided

that there were too many Mexicans in the U.S. and started round-
ing them up even though they were there legally, like his family, with businesses and homes and papers to prove it. Then they
shipped all the Mexicans they could round up back to Mexico.
Then he'd switch to twenty years later when the U.S. was at war,
and the U.S. government was begging for millions of Mexicans
to go there and work. Then he'd say that today if you go out to all
the big ranches and farms in the United States, you'll see that their
workers are mostly illegal Mexicans, doing the work that white
people won't do. The U.S. government knows that, the politicians
know that, he'd scream, but no one does a damn thing about it
because big, big money is involved."

Joey kept talking, but I wasn't listening. I wasn't interested in
any of that stuff. I just wanted to make sure that I knew how to
get back across the border with my money and pills. And the line
to the bridge was moving inches at a time. It was cold and dark
and it seemed like we'd never get to the bridge.

"What's going on, Joey? How come we're not moving?"

"Until we get to the bridge, it's gonna be like this. People are
sneaking into the line everywhere. They're family and friends
of the folks already in line. It's always this way. The ones who
are sneaking in today will be the ones who'll be letting others in
tomorrow."

"Then why did we have to get in line so soon? Why didn't we
just wait until the end of this line and get in then?"

"Just look at the line behind us. Can you see an end to it?"

The streetlights showed a line that went on and on into the darkness behind us.

"They're sneaking in back there too. It's kind of like an agreement they all have. Whoever gets in first is going to let his family
and friends in later."

The line did move slowly but steadily once we were on the
bridge. But it was tight. We were packed six across and there were
rows and rows of people in front of us and behind us.

"All these people are going to work?"

"Oh yeah. Every day, all the time. Going to the good old U.S.A. to do shit work for shit wages."

"How do they get past the Border Patrol on the other side of the bridge?"

"They've all been issued three-by-five, plastic work cards with their photos on them. They just hold out their cards, and the guard usually just looks at the card and at them and waves them through. But notice that almost no one is carrying anything with them. And that's what you should really pay attention to. Because once you get past the first guard, you go on to a second station where everything you're carrying is put on a table and opened and searched by the guards and you're given a much closer look."

When we reached the end of the bridge, people had a choice of going either up or down a flight of stairs to one of two guard stations.

"You want to go up or down?"

"I don't care. Which is faster?"

"Let me take a look." He stepped out of the line and looked on both sides and then came back and said, "Let's go upstairs. I know the guard up there. Went to school with him. There shouldn't be any problems there."

Gradually we made our way up the stairs to a dark-skinned guard in a dark-blue uniform who was sitting behind a table. He was looking at small, white cards people were holding out to him, looking at the cards first and then at the people and then letting them through to the other side. When we reached the top step and were next in line Joey said, "You better have a look at what's going on back there."

About fifteen feet behind Joey's guard friend were two guards at two tables, and they had a young guy stripped down to his undershirt and underpants as they went through his open travel bag and every item that had been in it. I didn't like it but before I could say anything, the guard next to us said, "Come on up, Joey."

Joey nudged me toward the guard's table and said, "Teddy, I want you to meet Jimmy Ramirez, a very good friend of mine. He was born and raised in California...L.A. He came down to visit me and I was showing him the other side, you know, my grandma's pad and all that, and now we're heading back into Laredo."

"Good," the guard said nodding, "now let me see your passport, Jimmy, if you have one, or your visa if you don't."

"What?"

Joey jumped in. "Teddy, the guy's a good friend of mine. He came down to visit me in Laredo, and I never told him to bring a passport or a visa to come to Laredo. Nobody's ever said you need a passport or a visa to get into Laredo. It was my big idea to show him the other side. I never guessed that he didn't have a passport or visa. Cut us some slack, Teddy. I've never had to show anything and I pass through here every day almost, sometimes twice a day."

"Yeah, but everybody knows you, Joey. Everybody knows you were born here. I've known you since we were five years old. But your friend's not in the same position."

"Talk to him, Jimmy, say something to him."

"Like what?"

"Anything. Show him you don't have an accent and you had to have been born and raised in the U.S."

"I don't have an accent, Teddy. I've never had an accent. This is the first time I've been out of the States. I didn't know..."

"Look, I can't rely on whether or not you have an accent. We have tons of people who were born in Mexico and went to the U.S. when they were babies or young kids. None of them have accents and they speak as good as you or me. That doesn't make them U.S. citizens. My job says I have to see a passport or a visa."

"I don't have one."

"Then you'll have to go back to Mexico."

"How?"

"Just turn around and go through that line back the way you came in. If you don't want to do that, I can put you in a holding cell until early tomorrow morning and someone from here will drive you over there."

"You gotta be kidding, Teddy."

"No, I'm not kidding, Joey. And I'm keeping all the people behind you guys waiting."

I thought of my bag in the locker. "OK, I'm going."

"Don't forget, Jimmy, we got that doctor's appointment at 11:00."

"I won't forget." And I started pushing against people who made it easy for me to get by them and head back to Mexico. As I pushed, the image of the man in the undershirt at the two tables wouldn't leave me. This trip into Laredo and Mexico was becoming a nightmare. There was no way I was going to cross into the States with that bag, with or without a passport. Once those guards behind Joey's friend opened my bag, the money would be theirs and I would be in prison. I had heard of people crossing with phony visas and passports, but that wouldn't do me any good because I would have to leave the bag behind. That was something I could never do. I had heard about *coyotes* for years. They could get you across and to the nearest big city safely for a few thousand dollars. Here it would probably be San Antonio. Money would be no problem. If I didn't have to wait for the pills and Joey, I probably would have started looking for a *coyote* then. No matter. I had to have those pills, and Joey would be better than me at finding a trusty *coyote*.

Once I got off the bridge, I went to the store. It was almost 8:30. I didn't care what time it was or who was going to be inside or outside the store or at the check stands. I was going to open that locker and take out a few more hundreds to start the search for a *coyote*. As it turned out, only one of the check stands was open. That didn't matter. I would be taking out my bag for good in just a few hours. I went straight to locker number six, opened it, unzipped my bag and took out a few more bills, zipped up the bag, locked the door, and went out into the street to find a place to wait for Joey.

I walked around in circles for a while thinking and rethinking my situation. The answer was always the same: a *coyote* to get me and my money and pills across the border. I only needed to get to San Antonio. Once I was there, no one would think I was a wetback. A *coyote* could probably get me there that night. Finally, I went to a park across from the doctor's office and sat on a bench in the shade waiting for Joey.

Just before eleven, Joey came walking down the street. "We'd better get into the doctor's office. The line there has probably already started."

"I need to talk to you, Joey."

"We can talk after we see the doctor. I've got all afternoon to talk. But I don't want to piss away a half hour waiting to see the doctor."

There was already a couple sitting in the chairs closest to the doctor's door when we entered that dark hallway. In a few minutes the doctor was at the door. He motioned to the couple and then saw us and nodded and smiled.

"You think he got the pills?"

"I'd put money on it."

"Why?"

"You saw the way he smiled at us, didn't you? Besides that, he really liked you. Most of the guys I bring in here are pretty strung out, and I think he thinks they've got no one to blame but themselves. You're not one of those guys. Didn't you notice that he didn't even ask for a penny up-front? With those guys he always asks me for something up-front. Because he doesn't trust them, doesn't want to waste his time and money getting drugs for them and then find out that they're not really interested or don't have any money. With you, he didn't even mention money, not a penny."

For a moment I wondered how much the doctor would charge me...but only for a moment because my bag flashed big in my mind. I had thousands and thousands of dollars stuffed in that bag. It didn't matter how much he charged me.

A few minutes later the door opened again and the doctor let the couple out and nodded to us. Inside he pointed to the chairs at his desk and went around to his chair. Once we were sitting, he looked at me and said, "I'm sorry, Mr. Ramirez, but I haven't been able to get the pills."

It was like I hadn't heard him or didn't want to hear him, because I looked at him and waited for him to say something else, something different.

"When can you get them, Doctor?" Joey was quick to ask.

"That's the problem. I'm not sure I can get them at all. You see, there's none in stock here that I could locate anywhere. That's because the wealthy have long since taken their mentally ill to Monterrey where there are psychiatrists and medical facilities for them, and I'm sure Zyprexa is available there. Those medical facilities in Monterrey are designed to deal with the mentally ill of rich people. The poor and the middle class here keep their mentally ill at home and deal with them as best they can."

"Where's Monterrey?" I asked.

"It's four hours south of here by bus," Joey answered.

"The distance isn't a problem. The problem is that you cannot simple go to Monterrey and buy Zyprexa over the counter at a pharmacy like you can with many other drugs. With Zyprexa, you can only purchase it if you have a prescription from a psychiatrist."

"Yeah, but me and Jimmy can get on a bus to Monterrey this afternoon and go see a psychiatrist tomorrow morning and get a prescription and have the pills by tomorrow afternoon. Isn't that right, Doctor?"

Except that I had had it with Mexico. I wasn't going an inch farther into Mexico. I didn't trust anything in Mexico. And I was heading back to the States as soon and as fast as I could. And with all that money in my bag, one way or another, I'd get those pills.

"I don't think it's going to be that easy, Jose. Any psychiatrist is going to want to do a thorough physical examination of your friend. He's going to want to get into his and his family's medical history and any history of mental illness in the family. Only then will he write a prescription. And I doubt that he could complete his examination in one visit."

"Well, maybe after a couple of visits we can..."

"Stop, Joey! I'm not going to Monterrey or anywhere else in Mexico. I'm going back to the States."

"How easy is that gonna be, big boy?"

"We don't need to talk about that here. Let's go."

"Well, at least say goodbye to the doctor."

"I don't have to say it. He knows I'm leaving." I nodded to the little man, got out of the chair, went to the door, and started down the hallway. Joey caught up with me before I got to the front door.

"What the hell do you think you're doing?"

"Can't you see what I'm doing? I'm leaving. The man doesn't have any pills for me."

"You're leaving, huh? And how in the fuck do you think you're gonna get out of Mexico with no passport or visa? Especially if you're thinking of taking that bullshit bag of yours with you."

"I'm not going over that bridge. I'm going to the border and find me a *coyote*."

"You're gonna find you a *coyote*? Are you fucking crazy?"

"Stop right there, Joey. I'm not giving you another dime. Your doctor didn't get those pills for me, so I don't owe you nothing. And I'm not gonna pay you to find me a *coyote*. I know of a lot of people on the other side who used *coyotes* to get across. It never seemed to be that hard."

"Look, I'm not asking you for another dime. The doctor didn't come up with the pills so you don't owe me nothing. But if you go running down to the border by yourself looking for a *coyote*, you're making a big mistake. You don't have any idea what's going on down at the border and you're gonna get hurt real bad. I'm not trying to get any more money out of you. You've already paid me two hundred dollars and I'm satisfied. That's way more than I make off of most of my customers. But if you're really set on running down to the border and getting you a *coyote*, then go right ahead. But before you go, just let me tell you a few things about what's really going on down there."

I still didn't trust or like the little bastard. But a lot of what he had told me turned out to be true. And the truth was that I didn't know anything about getting a *coyote*. I stopped walking and talking and just turned and looked at him.

He said, "Come on. Let's go over to the park where you were

sitting and talk for a few minutes, and then you can go down to the border and get you a *coyote.*"

We found a spot in the shade and sat down and Joey began. "About six years ago the U.S. and Mexico got together and decided that they were going to put an end to the flow of drugs going from Mexico to the United States. They called it the War on Drugs. Four years later 60,000 Mexicans were dead and drugs were still flowing from Mexico into the U.S. Mexico's crackdown created new drug routes and new gangs of *narcotraficantes.* There was a lot of infighting and violence among the new *narcotraficantes* for control of the drug routes.

"After four years, the Mexican people were convinced that the War on Drugs was a big, ugly joke and wanted it stopped. The talk on the street was that the government had reached an agreement with the main drug cartel letting it operate free from government interference in exchange for the cartel's stamping out the violence and slaughter of the new *narcotraficantes.* Those groups were soon put out of business and they went into new illegal businesses.

"One of the businesses the old *narcotraficantes* took over was the work of the *coyotes.* Now they are the *coyotes.* This is where you come in...because some are vicious, ruthless, and violent. Remember that, when you go down to the border looking for a *coyote.* But there are some who have been at it long enough to realize that robbing and killing their customers is no way to run a business. It is those *coyotes* that you want to locate and use to get across."

"How do I find the good ones?"

"Not by running down to the border and asking for the good ones. It's by asking people who have had experience with *coyotes,* who know what's happening down there at the border."

"How do I find these people?"

"By asking around, not just in one afternoon but over a few days or a week. After a few days, I'm sure you'll get an idea of who you should be dealing with."

"I don't have that kind of time. You know that. I'll be out of pills in three days."

"The word on the street is that the *coyotes* are now charging five thousand dollars a person to get you across the river and up to San Antonio safely, which is about three hours from here. Have you got five thousand dollars to give them right now?"

"Yeah."

"OK, so just picture this. You go down to the border and find a *coyote* who's in the business and tell him you want to go across the river. The first thing he's gonna do is ask you for five thousand dollars. If you give him five thousand dollars right then and there, you'll never see San Antonio. Maybe you'll see the other side of the river, if he's kindhearted enough to put you on one of those rafts with twenty other people and then just tell you goodbye."

"A raft?"

"Yeah, there's hundreds of people at the border from El Salvador and Honduras and Guatemala who are running away from gangs in their countries and trying to cross the river into the States. They don't have much money. What some of these *coyotes* have done is nail a bunch of beat-up boards together and call them rafts and then take all they can get from twenty or more of these people. They put them on their rafts and then wait until night to push them out into the river and paddle them across to the U.S desert on the other side. So if you give one of these *coyotes* five thousand dollars up front, you can almost bet on being put on one of these rafts and you can kiss San Antonio goodbye."

"What if I tell them that I don't want to go on one of their rafts. I want them to take me to San Antonio?"

"That could get you a bullet in the head and your body dumped in the river."

"People keep using these *coyotes*?"

"Yeah. But I'm just telling you what I've heard has happened to people who have walked up to one of these *coyotes* and handed over five thousand dollars to get them across to San Antonio. What the ones that do get to San Antonio do is agree to pay the *coyote* five thousand dollars but only give him say, two thousand dollars down with the understanding that once they get to San Antonio safe and sound, they will call their family or friends who will pay or send the balance. That's what I think you should do. Except you don't seem to have anybody waiting around for you to call them once you're in San Antonio"

"So that's how you're planning to worm into me again, Joey?"

"Jimmy, I don't need to be worming my way into you or anybody. You were all set to run down to the border and get a *coyote*. I actually felt sorry for you because you don't know the first thing about what you were gonna try to do. And you were gonna get hurt big time. So I told you how it really is to help you, not hurt you. Instead of thanking me, you shit on me. I don't need that, Jimmy. I'm gonna get outta here and I wish you luck. *Hasta luego.*"

He turned and walked away. With each step, I knew I needed him more than ever. When he was half a block away, I jumped off the bench and ran after him.

"Joey! Joey! Hold up, man! You gotta understand. It's just that I'm so paranoid behind the pills and the bridge and crossing and my money that I'm not me. You gotta help me, please. I gotta get across that river tonight. I only got three pills left and tomorrow it'll be two, and it's gonna take some time over there to buy my way to more. I'll pay you whatever you want. I've got to get to San Antonio tonight!"

He looked at me like I was a piece of shit.

"Joey, I'm sorry really! I'm just scared, really! You don't know what those voices are like. I've got to stop them before they start."

He didn't say a word. His look wasn't changing.

"Joey, I'll pay you whatever it takes to get me a *coyote* that can get me to San Antonio tonight."

He looked away and thought.

"Please, Joey. There's nobody else here but you that can help me. How much do you want? You name it."

He looked at me again. He was calculating. "OK, I'll help you, even if I think you're a fucking punk. But it ain't gonna be cheap. It's gonna be a lot of money and I'm gonna want it all up front."

"I can do it. Just tell me how much."

"Alright, listen careful. 'Cause later I don't want you saying you didn't understand. You got five thousand cash for the *coyote?*"

"Yeah."

"And I'm gonna charge you two hundred to find you a *coyote* we can both trust."

"OK."

"Once I give him a deposit of two thousand, I'm gonna have to catch a bus up to San Antonio and hang out in the bus station and wait for you to call me when you're safe in San Antonio. Then I'll meet you and the *coyote* and give him the rest of the money. My trip to San Antonio is gonna cost you five hundred more. The whole thing comes to $5,700. Correct?"

"Yeah."

"And you agree?"

"Yeah."

"You got the $5,700 on you?"

"No, but I can get it."

"Where is it?"

"In my bag in the locker."

"I thought so. How many times since last night at the restaurant have you gone to the store and checked on the bag?"

"Three."

"Three! Holy shit! I knew it! Didn't I tell you not to be checking on the bag? That people in the store would get suspicious?"

"Yeah, but I didn't know if I had really locked it or not the first time I put it in."

"Those lockers are for people shopping in the store. They're not there for street people to be storing things in. If the store people see you going back and forth to the locker without buying anything in the store, they're gonna get suspicious and tell the store manager. And the manager's got the key to all the lockers. If he hears about you going in and outta the store to that locker without buying anything, he sure as hell is gonna check that locker. And guess what he's gonna find in that locker? Your bag. And then he's gonna check it. You see what I'd be worried about if I were you?"

"Yeah."

He looked up at the gray sky for a while and thought. Then he turned back to me.

"A little change in plans. Let's walk over to the store together. You go in and I'll wait outside. This time you actually buy a big bag of groceries, dry stuff so it doesn't get your bag all wet. Then go to the locker with all your groceries and put them in the locker and take out just $2,200. The two thousand I'll use as a down payment for the *coyote* and the two hundred will be my finder's fee. After I find us a *coyote,* I'll come back for you and we'll go to the store together and get your bag out of the locker. Then you can front me the rest of the money, the three thousand five hundred, and we'll go down to the border and I'll introduce you to your *coyote.* I'll leave you with him and I'll cross over the bridge to the bus station to start my trip to San Antonio. I'll have a cell phone by then and I'll give you and the *coyote* the number."

We went to the store and I went in and bought some groceries. I put them in the locker and took out $2,200 from the bag. When I came out of the store, we walked to a church. In the back of the church, I gave him the deposit and the finder's fee. He told me to go back to my room and wait for him there. He thought he would have a *coyote* for us by five or five thirty and would come for me then.

"Whatever you do, don't go back to the store again until I come back for you," he warned me several times.

It was 11:45 when I got back to my room. Joey had said that he'd be back for me between five and five thirty. It was going to be the longest wait of my life. Did I trust him? More so than ever. I had been ready to give him $5,700. Instead, he took only $2,200. If he was going to burn me, he would have taken the $5,700 and run. What he took was proof enough for me that he was being straight.

Still, those five hours could have never moved slower. It was 11:49. I had to stop looking at my watch. If I kept looking at that thing, it would drive me back to the voices with or without the pills. I had to look on the bright side. If Joey got back by five, I could be in San Antonio by 8:30. With that bag full of money, millions maybe, I was sure to get some Zyprexa in San Antonio before my pills ran out. Joey knew how to hustle. He could get me some, even if I had to pay him a few hundred more. A few hundred more was nothing. It was 11:52. I really had to stop looking at my fucking watch.

I realized that I was pacing back and forth and I worried that the people below me might start wondering what I was up to. I lay down and worried that I might fall asleep. So what if I fell asleep? Joey would wake me. I had the key to another five hundred for him. There was no way he wouldn't wake me. I lay there wondering how I had gotten myself into this mess. I just tried to remind myself that I was probably a millionaire now. And once I got out of fucking Mexico and got my pills, I'd start living like one. No reason not to. The cops and Billy's friends had lost all trace of me by now. And who in the hell would ever think of looking for me in San Antonio, Texas...? Nobody.

I fell asleep. It was 4:23 when the maid knocked and asked if I wanted room service. I jumped out of bed thinking it was one of Billy's friends and yelled, "No! No! No!"

"Are you OK, sir? Is everything alright?"

It was then that I heard her and that I knew it was the maid, and I saw that my shirt was soaked with sweat.

"Do you want your room cleaned, sir?"

It was 4:24. I wanted to get out of that room. "Just a minute. Let me change my shirt."

I went downstairs telling her to call me when the room was ready. I sat on a bench next to the office facing the stairs. There was no other way to go upstairs. If Joey came early, I would meet him there. At 4:40 the maid leaned over the upstairs railing and said that my room was ready. I decided to stay where I was and meet Joey there. The minutes dragged past before I realized that I was sitting in the late afternoon shadows and I was cold. At 5:01 it was too cold to keep sitting there and I went back to my room. Joey would be there any minute. I watched the second hand circle and circle the numbers on my watch until it was 5:15, and I decided that watching the second hand was doing me more harm than good. I promised myself that I wouldn't look at my watch again until it was completely dark outside. But I looked again at 5:31. Now I was worried. Joey had never been late. My guess was that the *coyotes* wanted more money than Joey had, but he had no way of getting it since I had the key to the locker. At 5:45 I went downstairs to wait but after a few minutes decided to do the only thing that made any sense: get my bag out of the locker and go down to the border and find Joey and give the *coyotes* the money they wanted.

I hurried upstairs and got my jacket and made sure that I had the locker key and my vial of pills. Once on the street, I broke into a run but stopped as soon as people turned to look at me. I was going to have enough attention in a few minutes with my bag. I didn't know how to find Joey but I was sure people at the border could direct me to the rafts and the *coyotes*. I kept thinking that I should never have let Joey go without the full five thousand. Somebody might have already decided that two thousand wasn't good enough and was taking that out on Joey.

Half a block away, I could see the supermarket. I took the key out of my pocket. I was going to open that locker and take my bag out no matter who was near or looking at me. I had to hurry. God only knew what had happened to Joey. In the store, I jumped over the low brick runner that separated the lockers from the aisle. The closest checker looked up at me. I didn't care. But I was nervous as I jiggled the key around the lock's opening. Finally, the key slid in and I yanked the door open.

My bag was gone!

I looked at the key: number six. I looked at the locker door: number six. But my bag was gone! It had to be my locker because the bag of groceries I put in there that morning was still there. But my bag was gone! I screamed and screamed. People came running.

A checker asked, "What's wrong?"

I tried to answer but I couldn't talk. The only words that came were, "My bag! My bag!"

The manager came.

"My bag! My bag!"

"Your bag is there."

"Where? Not that bag! My bag!"

"Your bag is there."

"You bastard! You have a key! You stole my bag!"

"Your bag is there."

I lunged and grabbed the manager.

"Call the police! Call the police!" people screamed.

The police! The police! I let go of the manager and ran out of the store.

I ran as hard and as fast as I could for a block and then stopped. I was out of breath and I had a sharp ache on my right side. I glanced back and didn't see anyone chasing. I turned completely around just to be sure. No one was chasing me and there was no one on either side of the street except me. I started walking as fast as I could, which wasn't going to be fast enough.

I HAD to find Joey. That son of a bitch back there at the store had stolen my bag and now he was threatening to call the police on me. I didn't know what to do. I had to find Joey. He was the only one who could help me. A cab slowed and the driver looked over at me. "Yeah! Yeah!" I yelled. "Taxi! Taxi!" And he pulled over.

"Where to?"

"I have a friend who's trying to get a raft to take him across the river. He's meeting with some *coyotes* right now. Can you take me there?"

"Señor, I don't know anything about rafts and I don't want to know anything about rafts. That's something I don't need to get into."

"Well, do you know where the *coyotes* hang out? Where can I meet some?"

"Same answer, señor. I don't know any *coyotes* and I don't want to know anything about *coyotes*."

It occurred to me that without my bag, I didn't have enough money to hire a *coyote*. I didn't have enough money to get out of Mexico. And how would I live in Mexico without money? I had to find Joey.

"Where can I find out something about the rafts and the *coyotes?*"

"At the bridge. There's always people there who think they know everything about everything. Some of them do know a lot. But a lot of them don't."

"Take me to the bridge."

He drove on straight ahead. After a while the road seemed to end, but instead it veered off to the right. A block or two ahead the area was brightly lit and there were people milling around in the street.

"What's that up ahead?"

"The bridge."

"The bridge? What are all those people doing in the street?"

"They're just socializing, visiting, having a good time. Some are trying to hustle a few pesos if they can. It's like this every night."

"How do you get through?"

"Slowly. They'll move and some will bump against my car as I pass. I usually let people off on this side of the crowd because most of the time they can get through the crowd quicker than my car can. Anyway, there ought to be a lot of people in that crowd who can tell you where the *coyotes* and their rafts are."

"Maybe I should get off here then."

"I would. By the time you work your way to the other side of this crowd, someone's going to be able to tell you where the rafts and the *coyotes* are."

The people in the street and on the sidewalks were people of all ages, walking around aimlessly, talking and laughing, some with cans of beer in their hands. I saw a woman working the crowd but getting little attention. I chose a man who had the attention of three other men. I tapped him gently on the arm. He paused and turned to me, and I said, "Excuse me, I'm trying to find the rafts...the place where the rafts are that go across the river." He frowned and turned back to the others and continued talking to them. They laughed and I stood embarrassed, and then I walked away as if I hadn't stopped at all.

Farther on, I saw a cop who was standing in the middle of the crowd looking in different directions briefly laughing and talking to people he seemed to know as they passed him. Before going up to him, I thought of how best to approach him. "Excuse me, Officer, but I don't live here. I'm just visiting. But even where I come from, I've heard a lot about people crossing the river from here on rafts. I'm curious. Do you know where those rafts are located?"

"Young man, forget being curious. Those rafts are none of your business and believe me, you don't want to make it your business."

I had to find Joey. I needed that bag. I needed money. I had some hundred-dollar bills on me, but what would I do when they were gone? If I didn't find Joey, I'd be in deep shit.

"It's not that I want to get involved with the rafts or use them,

Officer. It's just that I'd like to see what that raft business is all about from a distance."

"Young man, do yourself a favor. Forgot about those rafts. That's not child's play over there."

He had looked to his left when he said "over there," and I moved in that direction. I didn't like his warning. But he was a cop and the way he saw things had to be different from the way I saw them. If I couldn't find Joey, if something had happened to him at the rafts, there'd be little reason for me to keep on living. I'd be trapped in Mexico with no money and no pills. I didn't think I could live through another set of voices and this time they would be endless.

Before I knew it, I was at the foot of the bridge on the Mexican side. I saw the machine I had avoided yesterday and the two Army guards next to it, just beyond the gates. I rushed to the gates and yelled at them, "Remember me? Remember me?" They turned to me, the same Indian, jungle faces: sharp noses, thin lips, deep-brown skin, and startled eyes. "It's me! Remember me from yesterday morning? I had the big suitcase and my friend gave you money so that I wouldn't have to take my suitcase through your machine! Remember him? Remember me? Remember that?" The whites of their eyes had gotten bigger; their mouths were open like they were remembering. "It's me without the suitcase from yesterday! Remember my friend? Have you seen my friend? Have you..."

Before they could answer came a shout, "Hey what the fuck do you think you're doing?" from outside a small office. A captain or major or something was yelling at me. "You better get your ass moving before I put it where it can't move!"

"Officer, I just wanted to..."

"Did you hear me? Move! Or I'll put your ass in the cell here!"

I hurried back into the crowd and kept moving. I couldn't afford to get locked up now. I had to find Joey. I was past the American side of the bridge and the crowd was thinning out when someone said, "Hey, I hear you're interested in the rafts."

It was a thin man in an old leather jacket who was nodding to me.

"Yeah, I need to get there. My friend's there. I need to get to him."

"That's my taxi over there," he said pointing. "I can take you out there but it's gonna cost you two hundred pesos. You got two hundred pesos?"

"Yeah, I got two hundred pesos."

"Then let's go."

In just a minute or two, we were outside the town or at least the beginning of a long stretch where there were no lights. He was driving fast and I couldn't tell what direction we were heading, except that I thought it was along the river because I thought I could make out trees on my left and nothing on my right.

"Where are we going?"

"To the rafts."

"Are they this far out?"

"They're farther still."

"Why so far?"

"I guess that way nobody bothers them and they don't bother nobody."

A little while more and he slowed and pulled over and stopped. "I'd like to get paid my two hundred pesos now."

"Why?"

"Because I don't want to get mixed up with you having to pay somebody something when we get there."

"I'm not going pay anybody anything."

"Just the same, I want to get paid now."

"OK." I handed him two hundred pesos."

"Thanks."

"How do you know these people? How do you know where this place is?"

"Everybody knows."

"Then why do the people in town act like they don't know?"

"That's their business and this is my business."

A few minutes more and he slowed and left the road and crept onto a very bumpy road on my left. His headlights showed a dirt road with deep holes everywhere.

"Are we almost there?"

"Almost."

Then in the distance, in the darkness, I could see lights. "Is that the place?"

"Yeah."

"Are those lights from a town or a pueblo?"

"No."

"Then where are they coming from?"

"From generators."

"Generator lights?"

"Yeah, generator lights."

Then it occurred to me that I had no idea where we were or how far from Nuevo Laredo or Laredo we were. "How much are you gonna charge me to take me back?"

"Are you going back?"

"Yeah. Do you want the two hundred pesos now too?"

"No because I'm not sure I'll be taking you back."

"Why?"

"Because they're going to want to know who you are and what you're doing out here and who sent you out here and what you really want. And that's gonna take some time."

"I'm going back."

"Good. But I don't want to wait around until you're ready to go back."

"All I want to do is find my friend and talk to him a little, and then we'll be going back."

"It's not going to be that easy. It's going to take you a lot longer than you think. It always does. They're going to check you out real good. But not to worry. There'll be another taxi coming out here soon. There always is. No matter what they say in town. So save your money."

We drove slowly, and the lights were getting closer and closer. Now I could make out trees on both sides of the bumpy road. We stopped. "What are we stopping for?" The driver didn't answer. Instead he rolled down his window. There standing next to him was a man with an automatic rifle. From the other side of the car a light flashed in. Another man with an automatic rifle strung across his chest was holding a flashlight.

"I'm bringing you another one," the driver said.

The flashlight ran across the inside of the car until it came to me and stopped. Both men looked in at me for a moment and then the man next to the driver motioned us by him. The lights got closer until finally we came to a big clearing that was well lit.

"What's that? What're all those people doing behind that wire?"

"Those are people from El Salvador, Guatemala, and Honduras. They're running from the violence and chaos in their countries and they're trying to get to the United States. But they have no papers and very little money."

"What are they doing in that cage? There's men and women and kids in there and I can even hear babies crying."

"There's actually two cages there. The people in the big cage are waiting to see if money comes for them from families or friends in the United States or from the countries they left behind. The ones in the smaller cage have had money come for them, and they're just waiting for more people to be paid for so they can fill up a raft and leave tonight."

"How much are they charging?"

"Three hundred dollars a person. Babies and kids under twelve go free."

"Three hundred dollars to go where?"

"Across the river."

"What's over there?"

"Desert. The same as what's here."

"Where do they go once they're in that desert over there?"

"Probably to the closest town or to people that will help them. When you think of how far they've come, they must be pretty good at keeping going. Mexico doesn't want them here and hasn't made it easy for them to get here. And yet, here they are. They've been able to reach the U.S. border."

"How long do they keep them in those cages?"

"In the big one, ten days. In the little one, usually less than a day.

They have several other cages too. They're well organized. They were a drug cartel before that business was taken away from them."

"How are they organized?"

"The word has spread that this is the way to cross to the United States. So they always have people coming. First the *coyotes* here have to decide whether the people who have come this far are worth feeding and sheltering for ten days or whether no one will ever send the three hundred dollars for them. If they decide they're not worth the risk, they'll send them on their way, reminding them of all the unknown bodies that have been uncovered in the desert, so they'd better be on their way. The ones they keep, they stamp with different markings that tell them how long the travelers have been here. They can only be here for ten days, no more. If they haven't received money for anyone after ten days, they put that person out in the desert too, to find his own way across. Once they receive money for those in the ten-day cage, they put them in the small cage until they have twenty-five. Usually they can fill one raft a day and send it across at night. That's twenty-five people on a raft. Twenty-five people at three hundred dollars each is a pretty good piece of change, especially when you consider what the dollar is worth next to the peso. But then the *coyotes* who say they can get you to San Antonio are now charging five thousand dollars. Very few, if any, of the folks coming on foot from other countries can come up with that kind of money."

We had been parked for a while and nothing had happened. "What are we waiting for?"

"For the man to come down and talk to you."

"Who's the man?"

"Nobody talks about that."

"What's the man waiting for?"

"He's probably counting his money. We better get out of the car. They're going to want to search it."

"For what?"

"Ask them."

We got out of the car and stood beside the driver's door facing toward what had to be the river. We waited. The night was getting colder. I had always thought the desert was hot. The days here still got hot, but now in mid-November, the nights were cold and the jacket I was wearing wasn't much help.

"Why are *you* waiting? I thought you said you had to go."

"I can't go until they search the car and say it's OK for me to go."

"Why are they going to search the car?"

"You better ask them. I don't know."

"Once they search the car, why can't I go with you?"

"Because they're going to want to question you."

"About what?"

"I don't know. They're very suspicious. They're always afraid that other people are going to try to set up more businesses like theirs along the river."

"Have people tried that?"

"I don't know, but they had a drug business taken away from them by the big cartel, and I guess they lost a lot of money in the process. So they're suspicious now."

It was getting colder and I was beginning to think that I had made a mistake coming, only to remind myself that without Joey's help, and he was probably with the man now, I'd never see my bag again or all that money and then I couldn't get my pills and I might never be able to get out of Mexico. And what would I do here without any money?

I heard them before I saw them. Then a short, squat man and a taller, thin man with an automatic rifle strapped across his chest came up next to us. Joey wasn't with them.

"*Buenas noches, mi jefe,*" said the driver.

Mi jefe? Where the hell was Joey?

The short, squat man grunted something and tilted his chin to the back of the car. The driver went to open the trunk as the tall man leaned into the car with a flashlight. When the trunk door slammed shut, the tall man said, "It's all clean." And the short, squat man said, "You can go," to the driver, who quickly got in his car and drove off.

Then the short, squat man turned to me. "What are you doing here?"

"I came out here looking for a friend."

"You have a friend out here? He lives out here?"

"No. My friend was supposed to come out here and talk to you about getting me to San Antonio."

"We don't take people to San Antonio. We take people across the river."

"Maybe I came to the wrong place."

"Maybe you did."

"My friend told me that he was going to get me a *coyote* that had a raft business or used a raft business that would get me across the river and then on to San Antonio."

"We have the only raft business along this river and I intend to keep it that way. We don't take nobody to San Antonio. We only take people across the river and not a millimeter farther. So somebody's been shitting you or you're not telling me the truth."

"Why would I lie to you? Why would I do that?"

"You know exactly why you were sent here, don't you?"

"I don't know what you're talking about. Nobody sent me here. I came out here looking for my friend who was supposed to be making arrangements for me to get to San Antonio."

"Do you have five thousand dollars?"

"Not on me."

"I didn't ask you if you had five thousand dollars on you. I asked you if you have five thousand dollars."

"I did but I don't know if I do now."

"You know that *coyotes* in town are charging five thousand dollars to get you to San Antonio, don't you?"

"Yes, I know that. That's what my friend told me."

"And you know that they don't use no fucking rafts to get you there, don't you?"

"No, I didn't know that."

"So you come out here trying to tell me you're ready to go to San Antonio, but you don't have five thousand dollars?"

"I had a lot of money in a bag but I can't find the bag now."

"So, you came out here without five thousand dollars, right?"

"Yes."

"And you want me to believe that you had a friend out here getting you ready to go to San Antonio even though you don't have five thousand dollars?"

"I had five thousand dollars in a bag, and a lot more."

"And you can't find the bag now?"

"Yes."

"Who sent you out here, *pendejo?* Or do I have to ask?"

"Nobody sent me out here."

"Search him!"

The tall man searched me, taking my money and my vial.

"Give me that and put some light on it."

It was a quick count. "Huh! Four hundred dollars in American money and a hundred and twenty pesos and a few pills to get loaded on. Rodrigo deals in American money. That's all he touches and usually only in hundred-dollar bills. I don't know if I should kill you or send you back to Rodrigo with a message. What do you think I should do?"

"Don't kill me! Don't kill me! Please don't kill me!"

"You're lucky you had those four hundred dollars in American money because first, it tells me who sent you, and second, it will pay for your passage across the river. And third, when you get back to Rodrigo, tell him that the next time he sends a stooge like you out here, we're going to go into town looking for him. And that stooge better not be you the next time or there won't be a next time for you, believe me."

WE WERE halfway across the river before I realized that I was lying facedown, coughing and choking on water that was coming up between the spaces on the boards. My head was ringing with pain. Someone was sitting on my back and someone was sitting on my legs. There were people squeezed all around me, either sitting or kneeling. Their body odors were strong and they were all talking, or so I thought at first. Then it was clear: I was on a raft crossing to the other side of the river and the people were all saying the rosary. My head felt like it had been split open. I tried moving, but there was no moving with that weight on me. Maybe I passed out again because the next thing I knew, the raft bumped to a stop and people began moving, struggling, fighting to move, and splashing in the water everywhere.

A man behind me shouted, "You better get up and get off this fucking raft before I throw you off."

I struggled to get up but couldn't. Instead, I crawled to the front of the raft, hoping he wouldn't throw me into the water. When I got close to the front of the raft he came up behind me and kicked me and then pushed me off into the water. I couldn't swim and I panicked until I felt that my hands and knees were on ground under the water. I felt the raft moving away and looked for the others. But there was no one else around. I crawled out of the water and up a bank and then collapsed next to a tree. The midmorning sun woke me, burning hot on my legs and arms and the back of my neck. I looked down the bank where the raft must have landed. No raft. I looked around for people. No people. But there were signs of people everywhere. Rags and old clothes and parts of old clothes and papers and cardboard and plastic water bottles and worn-out huaraches all over the bank where people must have climbed up to the flat, white hardpan. Even prickly bushes on both sides of the bank had pieces of rags stuck to them.

Slowly it came back to me. I had come to the river looking for Joey and instead had been beaten and robbed by ex-*narcotraficantes* and thrown onto a raft that crossed the river. I had to be in America again. But I could see nothing and no one around. Except for the river and an occasional bird, there were no sounds. Where was I? How far from Laredo? How would I get there? How much money did I have? I felt in my pants pockets. Nothing. They had taken every cent. And they had taken my pills, too. "Holy shit! My pills are gone!" I shouted. "My pills are gone!" I screamed. No one heard me. What I heard was the thought that was ringing in my head over and over again: *The voices are coming! No pills and the voices are coming for sure!*

I thought back to my last day at the hospital. "What if I lose my pills?"

"Not to worry," she had said. "You can always get a replacement here. And anyway, no matter what, you won't begin to feel the affects for a few days."

"A few days." What are a few days? Three, four, five days? Two at the very least. "That's more than enough time to get a replacement," she had said.

Two days, two days, at least two days for sure. I could get to Laredo in two days. Two days to get my pills. Half a day to Laredo and then I would go to a hospital and lie in their lobby and twist and scream that I needed Zyprexa. They couldn't turn me away. Not if I just screamed and screamed.

Two days. The thought wouldn't leave me. And then I realized that I hadn't eaten in two days, and on an empty stomach the Zyprexa would work itself away faster, wouldn't get wrapped up with anything else in my stomach, would disappear twice as fast, and free the voices that much sooner. I had to get something to eat. But where? I had to get to Laredo, or at least to a road to Laredo, or at least to someone's house where I could beg for something to eat...or drink, because I hadn't had anything to drink for two days either. A stomach without food and water would eat up the Zyprexa at its fastest.

Then I realized how thirsty I was. Like it or not, I was going to have to drink from the river, even if it was polluted. There was no way I could make that walk to Laredo without water.

I looked down at the river. I could see nothing in it other than its movement, its flow. It was moving from my left to my right. Laredo had to be on my right. People built towns in places where the water flowed to them not away from them. I couldn't see any debris in the water either, which also told me that Laredo was on my right. Because if the river had already passed through a town the size of Laredo, I would be seeing debris. And I was seeing none. Walking an hour, or two at the most, I would probably get to Laredo. I wanted to be on my way, but first I had to drink.

I went down the riverbank, hoping to see the bottom of the river, thinking that might tell me whether the river was polluted or not. I couldn't see the river bottom. The water was too dark, which wasn't a good sign, I thought. But I had to walk to Laredo. I had to take my chances.

I knelt down at the edge of the river and put my hands in the water. Slowly I lowered my head until my nose was an inch above the water. I sniffed and sniffed but couldn't smell anything but water. I dipped the tip of my nose into the water and let the water run up and down my nostrils. Still no smell of anything, and, better, no sting in my nostrils from any poison that might be in the water.

I drank, holding and swishing that first mouthful around and around in my mouth, still worried. I swallowed and stood up and planted my feet solidly on the river bottom, alert for any sign of dizziness. I stood motionless for several moments, maybe minutes, and nothing happened. Then I sank to my knees again and drank and drank until it felt like I had ten gallons of water in my stomach. It was time to be on my way to Laredo.

As I started up the bank, something sticking up in the water caught my attention. I went over to it and picked it up. It was a smooth, iron rod about a foot and a half long. I had no idea how it got there or whose it was, and I was about to drop it when I thought that I might need it on my way to Laredo. There was no telling what I might run into on my way.

As I began my walk to Laredo, the sky was a bright blue, clear except for some dark clouds far off in the distance. The land, as far as I could see it, was hot, hard, white, and empty except for an occasional treelike bush that stood about five-feet high and three-feet wide. As I started in the direction of the river flow to Laredo, I was wearing the same boots, pants, and T-shirt that I had bought in a Los Angeles Walmart five days before. I had nothing else except the iron rod that I was holding at my side.

I planned to walk a foot or two next to the river's vegetation and trees, where it would be cooler, all the way to Laredo. I knew nothing about heading north, west, south, or east, the way some people talked. All I knew was that sooner or later, the river would take me to Laredo. I walked and walked, having no idea how long I had been walking, until I started to tire and each step was getting heavier and heavier. Then I noticed that I was getting less and less shade under the trees. It took me a little while to figure out that the sun was going down on my right giving me less tree shade. It had slid down enough to convince me that I had been walking a long time and should be seeing signs of Laredo.

I walked out onto the hardpan looking in every direction, nothing but the white, hot hardpan for as far as I could see. As I stood out in that sun, I felt hunger pains and I also knew that I would have to drink more water soon. Tired, I decided to rest, to sit down at the river's edge again and at least drink some more water.

As I walked back to the river, I was puzzled. Laredo or houses or buildings had to be somewhere nearby. But they weren't. The taxi ride from the border to the river crossing hadn't taken that long. Of course, that trip had been by car. Still, it seemed like I had walked a long, long ways and there should have been some sign of Laredo by then. Laredo couldn't be that far away. When I reached the vegetation next to the river, there was no clear path down to the river. I tried walking through the vegetation, but the shrubs and bushes were very prickly, piercing through my pants and scratching my legs. On my third try, I led with my iron rod, slashing hard at the vegetation, beating back a path.

I sat at the edge of the water and took off my socks and shoes and put my tired and sore feet in the cool water. I leaned back until my back was on the bank. Looking up at the sky, I felt refreshed knowing that I couldn't have that much farther to go and that this rest stop would easily get me there. I might have dozed, but I wasn't sure, although I knew some time had passed when I sat up again intending to drink.

I was on my knees leaning toward the water when I saw it. I straightened up. Debris! What looked like a candy-bar wrapper, floating toward me. No, it couldn't be. Where had it come from? How did it get into the river? But it was only one, I told myself, and I had better drink and get back up on the walk before it got any later. I got up and saw more candy wrappers floating toward me and a plastic bag and two plastic bottles, too.

When they reached me and passed me, I screamed, "No! No! It can't be!" But there were more coming, single items for sure, but not to be denied. I turned and slipped and slid up the bank and my path as fast as I could and put on my boots, wanting to get away from the proof that I was lost. On the flat, hot hardpan I kept shaking my head. No wonder I couldn't see any signs of Laredo. I had gone the wrong way! I was lost! Lost! Lost!

I knew then that I would have to get back to the place where I had started, where the raft had come in. Because another raft would be coming in during the night, and I could go with those people to wherever they were going to survive. And once I was out of that wasteland, a road or a house would lead me to a hospital before the voices began. But I had to get there before dark or I would never find the landing place again. Tired, hungry, thirsty, and sore, I limped along as quickly as I could.

The dark clouds I had seen far off as I had started were now overhead and scattered. A strong wind had come up, and when the clouds were overhead blocking the sun, I began shivering, shivering so hard that my teeth were clattering. The sun was slanted now and I prayed for it to shine directly on me, because without it, the wind was freezing cold. Yet no matter how cold and tired and sore I was, I kept moving as fast as I could toward the landing place.

When I finally reached it, the wind was still strong and I was shaking so much that I felt like I was about to collapse. I had to find shelter. I hurried down to the river but the wind was there too, and, as the sun was setting, the riverbank felt colder than the hardpan. I scrambled back up the bank and saw a lone tree-bush bent almost in half by the wind. I ran to it and threw myself down against its lowest branches, which cut the wind some, while the top half of the bush seemed like a cover over me. Despite the bushes' prickly branches and leaves, it was the best shelter I could find and much better than standing or laying in that wind. But some wind was still getting through the bush, still making me cold, and with the sun setting, I worried that the wind was going to get much colder throughout the night.

I worried, and just as the sun touched down on the hardpan far away, I remembered and saw all the debris that the raft people had left on the riverbank and the bushes above it. I hurried to the riverbank and gathered as much of the rags and old clothes and plastic and cardboard as I could, and then I hobbled back to the tree-bush. With the help of the wind I fastened the debris onto the front side of the bush's stickers and sharp edges. The attached debris was now blocking a big portion of the seeping wind. But as I lay there again, I felt I could do better and went back to the bank as it was getting dark and I got more debris and hung that too. I couldn't help but think that the tree-bush looked kind of like a Christmas tree. No matter how it looked, it was almost completely cutting off the wind. I was still cold as I lay at the base of the tree-bush, but nothing like before, and I knew I could lay there until the raft came. I was soon asleep.

A crash in the vegetation woke and startled me. I reached for my iron rod and sat up. I thought another raft had come. I waited for the sounds and voices of people, but there were none. Something was, or had been, in that vegetation, something huge enough to have made that sound. I listened. I strained to hear. I could hear nothing except absolute silence in absolute darkness. I had never seen darkness like that before. Always at night there had been a trace of light somewhere. I turned, facing the vegetation. There had to be something in there. Minute after minute slipped by. I heard nothing, saw nothing. I felt hunger pains that reminded me how thirsty I was. But there was no way I was going down to the river in that darkness to drink. There might have been some berries in that vegetation. I would never find them in that darkness, nor would I try. With the wind still howling, I wasn't about to leave my tree-bush.

I don't know how long I sat up trying to see or hear something in that vegetation. I was very tired and part of my mind said I needed to rest...I needed to lie down and sleep. Another part said that I needed to stay up, stay vigilant, protect myself, and be ready for whatever was in that vegetation. I tried laying down and at the same time I tried staying up. My body struggled with itself until I finally collapsed and slept.

I don't know how long I slept again before I felt the first bug. All of a sudden, I opened my eyes in that darkness. There was something on my left cheek, and I was more than awake. It was resting lightly on that cheek. For a moment I thought and hoped that it might be my fingers, but my hands were nowhere near my face. Maybe it was a leaf? It wasn't a leaf. I was afraid to tighten or stretch my cheek. Any movement could lead to some disaster. My mouth was open. I guessed that I had been breathing through my mouth while I was sleeping. I didn't want to move my mouth either. But how long could I keep those parts of my face motionless? I didn't know and I didn't care. I wasn't moving them.

Then it moved, and I screamed and slapped the side of my face hard with my open left hand. I thought I had hit it but I wasn't sure. I sat up and gripped my iron rod, and with my open left hand, I patted the ground on every side of me. Nothing. I brought my left hand up just under my chin and then, dropping my rod, with the fingers of my right hand, I brushed gently across the inside of those left fingers and palm. If I had hit whatever was on my face with my open hand, there had to be traces of it on the inside of that hand. Nothing. I gently rubbed the fingers of my right hand against my right cheek. Maybe it had left traces there. Nothing. I sat up for a while hoping that the insect or spider or whatever it was would come again while I was fully awake so I could put an end to it then and there and go back to sleep. But it didn't return.

The moment my mind left the insect, the thirst and hunger returned. When the raft came, some of those people would surely share with me some of what little they had. Had the raft come? Had it already come while I was asleep? No, there would have been a lot of noise, far more noise than the noise in the vegetation that had awakened me. I had no idea what time it was. But I did know that sleeping passed the time without dwelling on the hunger and the thirst that were plaguing me. I lay down again.

I slept again until I felt that bug or spider on my right cheek. Its movement woke me, and in that moment of waking, I swung hard with my right hand at my right cheek. This time I hit it. There was no mistaking that. I knew I had knocked it off my cheek but I felt the cheek anyway. Nothing. I got up and knelt down and with both hands patted the ground all around me, knowing that it had to be there some place. But there was nothing there. I decided to sit up motionless and awake until it returned, knowing that the minute I lay down and fell asleep again, it would return. I don't know how long I sat up, but it was a long time. It didn't come.

By then, I was convinced that it would only come when I was laying down and it thought that I was asleep. I lay down again, promising myself that I would stay awake and motionless until it came. Sure enough, it came, on my left cheek again. This time I swung and cupped it in my left hand. "I got it! I got it!" I yelled. It had size, like a small ball. I squeezed it and squeezed it. I could feel its shell cracking. I squeezed harder, so much so that it slipped out of the bottom of my hand. "It slipped out!" I screamed.

I got down on my hands and knees again and felt all around until I finally felt it under my right hand. "I've got it! I've got it!" I grabbed it and began squeezing it with my right hand, which was stronger than my left. I felt the shell cracking again, breaking, becoming powder. When it was just powder, I brought my right hand up near my eyes to somehow see it, inspect it in that darkness. Carefully, I opened my hand and, unable to see anything in that darkness, I felt my palm with my left fingers to get a sense of it. But there was nothing there. "There's nothing there! There's nothing there!" I screamed. I started to cry and fell forward next to the tree-bush and cried and cried.

The sun was burning my back and the back of my head. I felt like I was on fire. I got up and stumbled as fast as I could to the riverbank and into the water. I sat in the river trying to remember and forget the night. Then I drank and drank from the river, hoping maybe to quench the hunger too. Even though my stomach was so bloated with water that I felt that I couldn't take another drop of water, the hunger pains wouldn't leave.

I sat in the water asking myself again and again if the raft had come. Had I slept through its coming? I couldn't have slept through all the noise of its coming. If the touch of a bug had woken me, how could the noise of a raft and all the people on it not have awakened me? A bug? What bug? Really, what bug? I shook the bug out of my mind. The raft and all those people couldn't have come and not awakened me.

I got out of the river and sat down on the riverbank to stay out of the sun. The voices could be as close as a day away. I remembered how they had haunted and taunted me, how they controlled and terrified me. I couldn't and wouldn't endure them again. I couldn't, I wouldn't. I was waiting for the people from the raft to lead me to Laredo or a road to Laredo or to someone who could tell me how to get to Laredo. It was my only way out now. But the raft hadn't come, and I was just one day away from the voices and I didn't know what to do. If the raft didn't come, what then?

A wind came up, and sitting in the coolness of the shade in wet clothes and shoes, it wasn't long before I started shivering. I wanted to get up and take those few steps up the bank to the sun but my stomach was hurting and I was feeling weak and dizzy. This would be my fourth day without eating. Still, I was getting colder and colder and the shivering had gotten so strong that my teeth were chattering and hurting again. I had to get under the sun. I stood and, leaning forward, took a step and then another toward the hardpan and then collapsed.

When I came to, the sun had moved from somewhere behind the tree-bush to a point in front of it. There was some shade behind the tree-bush but still enough sun next to that shade to keep me warm if I needed it. I had to get back to my tree-bush. I stood. The pain in my stomach was sharper, but I was able to stand up and walk up the bank and to the tree-bush, where I lay down partly in the shade and partly in the sun.

Sometime later, my hand touched that part of my iron rod that was still in the sun. I yelped and my iron rod said, "I don't want to be here anymore."

"You don't want to be here anymore? And where do you think you're going? You're my iron rod and I need you here for my protection."

"I'm not your iron rod."

"You *are* my iron rod."

"Not really. I was lying in the river as happy as I could be and then you came along and picked me up."

"I took you out of the water or you would still be lying there."

"You had no right to do that. I was content there."

"But I need you!"

"I don't need you. I want to go back to the river. I'm tired of being carried around by you everywhere you go and then being left in the sun."

"I can't let you go. Not now. Maybe tomorrow I can take you back to the river, but not now. Help me. I need your help. Especially when tonight comes."

"OK, until tomorrow. But that's it."

"Thank you."

I SPENT the rest of the afternoon lying next to the tree-bush thinking about the raft and what would happen if it didn't come and thinking too that maybe I wasn't awake or maybe I was. Because the afternoon was disappearing right before my eyes. I had to have been in and out of consciousness. As the sun was setting, I kept telling myself that I had to stay awake, and the next thing I knew, it was dark. I listened for the raft, but there was nothing to hear. I tried to see if there was any new refuse on the bank, but it was too dark to see anything. As much as I kept telling myself that I had to stay awake now that it was dark, most of the time I couldn't tell if I was conscious or unconscious.

Then Padre Ibarra was there. I don't know how he got there or when he got there. But he was there. He was standing over me dressed in a black cassock and a white surplice looking down at me.

"How did you get here, Padre? How?"

"I came because you needed me."

"Really? Or is it because the last time the voices broke me, you had just left me alone in that little Malaga church? Have you come just so you could leave me again just before they come...?"

"I'm sorry. But help me keep those voices away."

"It is not me you should be asking for help. It is God you should be asking for help. Get down on your knees and pray to Him. He is Good and He is Great and He will help you."

"You pray to Him for me, Padre. You're much closer to Him than I am. Tell Him I was your altar boy for many years. Tell Him about all the Masses I served with you that you said were to Him. How many days of Holy Obligation I was there with you. How many baptisms and church fiestas I was there with you. You tell Him all that for me, Padre. Because what I remember most now is the suffering I saw. The suffering was always there. People were always suffering. They were always coming to you with their sufferings. And when those people stopped coming with their sufferings, others took their places and brought new sufferings. And you kept saying what you just said to me, 'God is Good and God is Great.' But however Good and Great He is, the suffering never stopped. Those sufferings never stopped. And my suffering has never stopped."

"God's Ways and Wisdom can never be known or understood by man."

"Maybe not, but one thing man knows for sure is suffering. I took care of my grandmother for the last years of her life and she suffered and suffered and never stopped suffering right up to her last breath. And why, Padre, have I been suffering with this evil mind for years now? No, I can't understand God's Wisdom and Ways. And why does man have to keep on suffering? Why does God permit it? He is All Good and All Kind and All Wise and All

Great and All Powerful. He can stop suffering any time He wants. But He doesn't and He won't. Why must we continue to suffer? Why does He let the suffering go on?"

"So that man can gain His Eternal Happiness in Heaven."

"Otherwise, man goes to hell?"

"I didn't say that."

"And what about me, Padre? What have I done to deserve this illness and evil mind? If the voices come in the morning, I'll never survive. But tell me, you're God's agent, why me? Why have I been chosen for this lifelong suffering? To gain Eternal Happiness with God in Heaven? Is that what it's all about?"

"Your coveting and taking that filthy money was a sin, wasn't it?"

"And for that I'm given this lifelong punishment? You forget, Padre, that I had this curse long before I ever saw that money. And I took that money to avoid being arrested and sent to prison or being killed by Billy's friends. But long before and after I took that money, which I will never have, why me? What have I done to deserve this illness, this evil mind? You've known me for years, Padre. I've confessed to you many, many times. I'm not a big sinner. You know that, Padre. Why me? Why me?"

"I don't know."

Then he was gone, just as he had come, he had gone away. I must have known then that the raft wasn't coming, but the voices were. Still, I slept until the sun was on my legs, and I could hear the voices whispering behind the tree-bush. They didn't think I could hear them, but I did. And I got up and ran. As weak as I was, I ran and ran. I had to save myself.

And they ran after me, laughing and screaming.

You can't run from us. You don't even know who you are, do you? How can anyone who doesn't even know who he is run from us? Who are you? Tell us who you are! We know who you are but you don't know who you are, do you? Who are you? Tell us who you are! Have you ever really known or admitted, even to yourself, who you really are? You might have fooled everyone, you might even have fooled yourself, but you haven't fooled us. We've known all along who you are. Do you want us to show you again who you really are? Or will you finally open up to the truth and take a real look at yourself?

I kept running. They were always behind me, screaming and laughing. They were laughing at me, laughing at who I was, at who I really was, not at who I always said I was.

I ran from them over that hardpan. And no matter what I said or did or where I looked or how I covered my ears, they were there, loud and clear with their accusations.

You're nothing but a worthless piece of shit! You have no reason, no justification to be living! You've hid your despicable self from everyone all your life! But you can't hide who you really are from us! We see you clearly in all your worthlessness! You're just taking up space! You know what we want you to do! You know what you must do!

"No! No! No! I won't! I can't! I won't!"

You must!

"No! No! No!" I ran and ran. And as I was falling, I looked back and saw them for the first time, a big blue blur.

THEN I was in a Laredo hospital. I had no idea how I got there. The voices were gone. The doctors had injected me with Zyprexa. All they told me was that the Border Patrol had brought me there.

A day later, there was a knock on my open door. When I looked up from the bed, I saw a tall, young man in a blue uniform approaching me. I panicked. The cops had finally caught up with me.

"Who let you in here? You can't be in here!"

"Calm down. I just want to tell you how you got here. It's probably as important for me to tell you as it is for you to hear. Maybe more important for me.

"My name is Jason Ybarra and I'm with the Border Patrol. For the past four months my partner and I have been assigned to patrol an area east of here along the river in our four-wheeler. There's been a huge increase in the number of people crossing the river illegally. Most of the illegals are coming from countries below Mexico.

"Anyway, five days ago at about 10:15 in the morning, we saw you running and stumbling west in the desert, not far from the river. We assumed you were running from us. We turned our vehicle around and caught up with you and drove alongside you, about thirty yards away from you. We couldn't get any nearer because of the terrain. My partner was driving and after a while I decided that it would be easier if I just got out of the vehicle and apprehended you on foot.

"I caught up with you and realized that you didn't even know I was there, that you were screaming at something else as you ran. You were stumbling badly and just before you fell you turned, and the look on your face came as a shock. I knew I'd seen that look before and heard that kind of screaming before.

"You fell. Your face was twisted with terror is the best way I can put it. I cuffed you and then watched you writhe and kick on the hardpan. Your face was red and twisted with hate.

"I thought of my dad then and his never-ending fear that one day my sister might end up in the desert like you were then. She lives with my parents. She's always lived with them and probably always will because she refuses to take any medication. When she goes through one of her spells, in some ways not unlike what you were going through that day, my dad says he doesn't know what to do with her and is just thankful that he's three times her size.

"Anyway, I searched you and was stunned when I found one of my sister's handkerchiefs on you. You had either bought one or stolen one from her on a Sunday afternoon in old town where she sells them...or says she sells them. That's the only way you could have gotten one. I guess I was kind of dumbfounded. When my partner came, we put you in the back of the four-wheeler.

"When we got into our vehicle my partner said, 'Shall we take him to the Detention Center now or wait until we pick up a couple more?' I told him, 'We're not taking this guy to the Detention Center, we're taking this guy to the hospital.' 'What!' he said. 'Are you crazy? We're not supposed to be taking these people to the hospital.'

" 'Take a look at this.' And I showed him a receipt I had found in your back pocket. It was dated six days before from a Walmart in Los Angeles, and the pants and shirt and shoes you were wearing were listed.

"'So?'

"'He was in Los Angeles at a Walmart six days ago, and he's still on this side of the border right now. He's not an alien. He's not an illegal. It's my guess that he's a U.S. citizen who's very sick. And we're taking him to the hospital.'

"'How do you know he's very sick?' my partner said. 'You're not a doctor. And I don't want my ass chewed out just because you think you are.'

"'I'm pulling rank and I'll take whatever's coming if I'm wrong.'"

"So you're here in the hospital taking the medication my sister ought to be taking. You're a lucky man, Mr...Mr...?"

"Ramirez, Jimmy Ramirez."

Two days later, a man wearing a white shirt and tie came to my door and then into my room. "Hi, Jimmy, remember me?"

He wore glasses and had black, wavy, hair that was beginning to gray. I had no idea who he was. He wasn't a cop, or at least he didn't look like a cop, so I didn't think I had anything to worry about. I shook my head.

He smiled and said, "I'm Ben Chavez. I have a drugstore across the park in the old downtown. You came into my store about two weeks ago, I think it was, wanting a refill of Zyprexa. Remember?"

I did remember, but more than that I remembered how I had rubbed the label on the vial and I started to worry...except that his smile seemed warm and real.

"I was going to refill it but I couldn't find you on the Internet, and before I could say anything more, you left. Joey went after you but he came back saying that you didn't want to come back."

"Where's Joey?"

"I don't know. Nobody knows. He just kind of disappeared. Some people say he went to Nebraska to visit his mother, but nobody knows for sure. He was always saying that he wasn't going to stay here, that there were a lot better places to live in than Laredo."

Joey was gone. Joey had my bag and all the money. But how would I ever find him?

"Do you remember coming into my store?"

I nodded.

"You seemed to be having a hard time of it then, and I was concerned because the drug you wanted wasn't one of those drugs you can get high on. It was clear to me that you had other problems. But you didn't come back."

We looked at each other for a few moments. He didn't seem to have anything more to say and I didn't know what to say or what he wanted.

Finally, he said, "The Ybarras are good friends of ours. We've known each other for years. One of their boys is Jason Ybarra, you know, the Border Patrol officer who brought you to the hospital and came to see you the other day? He was telling me about you when I realized who you had to be. He told me that one of the doctors was very concerned about you because he was going to have to release you soon, and with your amnesia it might be a while before you can get on Medicaid for your medication and financial aid. They have to start a whole new file on you. And they have in fact been filling out the necessary forms for you to get you on Medicaid and financial assistance. But the process could take months and the doctor's worried about what you can do in the meantime.

"I've talked to that doctor as well. He's convinced that with the proper medication, you could be a very responsible person. He's prepared to prescribe that medication for you, and I've agreed to fill it until the program's in place.

"That still leaves you with everyday living expenses for two or three months until the financial aid comes through. Even then, you'll probably have to scramble to make ends meet. But for now, I've talked to my wife about you and here's what we're prepared to offer you. We have a small studio apartment behind the pharmacy that you can use for the immediate future. You can also have

Joey's old job at the store, cleaning, stocking, and doing odd jobs. That's two hours a day, six days a week, at three dollars an hour which will give you some income. I also have two or three deliveries a day that you can make on one of our bicycles. I'll pay you three dollars for each delivery and whatever tips you get are yours. Working in the store and making those deliveries should give you enough money to get by on for now."

As DETERMINED as I had been to find Joey and my bag once I was out of the hospital, by the third day at the store I knew that would never happen. And riding that bike around old town on deliveries gave me a sense of peace and security that I hadn't felt in a long, long time.

Then on my first Sunday afternoon, I walked down the same streets I had walked down weeks before until I got to that same corner. She was still across that street with her table and chair and handkerchiefs. I went over to her and said, "I need to buy a handkerchief."

She looked at me puzzled. "But I sold you one not too long ago."

"Yeah, but I lost that one."

"OK, which one do you want?"

I picked out one and she asked if I wanted her to sew my initials on it, and I said no and gave her a dollar and she gave me the handkerchief.

Then I said, "Would it be OK if I just sat here for a while?"

Puzzled, she said, "Yeah, if you don't talk too much and especially not about medication."

"OK," I said, sitting down on the curb, "I won't."

Ronald L. Ruiz is the author of a memoir, *A Lawyer* (2012), and four previous novels—*Happy Birthday Jesús* (1994), *Giuseppe Rocco* (1998), *The Big Bear* (2003), and *Jesusita* (2015). Born and raised in Fresno, California, Ron was educated at St. Mary's College, California, University of California, Berkeley, and University of San Francisco. He practiced law from 1966 to 2003 as a Deputy District Attorney, a criminal defense attorney, and a Deputy Public Defender. He was appointed to the California Agriculture Labor Relations Board by Governor Jerry Brown in 1974 and later served as the District Attorney of Santa Cruz County, California.